STROIKA

MARK BLAIR

Matador
9 Priory Business Park,
Wistow Road, Kibworth Beauchamp,
Leicestershire. LE8 0RX
Tel: 0116 279 2299
Email: books@troubador.co.uk
Web: www.troubador.co.uk/matador
Twitter: @matadorbooks

ISBN 978 1788035 187

British Library Cataloguing in Publication Data.
A catalogue record for this book is available from the British Library.

Printed and bound in the UK by TJ International, Padstow, Cornwall
Typeset in 11pt Aldine401 BT by Troubador Publishing Ltd, Leicester, UK

Matador is an imprint of Troubador Publishing Ltd

To Ben, Helena, and Sarah… and for Jackie, a thousand hallelujahs!

'We have to see and react to the times, otherwise life will punish us.'
Mikhail S. Gorbachev

AUTHOR'S NOTE

It is some twenty-seven years since the Berlin Wall fell. The millennial generation may have little to no knowledge of the Soviet Union. For others, perhaps those that are older, the world was a very different place when the Soviet Union challenged the West, seemingly everywhere, and battle tanks massed along the Iron Curtain that divided Western from Eastern Europe. The Cold War saw the world on a nuclear knife-edge balanced between two competing ideologies. It is strange today to think of a divided Germany, the Berlin Wall itself, and that people died trying to cross it to the West.

Stroika, a fiction that foreshadows the real events of August 1991, is set at a time of massive change, when the old Soviet Union was making way for the new and the Soviet Army was increasingly bogged down in an unwinnable conflict in Afghanistan. After only one year in office, the ailing Konstantin Chernenko was succeeded in 1985 as general secretary by the Politburo's youngest member. Mikhail Gorbachev had very different ideas to his predecessors. In 1986 he launched glasnost (openness) and in January of the following year his perestroika (restructuring) programme. Only by these means – open discussion and reform of the economic and political system – could, he argued, the communist system be saved. In the end, Gorbachev unwittingly set in motion a train of events that ultimately brought the Soviet Union to its knees and eventual collapse.

There are many competing articles and books on the subject of what actually did happen. Scouring second-hand bookshops for books written at the time and glued to my screen for many hours, I discovered that analysis is often contradictory and basic information sometimes hard to corroborate.

What is clear is the extent to which the Soviet people were deceived. Travel restrictions and little contact with the outside world shielded citizens from appreciating quite how far the Communist Soviet system had failed them; those that did challenge the status quo were silenced. In a mundane way, this was vividly brought home to me by the report of Yeltsin's visit to a supermarket in Texas in September 1989. The pure abundance of goods on display shattered his view of communism.

When Gorbachev assumed power, there was little real understanding of how a market economy worked and even less of how to transition a command economy into a modern, competitive one where goods were made that people wanted. Prices remained, by and large, fixed centrally. But there were a group of people who did understand, and they saw the opportunity, often functioning on the fringes of society. In the black market economy, that in many respects was the real economy, these budding, talented and, one has to say, brave entrepreneurs arbitraged the system and made fortunes.

In 1989, the Soviet Union comprised fifteen federated republics and occupied one-sixth of the earth's land surface, a staggering statistic. Its borders stretched for sixty thousand kilometres, the longest border of any country on the planet. Yet its economic plight was such that it could not feed itself and struggled even to distribute the food that it did have. In stark contrast, the Soviet Union's military budget had mushroomed, by some estimates, to one-fifth of national income, employing directly or indirectly one in five of the working population. Gorbachev appreciated this was unsustainable and, in the same year, shocked the Congress of People's Deputies by announcing that military expenditure was four times the published figure.

Glasnost and perestroika loosened the bonds that held both the Soviet Union and the communist bloc of Eastern Europe together. Increasingly, governments took an independent course as the central Soviet government began to buckle under the strain and dissent that emerged from within the ranks of the Politburo, the Soviet Union's supreme executive body.

In 1956 and 1968, Soviet troops had bloodily repressed uprisings in Hungary and Czechoslovakia. Thousands had died and thousands more had been arrested as political prisoners. Gorbachev recognised the time for change and began openly to encourage Eastern European governments to reform. The genie was out of the bottle. The year 1989 saw Eastern Europe consumed with civil unrest. In Leipzig, Monday demonstrations grew from a few hundred to a few hundred thousand. The question, of course, that hung in the air was whether the Soviet Union would respond in the same way it had done in 1956 and 1968.

The peoples of Eastern Europe and the world held their breath.

Stroika...

APRIL 1977

PROLOGUE

LENINGRAD

Miniature lakes form where the pavement has subsided. People hunch against the wet, making their way home, skirt familiar tarns, avoiding the kerb, wary of cars and trucks and soaking sheets. Grey turns to darker grey as the run-down façade of the Nevsky Prospect undergoes an unambiguous Soviet metamorphosis.

She rubs the wet off the dial. He is late, fifteen minutes. She takes cover under the overhang of a tall building, her eyes searching the crowd.

He is easy to spot. She can see him now, a hundred metres off, head up, running full tilt through the open spaces in the crowd. Two men some way behind are giving chase but the gap is widening.

A pedestrian inadvertently steps in his path. He slips, regains his balance. The gap between him and his pursuers closes momentarily. His hand moves inside his jacket, reaches for something. He is only metres from her now. She steps out into the pavement, directly in front of him, and braces herself for the impact. He sends her reeling.

Concerned passers-by help her up, ask if she's all right. Does she need assistance home? She says no, brushing the water from her coat; her gaze fixed a hundred metres ahead.

A car blocks his path. The men following grab him from behind. He doesn't struggle. He raises his hands, protesting.

They pull his jacket off, search him, find nothing, and drop it onto the wet pavement. A policeman arrives on the scene and quickly exits. A man climbs out of the back of the car and walks over to the small group. She can see him gesturing with his fist, a look of fury on his face. He lands a heavy blow to the man's arm and they release him, pushing him roughly forward. He stumbles and nearly falls. Empty-handed, they move off, leaving him alone and rubbing his arm.

Passers-by pay him no attention. He retrieves his sodden jacket and looks back, finds her and smiles. She smiles back, turns and walks away.

DECEMBER 1982

CHAPTER 1

LENINGRAD

Viktoriya made her way over to a small group of men seated at the far corner of the Muzey bar, their laughter and guffaws puncturing the general babble of the room.

'Viktoriya!' one of them shouted out, as hands reached for the beers she unloaded from the tray.

'This is Pavel Pytorvich Antyuhin, from Khozraschet, visiting us from Moscow,' said Roman, introducing the man seated next to him. He was dressed in an ill-fitting black suit, his hair plastered flat over his forehead.

'Economics must be economical,' Viktoriya quoted the general secretary.

Antyuhin looked impressed. 'You know about Khozraschet?'

He reminded Viktoriya of Brezhnev and his official portrait that littered the walls and offices of every municipal building: the familiar dark, bushy eyebrows and permanent facial expression somewhere between surprise and a frown.

'Viktoriya is an economics undergraduate at Leningrad State,' interrupted Roman.

'Maybe you should come and work for us when you have graduated?'

'Maybe,' she answered, only too familiar with the pick-up line. 'And what would you like to drink?' she said, smiling back.

'A beer… *Baltika*,' he said, pointing at Roman's bottle.

By the time she returned with his order, he had pushed back his hair and rearranged his tie.

'Are you free later for dinner… or tomorrow evening?' he asked before she could make a retreat. 'There is a new restaurant off Dumskaya. We could talk about your future opportunity.'

Viktoriya had heard of the new dining room reserved for party members.

'Perhaps another time.'

She did not want to offend him, nor did she want to spend an evening with some mid-level bureaucrat trying to get her into bed with the tenuous promise of a job.

Antyuhin looked disappointed, a little put out, as though he had expected her to say *yes* without hesitation.

'I go back to Moscow in a couple of days. I'm staying at the Baltic Hotel off the Griboedova Canal,' he added to impress her.

'I've got a lot on… exams coming up,' she replied, trying to be final.

Another customer signalled her across the room; it was the excuse she needed to make her exit.

★

By midnight most tables had emptied. Antyuhin had left half an hour before, making a big deal of slowly putting on his fur-trimmed Arctic parka and stuffing a cigarette packet back in his pocket, studiously ignoring her as the regulars waved her goodbye.

Just after one, the Muzey closed. Viktoriya threw on her short padded frock coat and headed out into the cold night air. She paused. Once elegant façades lingered sooted and mutinous over a deserted prospect, trembling in the flicker of a faulty street lamp. A mouse scurried by, leaving only the telltale trail of its tiny feet in the fresh snow.

At the next junction, Viktoriya vaulted a rusted pedestrian railing and crossed into Yusupovsky Park. A distant basilica, ice-capped, blinked and vanished. Snow, she thought, on its way. She could not remember the park being so perfect. Frosted willow and larch, skeletal against the moonlight, peppered a perfect white pedestal; park benches, once populated in summer, lay dormant and untenanted. A wedge of snow slid from a nearby branch and landed with a muffled thump.

Sticking out her tongue, she tasted the icy nothingness of winter. A lonely flake melted on her cheek. Viktoriya closed her eyes and remembered her mother's hand tightly clasped around her own, of scooping fresh snow and gingerly extending her tongue towards it until she encountered that numbing prickle.

Snow fell heavily now; what had started as a sprinkling blotted out most of the park. She squinted at a solid shape two hundred metres ahead. At first she wasn't sure if it was moving, or what it was, but as it passed under a park light she recognised the silhouette of a man, head down against the cold, hands thrust into his coat pockets. She pulled her coat tighter; maybe he was a road maintenance worker returning after a night shift, or a bar worker like herself making his way home. Hesitant at first, Viktoriya started down the footpath towards the approaching figure, telling herself that this was no different to any other encounter, two night-travellers bent on an opposite path. With each long stride, her confidence returned.

A few feet apart, the man looked up from the barely discernible footpath and stared her directly in the face. The words *good evening* died on her lips. She couldn't remember the name at first, only the fur-trimmed coat and that he worked for Khozraschet. She stopped, confused: wasn't his hotel in the opposite direction?

'Good evening, Viktoriya.'

He stepped sideways, directly in front of her, blocking her path.

'You really should have accepted my invitation. A pity… You remember me?' he said, grinning.

Her mouth went dry. She struggled to find her voice.

'Get out of my way,' she said as calmly as she could.

Snow swallowed her words; they dropped frozen

into the soft white powder thickening around her feet.

She turned to run and slipped, only managing momentarily to regain her balance before he threw his powerful arms around her, crushing her ribs, squeezing out all the air. Viktoriya screamed with the breath she had left, struggling desperately to free herself. She kicked him hard on the shin bone. He let out a muffled cry. Furious, her attacker released his grip and swung his fist hard into her solar plexus. Winded, unable to draw breath, she fell to her knees, frantically trying to find air before he was on her again. She managed a lungful before she felt his strong hands clench her feet and begin dragging her away from the path towards the towering yew border. She screamed, clawing at him with her free hands.

'*Be quiet!*' he whispered loudly. With that, he jumped on top of her, pinning her down as his fingers found her belt and worked their way round to the buckle. Recovering her breath, she attempted to push him off. This time he punched her in the ribs. For a moment she lost consciousness; the rough pulling off of her jeans jolted her awake. Violently, he entered her, one hand clawing her breasts while the other covered her mouth. Inert, shocked, fearful of another blow, she tipped her head back and stared up blankly at the snow-laden branches of an overhanging tree.

When he had finished he stood up. Terrified, she watched him zip up his trousers and extract a small wad of roubles from his back pocket. Counting out several, he paused, seeming to change his mind, and roughly stuffed the whole bundle into the pocket of her ripped and abandoned coat that he found at his feet.

He turned to leave, took three steps and stopped.

'You deserve a tip,' he said, and kicked her hard in the stomach, knocking the wind out of her a third time. 'And don't try anything when I'm gone, like going to the police, not unless you want your next job in Siberia.'

When Viktoriya found the courage to look up again, he was gone. Clutching her jeans, she crawled an agonising ten metres into the shrubbery behind a park bench. Wet snow forced its way up under her torn T-shirt, her bare legs and hands numb from the cold. Terrified he might return at any moment, she lay there motionless, struggling to garner her thoughts, to understand what had just happened, deciding what to do next. She couldn't stay there, not in those freezing conditions. A thousand thoughts crowded in. She willed herself to calm down, focus. She took a deep breath and held it before slowly exhaling, watching a steady stream of vapour condense and freeze into a small cloud. Gently, she stroked her bruised and aching abdomen. Blue with cold, she gingery pulled on her jeans and wrestled on her coat. With the back of her scratched and blooded hand, Viktoriya wiped away the tears that had begun to freeze on her cheeks. Going to the police, she knew, would be worse than useless. They would only say she asked for it. After all, what was she doing in Yusupovsky Park so late at night? Picking up customers? Wasn't Yusupovsky famous for it? They weren't going to arrest some party member whose connections might consign them to a posting in the Far East, and certainly not for an inconsequential young student. She had seen it happen before: the accuser becomes the accused, a university place revoked, a family member's job threatened.

Teeth chattering from cold and shock, Viktoriya climbed painfully to her feet. The sound of a lone, distant car horn drifted across the park. The snow had stopped as suddenly as it had begun; once again the moon cast its ghostly pall over the winter stillness. Skirting the frozen lake, now ornamented with the new fall, she traced the path to its beginning and exited onto a near deserted prospect. There was no sign of her assailant. Further up, workmen in orange overalls swung pickaxes at unforgiving tarmac next to a softly purring roadside generator. Hugging her torn coat, Viktoriya passed them on the opposite side.

Fifteen pain-filled minutes later, Viktoriya found herself in front of her apartment block. Four identical six-storey buildings of indeterminate brown enclosed a large floodlit square. A bronze statue of Lenin, clutching *Das Kapital* in his upheld hand, railed against oppression, oblivious to local drug dealers and alcoholics who routinely relieved themselves against his polished granite podium.

Viktoriya's ankle boots, wet and cold, sank deep into the drifting snow as she traversed the final twenty metres to the main door. Inside, two bare wires woven together replaced the switch that had been stolen the month before. Exhausted, Viktoriya battled the three flights of stairs to her bedsit share. When she finally managed to turn the key and push open the door, Viktoriya was blinded by the sudden switching on of the internal light.

'Agnessa, turn that off!' Viktoriya croaked, covering her eyes. Her head throbbed and she felt as though she would throw up at any second. She took a step forward and nearly fell. Agnessa caught her and guided Viktoriya past a small wooden dining table before gently easing her onto the sofa. Streetlights cast a jaundiced hue over the small and sparsely furnished room.

'You look terrible! Don't move, I'll be back in a moment,' said her flatmate.

Viktoriya didn't feel she could have moved even if she had wanted to do so. She began to shiver uncontrollably. Agnessa reappeared, helped her undress and towelled her dry before wrapping her in a woollen blanket.

'What happened?' her friend asked, her voice full of concern.

Viktoriya could not bring herself to say anything. She shook her head and held up her hand.

'I'll make you some sweet tea.'

'I need a bath,' Viktoriya managed to whisper finally.

Viktoriya watched Agnessa as she put on the kettle and placed two large saucepans of water on the hob to boil. How many years had she known Agnessa? Since she was six or seven? Primary school then Ten Year

School at eight. Their parents had lived on the same landing. Both their fathers had worked at the docks and often gone out drinking together, sometimes on a weekend binge. At fourteen it had been Agnessa she had turned to that night when her father had caught her in the face with a poker in one of his drunken rages, only narrowly missing her eye.

Reflexively, Viktoriya's finger traced the faded scar. Her headache was splitting now. She needed a painkiller, more than one.

'Before you go into shock,' said Agnessa, handing Viktoriya two Efferalgan and a mug of hot sugary tea.

'Thank you,' she managed to say, as feeling began to return to her half-frozen hands. 'I'm remembering this is not the first time you have played nurse.'

'It's what friends are for.'

Ten minutes later, Viktoriya lowered herself into a shallow tin bathtub of steaming hot water.

'You should see a doctor,' Agnessa said, staring at the terrible abdominal bruising that was beginning to show.

'I'll survive,' said Viktoriya, relieved to be washing the night away.

'Are you going to report this?'

Viktoriya shook her head.

'Bed,' she replied. 'That's what I want.'

Ten minutes later, bruised and exhausted but feeling a lot calmer, Viktoriya climbed into bed and fell instantly asleep.

CHAPTER 2

'What time is it?'

Viktoriya could hear him struggling to look at his bedside clock. Something crashed to the floor. She guessed it was the radio he always had precariously balanced there.

'It's 5.10 a.m.,' she replied in a matter-of-fact voice, as though calling him at that hour was not an unusual occurrence.

'Just a minute.'

Viktoriya heard Konstantin sit up. There was a muffled protest from one of his flatmates.

'Can you meet me by the Baltic Hotel, 7 a.m.? I'll explain later. I can't talk about it now, not here in the corridor.'

'Okay, 7 a.m.,' Konstantin repeated and hung up.

When Viktoriya had woken an hour before, she had lain there, not disturbing Agnessa, going over what she should do. She felt certain that this was not the first time her assailant had attacked a woman. He was just too confident, too sure of himself, sure that she wouldn't go to the police. For the same reason she hadn't gone to the police, she suspected neither had his other victims. Either way, whatever the truth about his past, Roman's drinking companion was not going to get away with what he had done or be allowed to assault her again.

That was when she had got up and called Konstantin. She could have called the bar doorman – he was ex-army – or one of her other male friends, but it was Konstantin she had instinctively turned to. He would *know* what to do.

Carefully, Viktoriya retraced her steps to the share. She wrapped some bread and cheese in a kitchen towel and, after layering up, headed out to the bus stop and the still dark square.

Light pooled eerily from overhead floods, the crunch of her footsteps magnified. On the far side a door banged shut with a *wumph*. A woman, heavily padded, wearing a bright red headscarf, materialised and quickly vanished down a side path. Viktoriya tightened her grip on the kitchen knife she had slipped into her trouser belt and peered anxiously about her.

The bus pulled in to her stop. A woman driver waved her in and quickly closed the door... warmth at last. Viktoriya cleared the condensation from the window, pulled off her gloves and brusquely rubbed her hands together.

As they skirted the Fontanka, smoke drifted from the chimneys of canal boats fixed to their winter moorings, hulls captive to slowly thickening sheets of ice; water dwellers, no doubt stoking early morning fires, preparing sweet tea and coffee, fending off the early morning cold. Life going on as it had before.

Here and there, workers began to appear along the wide pavement wearing thick padded jackets, ushankas and balaclavas. Once or twice, Viktoriya thought she glimpsed her assailant. Unnerved, she cast her eyes around the bus: a young woman with a suitcase bound shut with twine read a book; behind her, two men, a row apart, napped, heads lolling against the foggy window. She pulled her scarf up around her face and the flap of her fur hat across her mouth. Two stops and she disembarked. If anything, it felt colder than when she'd waited at the bus stop.

Next to an old church, now used as a warehouse, she found the hotel. It was small and, like most of Leningrad, well overdue a coat of paint. Faded streaks of pink, redolent of an era she could only imagine, emerged from under its grey rendered exterior. A sign above the door spelled in capitals: BALTIC HOTEL.

Sheltering under the buttress of the church, Viktoriya pulled the hood of her coat up over her hat and in between bites of bread and cheese sipped on the steaming hot tea she had bought from a street vendor.

A familiar whistle made her turn to catch sight of Konstantin striding purposefully in her direction.

'A sip of whatever you're drinking,' he said, standing in front of her holding out his hand. He pushed back his hood and swept a mop of jet-black hair off his face. She began to tremble as if the shock of what had happened was only now setting in.

'Are you going to tell me?' he said, staring down at her.

She wondered if he could tell what had happened just by looking at her, whether it was *that* obvious. She wiped her eyes and turned back to the hotel entrance.

'I was attacked last night on my way back from the bar.'

Haltingly, she told him. Konstantin listened silently.

'Just point him out to me,' he said coldly when she had finished.

Guests started to appear, some checking out with suitcases, others with briefcases ready for their day's meeting; a tourist studied his map for probably the hundredth time that morning, making an early start to the day's exploration.

By eight forty-five she was starting to think they might have missed him. Maybe he had checked out the night before, slipped by, or exited by another door. Konstantin showed no sign of impatience; he was smoking a cigarette behind her, propped up against the church wall. A halo of white cigarette smoke drifted by her and dissolved in the frozen air. She smiled for the first time since the previous night, turned and caught him studying her. In an hour they had hardly exchanged a word.

Five minutes later a taxi pulled up outside the hotel entrance. A man emerged from reception carrying an official-looking attaché case and climbed in.

'That's him,' she whispered.

Konstantin wrote down the cab telephone number displayed under the taxi sign.

'I need you to make a couple of calls. Then you can go home.'

'I'm not going home.'

He started to object and stopped. His mouth opened and closed without saying a word.

From his pocket Konstantin extracted a few kopeks and pointed at the payphone across the street.

'This is Inga from the taxi company. One of our drivers just collected someone from your hotel, a…' Viktoriya hesitated, 'I can't read his name. He left his briefcase on the back seat and he is no longer where we dropped him off. Is your guest returning to the hotel?'

'I will check. Yes, that will be Pavel Antyuhin. He is here for a couple more nights. You can leave it here. I'll be in all day.'

She replaced the receiver and called the taxi company.

'Hello, I'm calling from the Baltic Hotel. You just collected one of our guests, a Pavel Antyuhin. He has left some papers in reception. Can you tell me where you dropped him?'

There was a muffled conversation as the taxi booker covered the receiver.

'Yes, I have it here – 36 Italyanskaya.'

CHAPTER 3

Number thirty-six was a retail store reserved for party members selling household goods. It looked empty. The window sported a dusty white vacuum cleaner, a lamp with no shade and a random stack of pots and pans that leaned precariously towards the glass.

'We'll wait here,' Konstantin said, lighting up another cigarette.

Parking themselves opposite, hoods and scarves covering their faces, they had only a few minutes to wait before she caught a glimpse of their quarry. He had stepped forward from the rear of the store, a list of some sort in his hand, and was standing looking out onto the street. For one moment he seemed to look directly at her, but a second later he turned and walked back inside the store. He was broader than she had remembered him. His lank hair was swept back from his forehead, away from those thick dark eyebrows.

'Are you okay?' Konstantin asked.

She nodded, unsure about how she truly felt. Looking up at Konstantin now, she knew she had made the right decision calling him. He made her feel safe. The anxiety she had experienced earlier had been replaced by something else, a toxic mix of loathing, hatred and anger.

The sound of the door opening across the street made her start. Antyuhin had paused in its frame, making final adjustments to his coat and scarf. The store manager lingered awkwardly behind, no doubt anxious for his visitor to be gone.

'What now?' she asked.

'We follow him.'

They set off at a safe distance behind him, occasionally taking opposite sides of the street, arm in arm, a couple about their business. Antyuhin made two more calls before stopping on Kazanskaya for lunch, at a dismal-looking eating house with plastic-topped tables, a food counter displaying savoury pasties and a large soup tureen. They watched as he took his seat by the window with a steaming bowl and a large slice of dark rye bread.

'We haven't got long,' said Konstantin, his back to the window. They had moved to a café across the street where they could observe the eatery's exit. 'I'm going to make a call.'

With one eye on Antyuhin, Viktoriya watched Konstantin exit onto the street and stride up to a payphone not ten metres away. An old lady was speaking animatedly into its mouthpiece. Konstantin reached in and depressed the disconnect bar. She looked up, startled. Viktoriya couldn't see Konstantin's face, but whatever his expression the old lady thought better than to remonstrate. She picked up her bags and with an exaggerated shrug squeezed past him.

Konstantin fed the meter, dialled, looked over at her and winked, before whoever he was calling answered the phone. Stern-faced, occasionally shaking his head with what she presumed was frustration, the conversation lasted not much more than a minute.

Antyuhin was still seated when Konstantin returned to their vantage point across the street. He looked at his watch. She wondered how much longer he would remain there, when he suddenly stood up and started to put away the papers he had earlier taken from his briefcase.

They both got up.

'You wait here by the payphone.'

He pulled a notepad out of his pocket, tore off a sheet, and scribbled OUT OF ORDER and handed it to her.

'You know Lev and Ilia?'

She nodded.

'They won't be long. I'll call you the moment Comrade Antyuhin stops.'

Konstantin bent forward and rather unexpectedly kissed her on both cheeks.

'Mr Khozraschet is not going to get away. You have my word on that.'

'He's leaving,' she told him, squeezing his arm. Antyuhin had stepped onto the prospect. 'No... don't turn round yet... Okay, now. He's headed east.'

Konstantin set off after him on the opposite side

of the street, before turning back to look at her and mimic a phone with a hand held to his ear.

She took a last bite of the stuffed cabbage roll and then followed Konstantin out onto the street and fastened the OUT OF ORDER sign to the phone box with some gum.

The winter sun still on its northward journey had begun to dip. Shading her eyes, Viktoriya looked both ways down the prospect for Konstantin's two comrades. She vaguely remembered meeting them at a student party Konstantin had thrown at his share a year back. They were not so much his friends as *gofers*, collecting, by nefarious means, unpaid debts that Konstantin had purchased for next to nothing from unsatisfied creditors.

A tap on her shoulder made her spin round. For one second she thought it might be Antyuhin and that he had managed somehow to escape Konstantin and beat his way back to her. Lev and Ilia stood there, stupid grins on their faces.

'Kostya said to meet him here... didn't say anything else,' said Lev. Lev was well built with small deep-set grey eyes, his friend slightly taller, round-faced with thick lips, and the smell of alcohol and fish on his breath. Ilia was doing his best to hold a sausage roll away from his body as relish dripped down his wrist inside his parka jacket.

'We just wait for his call,' she said, indicating the public payphone.

Nearby, a gang of municipal workers scraped new snow off the pavement, piling it up in small mountains by the kerb. The temperature had dropped a good five degrees in the last hour. It was all they could do to keep their circulation going by clapping their hands and stamping their feet. Viktoriya bought sweet teas from a street vendor and made it abundantly clear she was listening for the phone and not to Ilia when he attempted to start up a conversation.

How long would it be before Kostya called? More than once she caught her two companions exchanging furtive glances, Ilia licking those thick lips of his as if she had induced some saliva reaction. At the student party, in the squash of bodies, she had felt him squeeze past her on his way to a refill at the kitchen bar. It had irritated her then, much as they both irritated her now. She would not have felt safe alone with either of them.

The strangled *tink-tink* of the public payphone made her jump. Lev cocked his head, doglike.

'That will be him,' he said.

Viktoriya picked up the receiver.

'Kostya?'

Konstantin asked her to pass the phone to Lev. There was a lot of head nodding and 'Yes, boss'. Finally, Lev replaced the receiver in its cradle.

'Mikhaylovsky Palace,' he said to his partner. 'The Palace Bar.'

This time Viktoriya was not in-the-know. Lev made no attempt to enlighten her, and she wasn't going to give him the satisfaction of asking; she just had to trust Kostya... that was all she had to do.

It was good to be on the move again. Fifteen

minutes later, under the towering walls of the palace, they stood across the street from the bar of the same name, whose grey shabby exterior matched its dilapidated surroundings. Only the wooden facia board above its door, lit by a single fluorescent tube, distinguished it from the entrance to any number of anonymous apartment buildings.

'The boss says you are to wait out here,' said Lev, and with that he and Ilia crossed the road and shouldered open the heavy door.

Light was beginning to fail. Viktoriya stared across the wide prospect at the bar door. Two men staggered out into the Arctic freeze. Morning time, drunks would be found frozen in doorways or curled up on the pavement, petrified, under a blanket of frost. Viktoriya shivered. How long would she have to wait? Standing there stomping her feet she felt exposed, and not just to the cold.

Two policemen rounded the corner and, seeing her, stopped. The taller of them said something she didn't hear to his partner, caught her eye and smiled.

'Papers,' one asked, as the other circumnavigated her.

This was the last thing she needed. Antyuhin might exit the bar at any second.

He studied her photo. 'ID photographs make us all look like criminals, don't you think?' he said wryly.

Viktoriya replied with a simple 'Yes', casting her eye across the street. She turned to look at the other policeman and caught him exchanging a sly smile with his partner.

A cough made them start. Kostya materialised as if from thin air and sprung onto the pavement. The policemen were no less startled than she was. Konstantin placed a proprietorial arm around her shoulders. She noticed one of the policemen place his hand reflexively on his revolver.

'Trouble, comrades?' said Konstantin, a broad grin on his face, more a challenge than a greeting.

The officer handed Viktoriya back her papers.

'I'd keep my eye on her if I were you. Leaving a pretty girl out in this cold is not too smart,' he said, directing his comment at Konstantin.

'I am sure that is good advice, comrade officer.'

The officer stared at him, twitched a grin and turned to his partner.

'Let's leave these lovebirds.'

'What was that about?' Konstantin asked her when they were gone. Viktoriya shrugged.

'Come, you'll freeze out here. There's a place you can sit out of sight. Your friend is busy at the bar.'

CHAPTER 4

The space was larger than she had imagined from the outside. A series of interconnecting smoke-filled rooms, each defined by a bare brick, high-vaulted ceiling, rolled towards a packed bar that extended along the back wall's full length. It was busier than the Muzey and much louder. Locals shouted at each other to be heard above the background babble.

Viktoriya took the seat next to Konstantin, who pointed at a heavily patinated mirror. At first she didn't recognise them; it was only when Konstantin pointed again that she made out the small group of men leaning against the bar. Ilia faced outward, with the other two turned half towards him. They were all laughing at some bad joke he was no doubt making. Antyuhin, vodka shot in hand, slapped him on the back and emptied his glass in one before turning back to the bar for a refill.

They made an unlikely threesome: Antyuhin, Ilia and Lev. Antyuhin, more and more drunk, shouted impatiently at the barmaid to refill their still half-full glasses. Viktoriya caught her rolling her dark eyes at someone out of view, as much to say, 'another night, another customer who will no doubt feel regretful in the morning'. Give them their due, Viktoriya thought, Konstantin's two enforcers managed to restrict their intake to a quarter of their new-found companion's.

Thirty minutes later, Viktoriya heard Lev shout 'Let's go' and slap his newly acquired friend resoundingly on the back. They split the bill. Lev tossed some roubles onto the bar and with Antyuhin between him and Ilia made their way out onto the street.

'Don't worry, I know where they are headed,' said Konstantin in response to her questioning look.

The two of them followed the tightly knit threesome at a short distance, Viktoriya with her hood up and scarf tightly around her face and Konstantin with his arm around her. Ilia led them left along Inzhenernaya Street under the grey and yellow façade of the palace towards the Griboedova Canal. It was ten thirty and well below zero.

'We can walk it from here. We need to wake up, get some fresh air, before the fun starts,' Ilia said loudly. Icy breath traced their path along a now deserted street.

'When you come to Moscow, you'll see. I'll introduce you to some *really* beautiful women,' Antyuhin bragged.

They crossed over to Mikhaylovsky Sad and entered the park by its southern gate.

'We can cut through here,' said Lev, 'it's not far.'

Their hanger-on followed them willingly enough, his alcohol fogged mind, she thought, no doubt focussed on the promise of young, willing, or unwilling, Leningrad girls. The park was empty. Benches placed along the gritted path stood forlorn, perfectly white, bounded by iced topiaries of yew. Ilia led the way, pausing occasionally for Antyuhin and Lev. At one point their companion slipped and nearly fell, saved only by Lev reaching out to grab him. Two hundred metres in, just short of the canal, Lev and Ilia stopped. Viktoriya's assailant staggered to a halt, confused by their lack of direction.

'Lost?' he asked, laughing.

'No, I don't think so.' It was Konstantin who spoke.

Antyuhin grappled with a voice he did not recognise, no doubt trying to fathom what it meant, when Viktoriya stepped into view. He appeared startled, bemused. He looked at his two escorts, who no longer appeared so friendly, and back to Konstantin and Viktoriya. She walked right up to him and pulled her scarf away from her face.

Terrified, he tried to force his way past, only to be sent sprawling on the path by Ilia's outstretched foot.

Grazed, covered in grit and ice, he begged to be let go.

'I have money...' He took out his wallet and waved it at them.

'I don't think Vika is interested in being compensated, are you, Vika?' said Konstantin with a smile on his face.

Viktoriya shook her head.

Lev and Ilia grabbed Antyuhin by the arms and

pinned him roughly to the ground as Konstantin extracted a razor-sharp flick knife from his coat pocket and slashed open Antyuhin's coat.

'Please...' Antyuhin begged, his eyes rolling around wildly.

Konstantin roughly shoved a handkerchief in his mouth and kicked him hard between the legs. He writhed in agony, twisting to free himself from his two captors.

'Your turn, Vika,' invited Konstantin.

Despite what he had done to her, she found herself unable to respond.

She turned away as Lev swung his boot into Antyuhin's ribs. She heard bone crack. When she turned to look again, Konstantin was rubbing a handful of snow into the face of an unconscious Antyuhin. He started awake, terror taking hold once more.

Ilia pulled off the man's belt and bound his hands tightly.

'Any last words?' said Konstantin.

Antyuhin started to babble incomprehensibly, his words strangled by the cloth he tried to spit from his mouth.

At a nod from Konstantin, the two men dragged Antyuhin the last twenty feet to the embankment before grabbing him roughly by his arms and his feet. On the third swing they let go. Ten feet below, his body crashed through newly formed ice and disappeared under a thicker sheet behind. They stood there in silence, not moving, staring at the water, watching the last ripples fade.

Ilia picked up the dead man's briefcase.

'Let's see what's in there,' said Lev. He flicked open the catch, pulled out a wodge of official-looking papers and passed them to Viktoriya, who was standing next to him.

'Pavel Antyuhin, Director Khozraschet North-West,' Viktoriya read out loud. 'They'll be looking for him now.'

'They can look as long as they like, but that river won't be giving him up until the spring thaw,' said Konstantin. 'He'll be perfectly preserved, of course.'

Lev pulled out a wallet and ID.

'Get rid of it,' ordered Konstantin. 'You don't want to be caught with that. You can split the cash with Ilia'

Viktoriya watched Lev divide the roubles and pocket the wallet and ID.

'It's safe,' he said, and patted his breast pocket. 'Don't worry, I'll dispose of it.'

JUNE 1986

CHAPTER 5

LENINGRAD

The door banged shut behind him. Misha pulled the
lock bar tight and slid over the interconnecting bolt
of the bauxite-coloured lock-up. Letting the two half-
empty duffel bags slide off his shoulder, he shone
his pocket torch onto the racking. He found what
he was looking for, struck a match and lit the candle.
Before long, several candles burned steadily around
the metal sarcophagus. Misha carefully unpacked and
placed jeans, T-shirts and illegally imported CDs in
their proper place behind him. A good day's trading.
For a Tuesday, the flea market at Apraksin Dvor had
been busier than normal. From the side pocket of
the canvas bag he pulled out a wallet and removed its
contents onto a wooden fold-up table: one hundred
dollars and a pile of roubles. Looking at the shelves,
he made a mental note of what he was running short
of. He must ask Viktoriya to get him some heavy
overcoats; it would be autumn in a few months.

The sound of a heavy fist banging on the container
made him jump.

'Who is it?' he shouted. He lifted his old service automatic from its holster on the table.

'Ivan! And you can put the gun away,' a barely audible voice responded.

Misha walked over, unlocked the door and swung it open. The damp late-summer afternoon air rolled in from the south across the Bolshaya Neva and Vasilyevsky Island. He took a deep breath, exchanging it for the stale atmosphere of the container.

'Coffee?' was all his flatmate said.

'Good idea.'

Misha turned and looked at the money on the table.

'Just one minute.'

He pulled the door to and placed the day's takings in an old combination safe bolted to the container floor under the racking. He closed the door and spun the dial once, tugging on the handle to make sure it was locked.

'Stefan's or Oleg's?' Ivan asked his friend when he reappeared.

'Stefan's today, I think.'

Misha liked Stefan's: the coffee was passable and probably was *actually* coffee. It was also a source of the rarest Soviet commodity: information. Street traders swapped stories, traded goods and alerted each other to the latest city crackdown.

Boats carrying coal, timber and building supplies chugged past. In the opposite direction, a barge, piled high with rubbish, stinking in the summer heat, glided by on its way out to sea. The waitress placed two steaming mugs of black coffee in front of them and a plate of piroshki 'Mushroom and pork today,' she said. Ivan reached for a pastry, took a bite and idly inspected the inside.

'Expecting to find something?' said Misha.

'You never know in this place.'

Misha studied his old school friend and wondered how much he ate in one day. Five foot ten and thickset, Misha guessed Ivan weighed at least a hundred and ten kilos.

'You should have one,' Ivan said, tucking into a second pastry.

'I will, if there are any left... I've been thinking,' said Misha, taking another sip of black coffee.

'Then we're probably going to be in trouble again.'

'I was at the Hotel Grand Europe last night,' Misha replied, ignoring him.

Ivan gave him a look. 'Not in those clothes I hope.'

Misha looked down at his worn leather jacket and faded denim jeans and shook his head.

'Look, things are opening up... all this talk of glasnost and... what was the word our new general secretary has been using?'

'Perestroika,' said Ivan, swallowing the last of his pastry and reaching for a third. Misha beat him to it. 'You think it will last? How many fancy policies have you seen so far that have come to nothing... zero?' Ivan added, unimpressed.

'We're free to travel...'

Ivan shrugged a *so what*?

'Don't you see? We have a huge opportunity.' His

friend just didn't think big enough. 'Start with the basics,' Misha said enthusiastically. 'People are crying out for everything… clothing… fashion, for instance.'

'And what do you know about fashion? Jeans and T-shirts, yes, but…?' said Ivan disbelievingly.

'Jeans? What do you mean? You can hardly get your hands on a pair, let alone anything decently made.' He looked at his own, where the stitching had come apart at the seams.

'Last night I talked to an Italian fashion manufacturer trying to find a way into the market. From the lookbook it seems right… perfect, in fact, and the price works. I've decided to pay him a visit, go direct… cut out the middleman.'

'And how do you propose to bring it in? You can't trust a carrier or customs.'

'Hand luggage… you're strong.'

Ivan pulled a face.

Misha pushed back his chair and stood up. He counted out some coins and put them on the table.

'Are you in?'

'Of course, you know me… I just hope I don't live to regret it.'

'You won't… I'll see you later. I'm going Gleb hunting.'

CHAPTER 6

Gleb hung out in only a few places. It didn't take long for Misha to find him: he was holding court in the back of one of the faceless cafés that nestled under the graceful and neglected ochre apartment buildings of Pirogova.

Misha counted two minders: one outside as he went in and a second at a nearby table just out of earshot of his boss. Misha ordered a tea while he waited for Gleb to finish with his current visitor, a wiry-looking middle-aged man busy leafing through a slim zip-up briefcase he had opened on the table. He teased out a sheet of paper, studied it briefly and handed it to Gleb, who examined it with a magnifying glass before nodding, satisfied with whatever it was. The minder caught Misha's eye and gave him a warning look.

Misha raised his cup and toasted his health.

Two minutes later the man with the briefcase left.

Misha lifted his tea and took it over to Gleb's table. Bearded with thick, heavy glasses, Gleb folded a wad of roubles and dollar bills and slid them into his front pocket.

'What can I do for you, Mikhail Dimitrivich – another internal travel permit?'

'Not this time – two exit visas and an import permit. How long will it take?'

'Three to four weeks,' said Gleb flatly.

Misha pulled a face. 'Two. No more.'

Gleb stared down at the table and rubbed his cheek. 'You could wait months if you used normal channels.'

'But I'm not.' Misha looked at him expectantly.

'Okay, but it will cost – one hundred a visa and the same for the import permit, half up front, US dollars.'

'Roubles?'

'Not interested. You know how it is.' Misha knew no self-respecting black marketeer wanted to be holding the rouble. He counted out one hundred and fifty dollars, handed them to Gleb and left.

Outside, Misha looked at his watch: seven thirty-five. He took the metro south and got off at Narvskaya.

Block upon block of anonymous sixties' apartment buildings stretched in every direction. Groups of youths loitered at apartment entrances and derelict exercise yards. A prostitute, who called herself Lily, waved as he passed and signalled he had company. Out of the corner of his eye he caught sight of a tall wiry teenager with a shaved head a few paces to his left. The crunching of grit alerted him of another to his right. Misha slipped his fingers through a knuckleduster deep inside his jacket pocket and spun round to face them. Better, he calculated, to confront them out here in the open than be jumped down some side alley or stairwell.

'Good evening, comrades.'

The two stopped a metre apart and a few paces behind. He hadn't had sight of the teenager's friend until then. Misha guessed him early twenties, a little shorter than his partner with the same shaved head. A snake tattoo curled its way round his forearm and silver studs decorated his nose and eyebrows. Stud-man was clearly the more powerful of the two. Broad-shouldered like a boxer, he wore a plain black sleeveless T-shirt to show off his overdeveloped biceps.

Stud-man took two steps forward and shoved his face inches from Misha's. His breath stank of beer.

'Enough of this comrade shit,' said Stud-man through gritted teeth and he went to grab Misha with his right hand.

Misha stepped back and in one swift movement swept his right leg under Stud-man, felling him heavily like a tree. He hit the ground hard. The knuckleduster broke Stud-man's nose and front teeth as he struggled to get up. Stud-man's friend froze to the spot.

'I suggest you pick up your friend and beat it.'

The boy hesitated until Misha took a few steps back. Warily, he helped a dazed and bleeding Stud-man to his feet and haltingly started back in the direction of the metro. When the two of them had disappeared from view, Misha returned to his course.

It took him only a few more minutes to reach the entrance to his building, a faded brown ten-storey prefabricated block etched with rust marks from broken guttering. An overflow pipe gushed water from the third floor, pooling on muddy ground with nowhere to go.

Ignoring the faulty lift, Misha climbed the five flights to his doorway. The key and a hard shove and he almost fell into the room. He switched on the unshaded light that hung above the kitchen table, walked over to the fridge and extracted a plateful of cold sausage and cooked cabbage. Grabbing a fork from the sink, he rinsed it under the tap, sat down and began to eat. He was hungrier than he thought.

The sound of a key turning in the lock and the door being forced behind him scarcely gave him pause.

'It's security,' Misha said without turning around. Misha felt a large hand grab his shoulder. He lifted the plate of sausage and offered it to his flatmate. Ivan took one and swallowed it in two bites.

'Have another; you need to keep your strength up.'

CHAPTER 7

The tricoloured flag, hanging limply in its wall
mount, identified the elegant three-storey house
as the Italian consulate. Could Italian bureaucracy,
Misha wondered, be any worse than Russian? That
morning, their answer machine giving opening times
had cut off its announcer midstream.

Ivan touched his shoulder and pointed in the
direction of a man in a car parked across the street.

'See, now they make their lists, later they arrest
us… Perestroika is just a ploy to flush out dissidents.'

Misha knew Ivan was only half joking.

Reception was a large tiled area on the ground
floor with sofas and the occasional chair scattered
around. Misha approached the reception desk and
took a number.

They only had to wait a couple of hours, a record
by Soviet standards. Misha threw down the copy of
Vogue he had been studying and the two of them made
their way to the door marked VISAS. He was glad
now he had put on his best and only suit, even if it
was slightly frayed around the buttonholes.

A dark-haired woman in her mid-forties, smartly

dressed, bid them to be seated. The nameplate on her desk displayed the name 'Valeria Gambetti'. He awkwardly straightened his jacket and caught her staring at him over her glasses as a headmistress might a delinquent pupil. The two of them must look very different to the apparatchiks he had seen in reception.

'And what kind of visa is it you are after?' she said in heavily accented Russian.

'Business,' Misha shot back confidently. He knew if he stumbled here it would all be over. 'Clothing… fashion,' he said, before she jumped to another conclusion, 'importing from Italy.'

Misha sensed her reappraising him. Her voice softened. 'You'll need an invitation.'

From a used and scribbled-on white envelope, Misha pulled out a fax from Venti Settembre signed by Luigi Crisi, their sales director.

'*Perfetto*! What else do you have? Passports, photos?'

Misha emptied the contents of the envelope on her desk: birth certificates, passports, proof of residence.

'*Bene*.' She sifted through them, made copies of what she needed and placed them in a file. She filled out an application form and had him and Ivan sign it in black ink.

'How do you want to pay? Roubles?'

Misha nodded.

'You'll be pleased to know you don't have to queue again. Just call again in a week.' She gave him a slip with a number.

Misha and Ivan stood up.

She held out her hand. '*Buona fortuna*! Good luck!'

Misha reached for hers. He would need all the luck he could get.

CHAPTER 8

'I don't know why you don't just take his money. He'd lend it to you if you asked,' Viktoriya said with some frustration. She could not understand why Misha was so stubborn sometimes. She fanned herself with Misha's procurement wish list. The summer heat was sweltering, the city airless. Even sitting at an open-air café on the Moyka made no difference.

'You *know* where he gets his money from. There would be strings attached.'

She shrugged. 'Hasn't the system made criminals of all of us?'

Surreally, a barge drifted by with a peacock on its deck in full iridescent display, its blue-and-green plumage cupped behind it like a shell. The waterman at the tiller waved at her.

'You don't seriously believe Konstantin makes his money through some small black market operation?' he said, more of a statement than a question. 'He's thick with the military here in Leningrad, ever since he got back from Afghanistan.'

'Moneylending, debt collecting...'

'And the rest… prostitution, drugs. No, I'd rather make it on my own… start small.'

Viktoriya looked at her old friend and narrowed her eyes exaggeratedly.

'I'll just have to work harder, faster.'

He would have to, no doubt, she thought. But Misha was not entirely wrong. She had stopped asking Konstantin how he made his money. He would tell her nightclubs, debt collecting, unofficial pawnshops around the city. The reality was that she didn't want to know. While Misha ran around on public transport and borrowed the odd vehicle, Kostya ran a fleet of Volgas, had his own large apartment close to Nevsky Prospect and a coterie of bodyguards. By comparison, she had only once ever visited Misha and Ivan's depressing flat share and vowed long ago not to repeat the experience.

'And how are you and Kostya getting along?'

'Good,' she answered ambiguously.

Viktoriya had never told Misha what had happened that night four years ago. Antyuhin washed up in the spring thaw as Kostya had predicted. The newspapers reported a random mugging. Kostya had never demanded anything in return, not put her under pressure; he had been attentive, considerate. It had been a good six months before she slept with him. He had just been assigned to an army intelligence unit and was about to fly out to Afghanistan. She had no idea when she would see him again or even if she would. They had gone to a party together, and while everyone else brought beer and vodka, Konstantin brought cocaine. She had snorted back a line and had sex with him in the cramped apartment bathroom, while people banged impatiently on the door.

'When do you think you can get me those items?' Misha interrupted her thoughts, pointing at the piece of paper flapping in her hand.

She looked down the list: one hundred pairs of jeans, fifty winter coats, three refrigerators, a single and three double mattresses. The list went on.

'A week... maybe two.'

She had her uses too, of course, she thought. Both Misha and Konstantin had recognised an opportunity when she had been appointed as a logistics manager to the main freight haulage business out of Leningrad. It provided Misha access to a whole new network of suppliers, and Kostya the perfect delivery mechanism for his regular shipments from Afghanistan. She was good at her job too. Bit by bit, her director, Maxim, had relinquished day-to-day control to Viktoriya, content with extracting his cut, assured that his private customers received a better procurement and delivery service than the state could provide its own citizens.

Viktoriya felt a nudge in her back. At first she thought the waiter had bumped into her, until she saw the bear-like figure of Ivan waving an envelope at her and Misha.

'The papers...' said Misha, a broad smile on his face.

Viktoriya suddenly remembered the small cylinder in her pocket and padded her jacket to check it was still there. It was a relief to be actually returning it after so many years. For nearly ten years it had lain buried under her mother's floorboards in a plastic bag, almost forgotten. Misha had never asked where she had concealed it, only if it were safe. She wondered why he wanted it now and what had prompted him to bring it out of hiding.

'I have to be going,' said Viktoriya, standing up.

She gave him a hug and slipped the palm-sized object surreptitiously into his hand before turning to Ivan and kissing him farewell on both cheeks.

'When are you off?' asked Viktoriya.

'As soon as I buy the tickets and confirm a time with Venti... I'll need a small van when we arrive back at Pulkova.'

Viktoriya rolled her eyes. 'Let me know your flight details. I'll have someone meet you.'

Misha lent forward and gave her kiss on the cheek. 'I knew I could count on you, Vika.'

'So does everyone.'

CHAPTER 9

MILAN

From his window seat, Misha traced the Neva east to the Gulf of Finland as pasture gave way to conifer and the city disappeared from view. Looking around the inside of the Ilyushin, he hoped its critical parts were in better shape than its visible internal workings. He tried again to fasten his seat belt and gave up. Ivan sat across the aisle in a seat that failed to recline, reading a copy of *Soviet Sport*. Still, he thought, its comfort compared favourably with the last time the two of them were in a plane together somewhere over Afghanistan, not long after their column had been decimated by a mujahideen ambush in some godforsaken valley. He wasn't so sure, though, that it was any less dangerous.

In leather jacket and jeans, Misha considered what an incongruous pair they made in a sea of dark suits. He checked for his shoulder bag tucked under the seat in front. Just about all he had in the world was zipped into the inside pocket.

A tall air hostess with long red hair stretched effortlessly across two empty seats and served him stewed tea from a heavy-looking ornate metal pot. Ivan winked at him. Misha was glad he had brought him. He could not remember a time when Ivan had not been around: fishing expeditions with Ivan's father on a Sunday morning, school, and Afghanistan where his own talent for trading had come to the fore. It was always Ivan who watched his back and kept an eye out for unwanted elements – Russians as well as Afghani.

Malpensa was packed, the lack of Cyrillic confusing. In the baggage collection hall, men in close-fitting impeccably tailored suits, deconstructed tweed check jackets and beautifully cut jeans, milled around conveyors. Women modelled stylish haircuts, trouser suits, short, close-fitting leather jackets, high heels and denim. The contrast with the Leningrad flight could not have been more startling. Russians in poorly fitting, uniform, black wool suits and heavy shoes dragged worn-out suitcases, reinforced with leather and canvas belts, onto airport trolleys. Misha cast a look at Ivan, who he could see was contemplating the same scene.

Luigi had told them to take the shuttle. Three came and went before they were able to get on.

'Well at least they have air conditioning,' commented Ivan once they had found their seats. The June heat was searing. As the shuttle made its way in heavy traffic along the Milano–Varese highway, Misha counted Mercedes, BMWs, top-down Porsches, Fiats and a dozen other makes tailgating bumper to bumper, cars he had never seen before. It was a far cry from back home: antiquated Ladas, punctuated with the occasional ZiL limousine or Chaika parade car.

After forty minutes, the shuttle began to weave its way through Milan's suburbs. Hoardings and billboards boasted breakfast cereals, coffee, electrical goods, and beautiful women with big smiles, hair products and perfume. Ivan pointed at a grocery store with fresh produce on display under a brightly coloured awning. They passed a supermarket and shoppers pushing trolleys laden with food and household shopping.

'Maybe we should stay here,' Ivan said across the aisle.

They had entered a fantastic world, a cornucopia, one which his countrymen were simply unaware existed. And yet, staggeringly, it was only a three and a half hour flight from Leningrad and Moscow. It was as if they had landed on an alien planet.

Ten minutes later, the shuttle pulled up at Stazione Centrale. The driver directed them to a bus stop. They caught the number forty-six, missed the stop, and walked the last two hundred metres to the two-star hotel recommended by Luigi.

Misha's room was small but the bed seemed comfortable enough. He threw his bag on the floor and walked into the bathroom… shower, basin, bidet… he slid open the shower's door and turned the thermostat to hot. Steaming hot water gushed from an adjustable-height showerhead. Impressed, Misha tried to imagine how a four star might compare, and thought of the understated opulence of the Hotel Grand in Leningrad.

They had the afternoon to explore; their meeting was not until the next morning. The receptionist recommended they start with the cathedral. They took the metro to Piazza del Duomo and walked to the vast gothic cathedral. Stained-glass windows cast brilliant blues and reds into its gloomy interior as people prayed openly at altars. They took the stairs to the roof and walked around the terrazzo, taking in the city below and the Alps to the north. Misha unfolded his map and took his bearings from various landmarks.

'This is where we want to head next.' He pointed at an area about a quarter of a mile from where they stood. 'The Quadrilatero, Via Monte Napoleone. It's the fashion district,' he added in response to Ivan's questioning frown.

The fabulous boutiques of the Via Monte Napoleone were a kaleidoscope of plenty and excess, dresses of every style: micro, mini, empire, shirt... in silk, chiffon, linen, tweed, suede and leather; shoes: pumps, flats, sandals and high heels; boots: ankle, over the knee, patent leather and alligator; the catalogue went on. Misha remembered a few names from the magazines he had thumbed at the Italian consulate, but most he didn't recognise: Alberta Ferretti, Pucci, Fratelli Rosetti, Salvatore Ferragamo, Cartier and Bulgari.

Shoppers explored narrow alleyways holding distinctive carrier bags, stopping occasionally to look into beautifully dressed windows.

They stopped at a small elegant café just off the

main street and took a table on the pavement out of the sun. A waiter brought them a menu. Misha counted ten types of coffee: espresso, macchiato, cappuccino, caffe mocha… and a dozen combinations of ciabatta, focaccia, and panini. His eyes lighted on the desserts: panna cotta, lemon polenta cake, tiramisu, and cheesecake. He ordered an espresso doppio and Ivan a cappuccino. They both decided on the strawberry cheesecake.

'Makes a change from Stefan's,' said Ivan, scraping the last of the froth from his cup with a spoon.

'No queues either, except outside that store.' Misha pointed to a line of Japanese girls waiting patiently outside Salvatore Ferragamo.

*

That night, Misha slept fitfully with his canvas bag tucked under his feet. In the corridor, people came and went. A couple made love noisily in the adjacent room.

In the morning, a shower and breakfast quickly restored him. From the buffet, Misha selected cereal, fruit, ham, cheese and crusty panini rolls. Not bad, Misha thought, for somewhere Luigi described as *basic*.

Not risking the underground system this time, they took a taxi to San Babila. Venti was easy to find. A young receptionist in a sleeveless, patterned silk top and pencil skirt brought them coffees.

A shout of '*Benvenuti*' echoing down the marble corridor announced the arrival of their host.

Luigi shook them warmly by the hand and asked them in broken English how they were finding Milan so far. Misha could have spent the next hour telling him but simply said 'Good'. Luigi flashed him a sympathetic smile.

'*Bene, Bene,*' was all he said and guided them down the corridor to the lift and first-floor showroom.

A tall olive-skinned model wearing a T-shirt, jeans and pumps greeted Misha in perfect Russian and introduced herself as Ilaria Agneli. This would make life a lot easier, he thought

Misha took out his camera – an old Zenith – and a notebook.

'Do you mind?' he asked Luigi.

'No, no, please,' said Luigi. 'Ilaria…?' He looked in her direction and she nodded.

She was a perfect fit for the collection. Disappearing and reappearing from the changing room, Misha simply voiced a *no* or *yes*. A *no* and she would quickly try on something else. A *yes* and she would stand there while he took pictures and chose fabrics. The more he saw, the more he thought the collection perfect for the Russian market. Venti expressed the latest catwalk styles at a price even the average Russian woman could afford. He tried his best to contain his excitement. And this was only *one* label. With more research he was sure he could find others. Ivan sat next to him sipping coffee, taking it all in silently.

At one point he caught Ilaria studying him as he made a note. Self-consciously Misha remembered how his fellow passengers had struck him at Malpensa, how poorly dressed they seemed in every sense of the word. He looked down at his ill-fitting jeans and clumpy matt leather shoes and felt embarrassed, humiliated. The Soviet system had at best failed its citizens and at worst deceived them, him included. He had had some inkling; after all, he was a street trader dealing in shortages. It was the scale of the lie that hit him now. The past two days had been a revelation. He no longer wanted to be a member of the great deceived. He wanted to experience the everyday, like these Italians. More than that even, wasn't he only scratching the surface? There was so much more to learn.

He was suddenly aware that the room had fallen silent and they were waiting for him.

'May I comment?' said Ilaria in Russian.

'Please,' he said. Luigi looked from one to the other, no doubt wondering what his visitors were saying.

'The colours you are choosing are very bright. I know we have *Roberto Cavali*, but Italian style is mostly about neutrals.'

'Yes, I can see that, but my guess is Russia has had enough of neutrals for a lifetime. Grey is the Soviet's favourite colour – almost everything is painted one shade or another: apartments, offices, factories… tanks. Russians love vibrant colours, ornate churches, and gold cupolas, pink and blue houses. They just haven't experienced them for a while. No, I think it's time for a change. Russian women are going to express themselves, like they haven't for generations, show off… we Russians are not a subtle people.'

And saying it out loud, he knew it was true. The new general secretary had opened the door... just a fraction... and if one had the courage to venture out, you would see the world as it is, not as you had been told.

Sitting there in his shabby clothes, he suddenly felt a lot better about himself. Ivan placed a hand on his shoulder. He was the modern-day explorer on the threshold of great discovery.

'*D'accordo*,' she said.

He could see that his conviction had hit home. She blushed faintly.

'Please, feel free to input. What you said was helpful.'

Ilaria quickly began to get the drift of what he was looking for. Subtle it wasn't – figure hugging, often short and overtly sexy it was.

Mid-morning, they took a break. Leaving Ivan struggling to converse with a young female showroom assistant, Misha grabbed a coffee and made his way over to Ilaria, who had just appeared from the changing room wearing the jeans and top she had arrived in.

'What part of Russia are you from?' he asked.

'I'm not. I've never been to Russia. My mother's Russian and has always spoken to me in her home language, but she left before I was born. To be honest there hasn't been much use for it until now.'

'You know a lot about fashion?'

'This isn't my full-time job. I'm a student, or I should say *was* a student at the Milan College of Fashion. I've just graduated. My mother and father are both buyers at *Rinascente*, one of the big retail groups.'

Misha took another gulp of coffee, trying to weigh up whether he should put the question to her he had in mind.

'Are you free for dinner tonight? I go back to Leningrad tomorrow.' He could see her hesitating; being asked out by showroom clients must be an occupational hazard, he thought. 'A business proposal,' he added, trying to reassure her. He saw her relax a little.

'And you can practise your Russian. You name the time and place'

'All right,' she said, giving in. 'Eight this evening.' She suggested a local restaurant not far from where he was staying.

For the next two hours she changed in and out of another dozen or so styles. Finally, they finished. He reckoned up the order.

'Are you going to pay in cash?' Ilaria asked him in Russian. 'You could probably get another 15 per cent off these list prices.'

From his satchel Misha extracted a wad of neatly bound US dollar bills, in varying denominations and condition, each totalling one hundred dollars. He stacked them carefully on the table and pushed them forward. He was making a bet with his entire life savings.

'Ask for twenty-five.' Misha gave her her due, she didn't hesitate in relaying his offer in Italian. Luigi punched at the calculator in his hand; more, Misha thought, to give himself time to weigh up his offer. It was a simple choice: cash up front, no risk, no agent's percentage, a direct sale into a promising new market – his first Russian customer.

'And tell Luigi that if this goes well I'll be back and I'll want exclusive distribution rights for his line in Russia.' Misha was looking directly at Luigi as he spoke.

Luigi put down the calculator. 'Did I tell you where I met Michael, Ilaria?' said Luigi. She shook her head. 'At the bar, in the finest hotel in Leningrad, doing his homework, talking with businessmen, picking their brains... I think he'll go far. *D'accordo!* Twenty-five per cent.' He grinned and held out his hand. They shook on it.

Misha counted out the agreed amount and pointed to several empty canvas bags next to Ivan. 'Please pack the order in these. We'll be back at eleven tomorrow morning to collect.'

Leaving Ivan to do his own thing, Misha spent the latter part of the hot afternoon absorbing Milan. He wished he had allowed himself more time now, time to map it all out: high street to high-end boutique.

He stopped outside a men's store. A beautifully cut suit had caught his eye in the window. He stood staring at it, hesitating. It struck him as strange that he didn't have to be a high party member to go in. In Milan he was as entitled as anyone. A smartly dressed doorman standing inside opened the door for him.

'Can I help you, sir?' asked a sales assistant the moment he stepped onto the marble floor. He was mid-twenties, Misha guessed, and wore a close-fitting black suit, white shirt, black tie and patent black leather shoes.

'I am from Russia,' said Misha in heavily accented English, hoping it would explain everything.

Misha pointed at the black suit in the window. The sales assistant led him over to the suit rail and, guessing his size, unhooked one.

'This is the same as the one in the window: *Zegna*, an excellent make. Would you like to try it on?' Misha tried not to wince at the price on the ticket.

Twenty minutes later, Misha left with a new suit, two white shirts and a new pair of soft leather shoes. It was an altogether new experience. The sales assistant could not have been more charming or the quality of clothing more extraordinary. He felt embarrassed thinking about the suit hanging on his door at home and determined to give it away at the first opportunity.

Back at the hotel, Misha wrote down everything he remembered while it was still fresh in his memory. By the time he had finished it had already turned seven fifteen. He quickly showered and changed into his new clothes. Standing in front of the wall mirror, he was shocked at how different he looked. Gone was the rough-looking young Russian; before him stood an entirely different character, well dressed, Italian style. He squared up to the mirror, ran his hands through his still damp, vaguely long fair hair, and over his unplanned designer stubble. The jacket fitted his broad shoulders perfectly, tapering at the waist. He tugged down his white shirt cuffs, leaving an inch or so showing, copying the way the mannequin had been dressed in the window. Any lingering uncertainty about spending so much money evaporated.

At a little before eight Misha seated himself at the bar of the restaurant where they had agreed to meet. He ordered a *Peroni* recommended by the bartender and wondered what Ivan was up to. Italian women, he knew, would have been his first priority. Sat there, facing the bar, enjoying his drink and air conditioning, Misha reflected on the last two days, the experiences it had brought and how a three-hour flight had delivered him to a new world, unimagined. The sound of a Russian female voice behind him jolted him out of his reverie.

'Penny for your thoughts,' she said.

He turned round. Ilaria was wearing high heels, black leggings and a diaphanous black silk top. Her hair was no longer fastened back but fell straight on her shoulders, her eye make-up subtle but smouldering.

He could see her taking in his new attire, reappraising him.

'*Zegna*,' she said, looking at his suit; a statement not a question. He was impressed.

He ordered a glass of Soave from the bartender as she swivelled onto the stool next to him, crossing her long legs only inches from his.

They touched bottle and glass.

'Ilaria,' he said trying out the name.

'Mikhail Dimitrivich.' She had heard Ivan use his first name and patronymic in affectionate frustration during the afternoon session.

'Misha… that's what my friends call me.'

'Misha then,' Ilaria repeated, introductions settled. 'And what do you think of Milan?'

'How long have you got? It is difficult to take in how much you have of everything... back home even basics are hard to come by... even things like shoes,' he added, thinking of the shoes he had brought with him, another item he vowed never to wear again.

'Back home,' he said again, his expression hardening slightly, 'there are shoe shops but often there are no shoes. If you find a pair that fit you, if you are *that* lucky, you buy them; if they don't fit, you buy them anyway and advertise a swap for your size in the newspaper.' He could see her struggling with the reality of what he said. 'Ask your mother, but maybe it was better back then.' Her expression softened a little.

'And what about pere—?'

'Perestroika... before we had a bad plan, now we have no plan. Shortages are worse than before... much worse.'

'But you have been allowed to travel. My mother told me how difficult it was in her time to leave. Isn't that a change?'

'Yes. It's just that hardly anyone has woken up to the fact, or they don't believe it will last... and maybe it won't. People fear that the hardliners will seize power again, especially now, when there is little sign of progress... they should see Milan! Maybe that would change their minds. The opportunity though is huge, for those willing to step into the vacuum.'

'Are you?' she asked.

'I'm here. That's a start.'

The restaurant owner arrived and led them to their table. Misha followed Ilaria, this time without the added complication of having to decide whether to buy what she was wearing.

Ilaria translated the menu for him. She described food he had never encountered before. In the end they plumped on bruschetta to share as a starter and seafood risotto and pumpkin ravioli as a main. Ilaria choose the wine – a dry white Verdicchio.

'And your mother, how did she get to be here?'

'She was a member of a choral group that travelled to Italy in the sixties. She met my father after one of the performances at a party and the rest is history.'

'And she's never been back?'

'No. She still has relatives in Perm. Her parents died some years ago.'

'That must have been hard.'

'She doesn't talk about it much. Somehow she put it all behind her, put down roots and a family here. Do you have a family back in Leningrad?'

Misha shook his head.

'My father was a refusenik.'

Ilaria frowned.

'He was Jewish… trained as a doctor. The authorities refused him permission to emigrate and then stripped him of his job. I only have vague memories of him. He found a job as a street cleaner and a month or two later was arrested for supposedly making a joke about some communist official… six years hard labour in a gulag. He died pretty much broken a couple of years after his release and my mother two years ago.'

'I'm sorry,' said Ilaria.

'Your mother was lucky.'

'Yes… and your friend?'

'Ivan is as close as there is to a brother to me. Our mothers met in the play park when we were barely out of prams… school… conscription… Afghanistan… you name it.'

Misha took a bite of the bruschetta that the waiter had placed between them.

'This is really good,' he said, and took another bite. It tasted so fresh. 'And the modelling, did you find them or they find you?' he said, changing the subject.

'Spotted at a college fashion show. Only showroom stuff, though, and the odd bit of catalogue work. This isn't my career of choice. But it neatly fills the financial gaps. It's good for contacts, though.'

That was something Misha did understand; if you didn't have *svyazi*, you were nowhere.

'Which brings me to the reason, the official reason,' he corrected himself, 'I invited you this evening. Would you be a buyer and fashion coordinator for me, run my Milan office, not that I have one at the moment… set it up? I can't promise to pay much to start, but as I've said there is a massive opportunity here, and not just one.' He had already begun to think of other possibilities. Wasn't Russia short of just about *everything*?

'To the Soviet there is no such thing as a *consumer*, only the proletariat, but when the *proletariat*,' he said mockingly, 'start spending…' He didn't finish the sentence. 'There are fortunes to be made… if you can leverage the system.'

'And what about you?' she cut in, half teasing.

'Oh, the biggest fortune of them all, of course,' he said, joking. It was not something he had thought about in any depth until now; making money yes, but not serious money. They fell silent for a moment. 'But not until you accept this job. That will be the first step. It will be hard work. As I say, not much pay to start… we wheel and we deal.'

'So, what do you think, Ilaria?' Misha knew he was taking a risk with someone he hardly knew, but he decided to go with his instinct as he had on so many other occasions.

'Do I get a contract or anything?'

Misha took a serviette and wrote down a number and signed it.

'Will that do?'

She looked at him, slightly embarrassed, before breaking into a broad smile.

'I think that will do fine. When would you want me to start?'

'Tomorrow. I'm heading back to Leningrad in the morning. If this goes down as well as I expect, I'll be back on the phone to you in the next few days and you can put together the next order with Luigi.

'And one more thing.' He reached into his inside pocket and fished out two small 35mm film cassettes.

'The shots from today?'

'Not quite.' He handed her the new-looking film case. '*These* are the photos from today. Can you get them back to the showroom and developed by eleven tomorrow morning?'

She nodded.

'And this one…' it was obviously a lot older than the first, the casing duller. 'Do you know a private photographer who could develop this? Eight by tens. Some of them may be partly exposed.'

'Yes, of course.' She looked at him questioningly. 'A bit cloak and dagger?'

'Maybe, but the less you know about this the better. When you speak to the photographer, make sure he understands you want the negatives and all the photos back. He's not to keep any copies.'

'Can I ask what they are of?'

'To be honest, I don't know, but the people who have been after them don't play around.'

CHAPTER 10

LENINGRAD

The return flight was uneventful. A distance that under the old Soviet had seemed almost infinite was suddenly commutable. Still, Misha did not think the average Russian would be making the journey any time soon.

In the baggage hall at Pulkova he and Ivan stacked six tightly packed canvas bags on two airport trolleys and pushed them towards the military customs point. An officer waved them over to a long steel table.

'Your declaration,' he said abruptly, snapping his fingers. Misha handed over the list of items and the invoice from Venti.

'Import permit?'

Misha handed him the permit. The officer looked at it briefly.

'Unzip the top bag.'

The custom's man rifled through its contents, glancing occasionally at the permit. He held it up to the light.

'This permit is a forgery. You will need to leave these bags here.' He handed back the invoices.

That nagging doubt about Gleb came to the fore. He shouldn't have trusted him.

'Come to my office. I will take your details. There will be a fine to pay,' he said, indicating a glass-paned wooden box.

Misha folded a fifty dollar bill inside the invoice and handed it back to the customs officer once inside the dingy cubicle.

'Officer, I am sure if you look again you will find this permit in order.'

The officer sat down, unfolded the invoices, pocketed the dollar bill and stamped the declaration approved.

'There you are, that's all in order,' he said. He pointed at an import permit taped to the cubicle window. Misha could see the difference. A large watermark in the shape of an asterisk was missing.

'You have my address' said Misha. 'If your girlfriend or wife would like an outfit, she can have her pick.' Misha wrote down his telephone number.

'That would be good, comrade,' the officer said, pleased with the added bonus.

'That Gleb, he's a chancer,' said Ivan as they wheeled their load through to Arrivals. 'You could have had the whole lot impounded.'

'Well I can assure you he is not going to get away with it.' Misha had to have people he could rely on, not risk losing everything because someone tried to shortcut him.

Ivan's friend Rodion met them at the exit. They piled the bags into the back of a heavily scratched and dented van with the words 'Leningrad Freight' on the side and squeezed themselves into the front. It didn't take long to negotiate their way through the city. They stopped at a building just east of Anichkov Bridge. One of Ivan's security contacts had suggested it, a small nondescript manufacturing unit that was no longer manufacturing. Alina, Rodion's girlfriend, had already assembled mobile clothes rails around a large empty office.

The three of them unpacked one of every style, while Misha wrote out and affixed price tickets. The main stock they sorted tidily on shelves in the second room. It was early evening by the time they finished. Misha decided to stay the night and slept on an ex-army canvas fold-up that Rodion seemed to procure from nowhere.

Next morning, Misha had Ivan put word out on the street that a fashion consignment was newly arrived from Italy, and by the afternoon the shelves had been cleared at many times the price Misha had paid. Only the sample styles remained hanging on the rails. Alina, who had been helping, look frazzled; the morning had been a free-for-all, with traders jostling each other for attention.

He counted her out fifty roubles. 'I have another job for you, if you are interested. I want you to go visit those people who left empty-handed and then the ones who bought, take advanced orders, 25 per cent upfront, US dollars, balance on delivery, 10 per cent for you, all right? Just traders – we need volume.'

Alina nodded enthusiastically. 'I'll be on it as soon

as I finish this coffee.' She was clearly pleased with the turn of events. 'When are you going to bring in the next order?' she asked, putting on her jacket.

'Let's see how you do on the sales side.'

Misha went out onto the street and found Ivan smoking a cigarette in animated conversation with Rodion. He handed him a wad of dollars.

'You were right about Gleb. I could have had my whole consignment impounded. The End. And I've been thinking... I do need security, plenty of it. I have a good feeling about all this – better than that. How about you running that for me... security? You know how it works. You've got contacts... Rodion, for instance.' Misha mentioned a figure in US dollars many times what he was making trading CDs on the street and nightclub security work. 'And you won't have to be sharing digs with me forever, not on that! What do you think?'

'Seems like I'm about to get paid for what I've always done for free,' he said smirking. 'Okay.'

'Good,' said Misha, delighted. 'Have we still got the van?'

Ivan pointed down the street at its tail poking from a side turning.

'Right... first job.' He looked at his watch – three thirty.

'We'll take the van, drop off the money at the lock-up, and then pay a call on Gleb.'

They parked one hundred metres down from the café. Misha recognised Gleb's man standing on the doorway. The three of them climbed out of the van and broke up, taking different directions. Ivan approached the café from the left, Rodion from the right and Misha from across the street. The guard on the door had no time to react. Rodion felled him with one blow to the solar plexus. He let out a loud *ouff* sound and collapsed onto the pavement. Inside, Ivan grabbed hold of the second minder, bending his arm behind his back and spinning him around so that his face was pushed hard against the rough plaster. Gleb, startled, jumped to his feet as Misha stepped forward, kicked over the table and punched him hard in the face, breaking his glasses. He fell heavily to the ground, gushing blood from his nose. Misha bent down, prised open Gleb's front pocket and extracted a wad of dollar bills. He counted out $300 – the price he had paid – and threw the rest back at him.

'I like to think I'm a reasonable man, but you let me down badly, Gleb. I could have lost my entire life savings, such as they are.'

Gelb stared at him. 'What do you want?' he said finally, trying to stem the bleeding with a handkerchief.

'Exit visas and import permits, real ones, free for the next six months. I'll send my man. Let me down and you won't live to regret it.'

FEBRUARY 1987

CHAPTER 11

SOMEWHERE BETWEEN VELIZH AND CURILOVO, 100 KILOMETRES NORTH OF SMOLENSK

'So, what happened?' Colonel Yuri Romanavich Marov asked the two men.

One of them pointed at a fallen tree, fifty metres ahead; it had been pushed into the roadside gully. By its size the colonel estimated it would have blocked the entire highway; the freighter would have had no chance negotiating a way round it. He walked over to a pile of freshly made sawdust and idly kicked his boot through it.

'They hit us with machine-gun fire the moment we stopped. The driver died instantly. We managed to make it to the forest. We got one of them.' His friend pointed at the twisted body in the middle of the open road not far from the fallen tree.

Yuri looked up at the MTV hovering overhead, momentarily blinded by its spotlight. He looked down at his watch, letting his eyes adjust to the darkness – one in the morning. Ten heavily armed soldiers formed a perimeter around the scene, facing outwards. Yuri walked over to the trailer-less Kamaz, slewed at a forty-five degree angle across the road. It was a wonder anyone had survived. The cab was riddled with bullets, its windows shattered and tyres shredded.

He nodded at the soldiers standing next to the two men to lower their weapons.

'They hooked up the trailer to a new truck.'

A sergeant searching the clothes of the dead man came up empty-handed.

'How many men?' Yuri asked.

'Eight... ten? It's difficult to say.'

'And what colour was the hijackers' truck and the trailer?'

'Red and orange. Their car was a dark sedan of some sort. I didn't get a clear look.'

'And what time did they hit you?' asked the captain.

'Ten forty-five, it must've been around then.'

One of the soldiers handed Yuri a map.

'What do you think, Captain? They must be somewhere within this circle.' The captain nodded agreement. He was probably twenty-seven or twenty-eight, thought Yuri, maybe only five years younger than himself. 'Order the other MTV to search here.' He pointed at the map. 'We'll take this highway. And, Captain, they are not to engage until they have orders from me.'

The captain turned to the radio operator and

passed on the new order to his lieutenant some twenty kilometres to the east in the second helicopter.

Five minutes later they were airborne again. Keeping low, the MTV followed the highway north towards Usvyaty. The Klimov gas turbos made normal conversation impossible. Yuri noticed several soldiers nod off, rocked by the motion of the MTV as it clattered through the night sky. A corporal idly stripped and reassembled his Kalashnikov, trying to outdo the private opposite.

The voice of the reconnaissance officer from the second MTV cut into his headset, loud and clear against the low-level shushing of white noise.

'We have sight of a cargo freighter, red cab, orange-topped trailer, dark car following... five men in the car.' He read out the coordinates. The flight captain tilted eastward and pushed the MTV to maximum speed.

'Rendezvous fifteen minutes, Colonel.'

Yuri ordered the second MTV to maintain a discrete distance and track with infrared.

'Captain, I want Lieutenant Ryzhkov's platoon to take up a position ten kilometres to the north on the M20 just above Pustoska.' Yuri read out the map reference. 'They are to stop them there. Remind him, Captain, they are heavily armed, probably ex-army. He is not to underestimate them... and let's try not to damage the trailer – not if we can help it,' he added wryly. He could only guess what the manifest was really worth... no doubt many times the number he had seen on the import papers.

The two MTVs deposited their cargo of soldiers at the reference point, touching down lightly before heaving away into a velvet black sky. Back up at fifteen hundred feet, bent over the infrared scanner edging the reconnaissance man aside, Yuri studied the scene below. This was going to be the captain's action. He had decided not to intervene. Soldiers unwound a heavy belt of three-inch spikes across the road while the sergeant stood in the middle, barking orders. The rest of the platoon fanned out along the highway as two snipers took up firing positions fifty metres behind the barrier. Yuri imagined them checking their night-sights, making last-second checks: safety catch, ammunition, a clear line of fire. One of them stood up and moved five metres to the left and settled back down again using a boulder to steady his aim. Ten kilometres to the south his MTV picked up the small convoy of two vehicles moving steadily towards them.

'There's a vehicle behind them, Colonel, two kilometres,' said the second officer, not taking his eyes off the ground radar.

'Inform Captain Chekhol,' was all he said. It was up to the commanding officer on the ground now.

He glanced back at the scanner and the ground directly below; nothing moved. They must be able to hear the sound of the diesel by now. His thoughts drifted back to the Peshawar Valley. He and another group of men had lain in ambush for a band of mujahideen, staring into the blackness, straining every sinew for any sound or sign of movement. There had been no overhead support then, no infrared scanners.

'Target one kilometre!' relayed the helicopter reconnaissance officer to the field radio operator on the ground. Yuri didn't have to look at the infrared to see the truck and its escort move swiftly below. The third vehicle had closed in behind and was trying to pull past them.

'Two hundred metres,' chimed the reconnaissance officer mechanically. 'Man and child in small sedan.'

They would die if they got caught in the maelstrom that was about to be unleashed.

Over the radio he heard the captain's voice. 'Snipers… at my command, third vehicle… tyres only.'

Through his headset Yuri caught the almost imperceptible growl of a fast-approaching vehicle. Suddenly the smaller vehicle pulled out from behind the sedan. Yuri watched it accelerate. It was level with the hijacker's sedan now.

'Snipers fire!'

Tyres shredded, the small sedan spun wildly out of control before crashing side-on into the trees. On cue, machine-gun fire ruptured the night air. The juggernaut surged over the chain barrier and began to swerve erratically. Yuri watched it cross the narrow roadside storm gully and ram a tall pine. The second car slewed to a halt fifty metres behind. Dense black smoke drifted skyward. The helicopter shifted position.

For a moment, everything freeze-framed, even the smoke pouring from the diesel engine seemed static, as if painted by a broad brush onto a perfect tableau.

Yuri was tempted to bang the scanner when someone below hit the restart button. The car's rear doors flew open, followed by the front. Four men tumbled to the ground. A hijacker rolled over and took aim at Yuri's MTV. There was a clunking of metal on metal as heavy ammunition ricocheted off the fuselage. The MTV turned. The flight captain's finger moved towards the weapons' control system as four men jumped to their feet and sprinted towards the woods. One died instantly, blown back against the now burning car a second before he reached the roadside. The survivors hurled their AKs into the undergrowth and threw themselves on the ground, arms outstretched.

Yuri's helicopter landed downwind of the acrid smoke. A soldier helped a man and young boy out of the wrecked Lada. Across the highway the two survivors were handcuffed and hauled to their feet.

'Give me their wallets, soldier,' said Yuri when he had come up to them.

Yuri pulled out a wad of roubles.

'Give this to him.' He pointed at the man climbing into the second MTV with his son.

'Casualties, Captain?'

'None, sir.'

He walked over to the trailer and waved for a soldier to open it. With a torch he began examining boxes. Soldiers stopped what they were doing and watched as he began shifting them around: computers, CDs. He stopped and smiled, delighted. He grabbed one box and then a second, passing them down to the nearest soldier from the duck board.

'I hope your men like Chivas Regal, Captain...
off-duty rations! Captain, that was an *excellent* night's
hunting.'

CHAPTER 12

LENINGRAD

Vdovin passed Konstantin a box of Cuban cigars. He took one, bit off the end, struck a match and lit it. Konstantin gave the cigar a long pull and exhaled in the direction of the general seated across the desk. He glanced up at a photograph of the general secretary looking down on them benevolently and back at Vdovin.

'Do you think he'll last?' Konstantin asked, wondering idly whether the general's jacket would burst its seams.

Vdovin shrugged. 'Glasnost, now perestroika. *We need democracy just like we need air to breathe.* Stirring stuff,' he scoffed.

Vdovin was *so* old school. Konstantin thought back to when he had first met him – 1983, Kabul. The general was a colonel then, head of the intelligence section and he a low-ranking intelligence officer. He remembered spending the best part of one week tracking the colonel's movements, looking for an opportunity to speak with him on his own. One had finally presented itself – a well-known local brothel reserved for officers. Vdovin was seated at the bar, a shot glass of vodka in his hand, eyeing up three heavily made-up young women. The colonel had barely given him a second glance. To Konstantin the choice was obvious. He had signalled to the youngest and prettiest of the three to join him at the bar. She was Tajik, no more than sixteen, with fine Persian features, brilliant brown eyes and straight black hair. He could still recall the scent of her over-sweet perfume. Vdovin had looked at him annoyed, his choice reduced by a third.

'Colonel, I'll trade you this beauty for ten minutes of your time – my expense.'

The colonel had looked at him quizzically, shrugged and grabbed the girl from him. Forty minutes later he had reappeared, flush-faced, tucking his shirt into his trousers, his jacket over his arm.

'Ten minutes then,' was all Vdovin had said, and he sat down at a table away from the bar. Ten minutes had turned into an hour. He had made drug dealing sound almost patriotic. The Afghanis would be free to grow and harvest their poppy crop in certain areas, and they in turn would leave the Soviet troops in peace. Russian government money would subsidise the farmers and he would manufacture and market the heroin. It was simple. Wasn't the whole military infrastructure at their disposal and intelligence packages given top-secret priority clearance?

In just four years it had made the two of them rich. He had returned to Leningrad and focussed on building his Soviet distribution network and expanding into Europe, and Vdovin had been rewarded with command of the north-west district and two hundred thousand men. He just needed the war to continue, they all did, all those monkeys in the chain: the general, KGB, the army, politicians. The list was almost endless.

The door opened and a secretary brought them two cups of coffee, retired, and shut the door behind her.

'We have a small security problem,' said the general, picking up his cup. 'Some lieutenant at Pulkova Airport nosing around noticed the last shipment and has been asking questions; seems he wants to get in on the act.'

'How did you find out?'

'KGB.'

At least Konstantin thought he could rely on KGB self-interest.

'They think you should deal with it.'

'Wouldn't it be easier to shift him to front-line duties?'

Vdovin shook his head.

'Okay.' Konstantin decided there was no point in arguing.

'And there's another matter, highly sensitive, they think you can help them with.'

Konstantin wondered who the '*they*' were that Vdovin constantly referred to.

'How well do you know Mikhail Dimitrivich Revnik?'

'We went to secondary school together. I bump into him occasionally. I haven't seen him in months. Why?'

'Well, the KGB want to take this offline. They think he has something they are after... sensitive photos, a roll of film, taken some years ago. You know the KGB, they won't elaborate.'

Konstantin shrugged.

'I'll make some enquiries.'

'You are to hand over anything you unearth intact – no copies.'

'I get the picture.' Not even he would pit himself against the KGB. It had a long reach and an equally long memory.

Konstantin got up to leave.

'Before you go... there's another big offensive underway.'

Not another doomed expedition, Konstantin thought. Success was only ever temporary. No one seemed to learn.

'There may be some disruption to our delivery schedule,' the general continued.

'General, that's for *you* to figure out. I have important customers waiting. I'm sure you can make it happen, offensive or no offensive.' He wasn't going to allow Vdovin off the hook.

'I'm sure I can organise something,' he replied, looking uncomfortable.

Konstantin was sure he would. This was business as usual.

'General, *you* do your job, *I'll* do mine.'

CHAPTER 13

NOVGOROD

'Mother, why don't you move back into the city,' Viktoriya asked, already suspecting the answer. It would be so much easier if her mother moved to Leningrad. She could get her a job at Leningrad Freight. Her mother had just turned fifty-five, was still attractive, but had had no particular man in her life, not since her father had disappeared. She imagined her mother happier that way. Her father had only made her mother's life a misery – sober for days before hitting the bottle and more often than not turning violent. Perhaps she didn't trust herself to make the right judgement again.

'It would be nice to be near you, darling, but you are working and no doubt busy in the evenings, as you should be, and I have my friends, my sister, all here. I think I'll stay put for now, but maybe later…' She kissed her daughter on the cheek. 'And how about you, is Agnessa still living with you?'

'No, she moved out last month. She moved in with her new boyfriend.'

Apart from Konstantin, Agnessa had remained the only person who knew what had happened to her that night. It felt odd to be living alone.

Her mother handed her a cup of tea. She took it over to the window and looked down onto a small square surrounded by a tall yew hedge. A workman busied himself with a wide spade clearing snow from a footpath towards a large circular flower bed that lay fallow at its heart. She watched his breath billow as he moved the spade back and forth, pausing occasionally to marshal his handiwork neatly at the path's edge.

'I like it here,' her mother said, gazing out of the window with her. 'I have everything I need... *and* you come and visit me.'

Viktoriya kissed her mother and took her nearly empty cup back over to the sofa she had been sitting on five minutes before. The apartment was a reasonable size, with a separate bedroom and double bed, a small kitchenette and a good-sized bath in the bathroom. The heating and plumbing worked too, as did the lift to the third floor... at least more often than not.

'And what about that boyfriend of yours – Kostya? He was always a handful, that one.'

'Still is... I don't know about *boyfriend*. We still see each other,' Viktoriya said, smiling. And in fact they still did see each other... occasionally on a more intimate level. She would finish back at his place or hers after a night at one of his clubs or a party.

'Well, be careful, Vika. You know what I think.'

'Yes, Mother, you don't have to repeat it. He's not like you think. He's always been a good friend.'

'And Misha… such a nice young man?'

'You know Misha, always up to something. No, he's doing fine.' Better than fine, she thought. 'He's not the street trader you remember.'

Her mother took a seat on the sofa. Her smile had disappeared. She tugged anxiously on the hemline of her dress.

'What is it, Mother?'

'There's something I've been meaning to talk to you about. I didn't want to raise it on the phone… I've heard from your father.'

'Father?' she said, shocked. She hadn't seen or heard of him in over ten years. Part of her thought, even hoped, he might be dead.

Her mother nodded.

'He has written me a letter.' Her mother unfolded a sheaf of paper from her pocket.

'What does he want?' With her father, it could only be bad news.

'Money… He says he's stopped drinking, found a labouring job with a building cooperative but has got himself into debt. Could I help him out? He says he'll pay me back.'

Viktoriya knew her mother had little in the way of savings. What spare cash she did have, Viktoriya had sent her, despite her mother's protests. She always maintained she didn't need it, but Viktoriya knew otherwise.

'Where is he living?'

'Leningrad, Smolninsky district. You haven't seen him?'

'No. I thought he'd left the city... How much?'

'Five hundred roubles.'

Five hundred roubles was over six months' pay for her mother.

'He asked after you.'

Viktoriya felt she did not owe her father anything; he had only made their lives wretched, but she didn't want him worrying her mother either, and this was something she could take care of, easily – pay him off and get shot of him.

'Mother, I'll take care of it.'

'That wasn't what I intended.'

'I know. But, really, I can handle this.'

MARCH 1987

CHAPTER 14

LENINGRAD

Misha drove his fourth-hand battered red Zhiguli into the icy courtyard behind his new premises, a nineteenth-century three-floor construction on Malaya Morskaya. Outside, a team of workmen busied tearing rusting balcony railings from first-floor windows and replacing them with modern glass balustrades, while another repaired lintels and the façade ready for painting. He parked to the side of the Kamaz, got out, and admired his car for at least the third time that day. Two men standing guard with Kalashnikovs acknowledged him as he approached.

'Rodion, where's Ivan?'

'In the warehouse, boss,' replied the taller of the two, waving the barrel of his machine gun in the direction of the warehouse door.

Men ferried merchandise past him from the truck. He stopped one of them and lifted up a neat compact box labelled Amstrad.

'If only I could get more of these,' he said. The

handler looked at him blankly. Misha replaced it on the trolley and continued into the warehouse.

Ivan saw him first. He was fifteen metres down the main aisle, talking with the warehouse manager who was busy ticking off items from a clipboard.

'Do you have the number of the agency you were talking about the other evening?' he asked him, deadpan.

'I do,' he answered with an amused look. He reached inside his leather jacket, extracted his wallet, retrieved a business card, and handed it to him. 'Leningrad Angels, and they are, truly.'

Misha looked at him blankly, and without saying a word he put the card in his back pocket. He climbed the steps two at a time to the first floor and stepped into the main building. Elegant rooms with long ornate French windows looked out onto the courtyard below. In one, a painter was put finishing touches to the new showroom. Half a dozen brands hung neatly grouped around the walls. Misha switched on the accented spotlights and turned the dimmer for effect.

Alina walked in with a cup of coffee and handed it to him. Misha recognised the two-ply cream cashmere roll neck from a new Italian supplier.

'Ilaria has been on the phone for you.'

He nodded. 'I'll call her back.' He twirled the dimmer again. 'Beats the old place.'

He took a sip of boiling hot coffee and winced at its bitterness before taking another. Below, two men with AKs slung over their shoulders lingered in front of the high steel gate. Misha watched as Rodion walked up to one of them and said something.

He turned back to the room and took the card Ivan had given him out of his pocket and looked at the graphic outline of a topless angel. He dialled the number. A woman with a sing-song voice answered the phone and asked him how he had heard of Leningrad Angels, did he have any *preferences*? 'A *friend*'... '*attractive*', and '*two*' was all he said in response, slightly disappointed with himself when nothing more definitive immediately came to mind. He agreed the money – US dollars of course – and gave her the name of the new restaurant: Canali, next to the Mariinsky Theatre.

How much was it all going to cost this time, just to open a currency account?

That morning he had appeared at the bank laden with small gifts and had asked to see a manager. He had sat there for an hour and a half mesmerised by the *clack clack* of a hundred typewriters and the elongated *zip* of the carriage return. A legion of clerks, sitting at grey metal desks, typed forms in triplicate. Eventually a manager had appeared. Heavyset, in a dark grey ill-fitting suit, Misha guessed him to be in his early forties. He had introduced himself as Grigory Vasiliev and led him to a wooden and frosted-glass cubicle.

'How can I help you?' he had asked, distracted. A clerk had entered without knocking and placed a form in front of him to sign.

'I want to open a foreign currency account, US dollars... to pay suppliers,' Misha had continued when the clerk had left. He chose to omit the bit about siphoning money off to a Swiss account.

Vasiliev had simply stared at him.

'You'll need Central Bank permission… three to four months, if you are lucky.'

That was when he had suggested dinner.

Misha made it to the restaurant earlier than planned. He took the Zhiguli and parked it on the embankment. As he stepped out of the car a sudden gust of Arctic wind forced him to take a step back. He grabbed the iron balustrade and looked down onto the canal. He shivered. Ice stretched in every direction, a silver filigree knitting snow-covered island to snow-covered island. A man wrapped up in a wool blanket, standing next to a bucket, stood over a hole cut in the ice holding a fishing rod in one hand and a lantern in the other. He wondered if he'd had any luck.

Canali made Misha feel he was back in Milan. Konstantin had done a good job, no doubt with input from Viktoriya. An open, custom-built, stainless steel kitchen gave on to a limestone floor dining area, where low lighting illuminated exposed brick and discretely placed tables.

At the bar, two women sipped champagne while balanced on elegant cream leather stools. The blonde caught Misha's eye as he stepped down into the restaurant from the entrance. No doubt the *Angels* he had ordered, he thought. She introduced her raven-haired friend as Sveta and herself as Dasha. Misha guessed them both around twenty. They were certainly dressed for the part. Dasha wore a short black tube dress and Sveta a diaphanous gold-coloured loose blouse over leggings. Misha took two envelopes from his inside jacket pocket and gave one to each.

No sooner had he finished explaining that he and, by implication, they were entertaining a business associate did the door open and Vasiliev appear. Gone was the ill-fitting crumpled suit Misha had seen in the bank. Grigory wore an expensive-looking three-piece under a half-open navy wool coat. A man of many parts, thought Misha. Grigory looked over to the bar, caught sight of Misha chatting to the two girls, and raised his hand in acknowledgement.

Vasiliev took an instant liking to the blonde Dasha. The girls turned out to be well educated and from cities east of Moscow; occasional escort work at university had gravitated to full-time after they had moved to Leningrad. They could earn more in one night than they could in a month in some boring and grim state factory or office job. The punters, they said, generally had more going for them than the loser boyfriends they had knocked around with in the past.

Outside, an old lady carrying an almost empty string shopping bag caught Misha's eye as she walked, stooping, past the side window of the restaurant. When he returned his attention to the group, he found Sveta studying him.

'I don't want to end up like her,' she said seriously.

'Well that makes two of us… Come on, let's eat.'

The maître d' led them to their table. Misha had asked for a private corner. As it turned out, it was a quiet night. Dasha sat opposite Vasiliev – who insisted on being called Grigory – and Misha, Sveta, whose long legs stretched under the table, occasionally brushing his.

They ordered food and a good bottle of Georgian wine. Dasha rarely broke eye contact with Grigory, constantly running her jewelled fingers through her long hair, flirting outrageously. Grigory was clearly enjoying himself. Why wouldn't he! Misha thought. Sveta sat quietly taking it all in.

'So tell us more about your business,' said Grigory, turning to his host.

'Import, about to move bigger into export... fashion, perfume, computers, you name it.'

'You have a tie-up with Leningrad Freight, I understand.'

'Yes, you are well informed.' He wondered how well informed. Did he know he was also bringing in merchandise across the border at Smolensk to avoid the prying eyes of the military customs in Leningrad?

Misha felt the tip of Sveta's high heel rub against his leg. She looked at him across the table in a steady gaze and smiled. It was hard not to be aroused. She was striking, now he looked at her again, with thick, straight shoulder-length hair, high Slavic cheekbones and wide, dark oval eyes that sparkled in the subdued restaurant lighting.

It was after coffee that Misha asked the two girls if they could wait at the bar while he talked to Grigory privately.

'Pretty girls, Grigory.'

The banker added his confirmation. 'Will they be staying?' he asked, clearly afraid Dasha might leave.

'That depends,' said Misha. 'What will it take to open that foreign currency account within the next two weeks?'

'Two thousand US dollars.'

Nothing came cheap, thought Misha. 'How about one thousand dollars and Dasha stays?' he countered.

Grigory considered the proposal.

'I'm interested in long-term business relationships,' said Grigory. 'I appreciate this might not be the case with Dasha.'

Misha watched Grigory take a sip of brandy and replace his glass slowly on the table.

'Can I ask you what you want to use this account for?'

Misha considered giving him a flat *no*, but the banker would have access to his account anyway. He'd see what he was doing, or at least guess.

'A number of reasons: firstly, paying overseas suppliers – the business is getting too big now to be making payment via suitcases; secondly, the rouble is headed in only one direction as far as I can see… who wants to be holding a currency worth less and less every day; thirdly, moving money to safer jurisdictions; and finally, receiving hard currency payment for exports.'

'Exports?'

'Hard currency assets: timber, fuel, nickel… oil. So I've told you about what I am after, what is it you want? Beyond Dasha, and, of course, helping me open a currency account.'

Grigory took another sip of his brandy.

'I am a banker. I've worked for state banks

overseas, London for three years. I know how money works. You've been to Milan. It doesn't take a genius to work out that Soviet banks are antiquated and that most have *no* idea how the international system works. There is opportunity in that.'

'Okay,' said Misha, warming to him. 'Like *what* specifically?'

'Investment banking... currency trading, for starters.'

'Well, the second part we can start to do now... once you have that foreign currency account open. Investment banking...?

'Buying state property... companies when they start selling them. It's going to happen.'

'Let's talk more, later, who knows...'

Grigory looked pleased with where the conversation had gone. He paused before asking: 'And why don't you get yourself a decent car; that red Zhiguli parked on the embankment is yours, isn't it?'

'I like it,' Misha answered defensively, and laughed. 'I think we should join the girls now and not waste any more time!' Misha looked at his watch; it was still only ten fifteen.

Misha stood up and Grigory followed him over to the bar. The girls were standing close to each other. Dasha leaned towards Sveta and whispered something in her ear, and whatever it was caused her to almost choke on her drink. She put down her glass on the bar and covered her mouth, her slim body shaking with suppressed laughter. Misha eyed her skinny frame balanced on pin-like stilettos and slipped his arm around her waist. She leaned back against him. His thumb massaged her hip through the silky fabric of her top as they watched Vasiliev and Dasha collect their coats. Dasha gave her friend a knowing wink before disappearing through the door, her escort in tow.

'Your place or mine?' said Misha, suddenly impatient to be in bed with her.

'I think yours. It *has* to be better than mine,' she said, squeezing his hand. He helped her on with her grey woollen coat and noticed its frayed edge around the lapel.

'You'll have to call in at the showroom, choose some samples,' he said, holding open the restaurant door for her. They were hit by a blast of freezing cold air.

'How long have you had this?' Sveta asked teasingly as she walked around the red car in mock admiration, avoiding the icy snow banked up on the kerb.

Misha considered how long it had taken him to acquire his first car and how many strings he'd had to pull to find this one, even if it was a hundred years old. He knew he could afford a much more expensive model now he was beginning to make serious money, but he didn't see any point in attracting unwanted attention, either from the authorities or the criminal fraternity.

'All I can say is that it's colder inside than out.' Misha walked round the car, tugged the door open and watched her slide in. When he turned back, he nearly stumbled straight into Konstantin. He was standing almost directly behind him, Viktoriya on his arm, three bodyguards behind him.

'Nice car,' said Konstantin.

'So everyone keeps telling me.'

Viktoriya stepped forward and kissed him on both cheeks.

'Misha is not into the cars like you are, Kostya.'

'Clearly not.' He pointed at the ZiL parked fifty metres away. 'You should get yourself one of those. And take my advice, you shouldn't be walking around on your own, not in this city.'

Viktoriya and Ivan had been nagging him about the same thing. He had doubled protection at the warehouse but he didn't want a band of men following his every movement.

'You probably need it more than me, Kostya. What's that old joke about paranoia?'

'Quite,' said Konstantin frostily. 'We should talk business, you and I, soon.'

'I think we're better off doing our own thing.'

'Pity, you need allies, we all need allies. Shall we go, Vika?'

'She's very beautiful, Misha,' said Viktoriya, casting a glance into the car, a wry smile on her face.

'I do my best. She's probably frozen by now.' He looked in the car. Sveta blew a cloud of iced vapour at him. 'I rest my case.'

Ten minutes later, Misha stopped outside his new apartment. Sitting there gazing up at its newly painted neoclassical façade, he sensed Sveta was considerably more impressed with it than she had been with his car.

'Your friend back there is very beautiful... old girlfriend?'

'Funnily enough, she said the same thing about you... no, school friends.'

'Really... I'm not so sure... and I know the other guy – owns that restaurant and a pile of clubs. You don't want to be mixing with him.'

'Good advice... I won't be.'

He felt the warmth of her delicate hand run down his inner thigh and up onto his crutch. Misha leaned forward to kiss her, only to be pushed back by an outstretched index finger.

They took the lift to the fifth floor. She leaned back against the mirror as he slid his hand inside her coat and ran his fingers down the outside of her silky leggings. This time she did not pull away. The over-warm corridor smelled of new paint and varnish. Sveta slipped off her coat and hung it over her arm as Misha inserted the key to his apartment door. The barrel lock sounded its familiar double dead clunk; Misha pushed open the door and waved her ahead. She eased past him, heels clipping the wooden floor, her body brushing his. Misha turned his head towards the switch and glimpsed the silhouette of a fast-moving object crashing towards his skull. He raised his hand reflexively. Sveta screamed, and whatever it was connected solidly with his head, triggering a fire-burst of yellow light and... blackness.

The first thing he experienced when he came round was a sharp stabbing pain to the left side of his head above his ear. He reached up and felt a sticky wetness. It was pitch black. For a moment he struggled to recollect where he was. His flat… a girl… Sveta. He pushed himself up onto all fours. The sharp pain turned to an insistent throb; unsteadily he climbed to his feet. The room began to swim. He squatted down for a moment and was violently sick. Struggling back on his feet he edged forward until he felt the wall. It took him a few seconds to find the light switch. He clicked it on.

At first he didn't see Sveta, but then at the end of the hallway, jutting out through the half-open living room doorway, he noticed her feet twisted at an awkward angle, one shoe partially detached hanging by a strap twisted round her ankle. Misha struggled along the hallway using the wall as a prop and pushed open the door. Sveta looked up at him with blank unseeing eyes, her neck terribly twisted.

The living room had been ransacked. Drawers lay empty and upended, contents strewn across the floor, the bookcase emptied a brand new computer he had brought home to experiment with, missing. The bedrooms and kitchen were more of the same. Even the contents of the freezer had been emptied onto the kitchen floor.

Misha stopped, walked back into the living room and looked at the sofa. It was on its side. The photographs... He ripped off what remained of the hessian underside of the sofa and came up empty-handed. He searched again, this time checking the floor in case the envelope had fallen out inadvertently or been abandoned. Nothing... they were gone.

CHAPTER 15

'Am I completely surrounded by idiots?' spat out Konstantin. He peered closely at the four black-and-white photographs: two men standing by a waterway, the prints heavily fogged, it was impossible to make out any discerning features. He couldn't imagine they would be of use to anyone. 'At least we have the photos, if not the negatives,' he added, somewhat placated. Maybe the KGB would get off his back now. He looked at the glass-domed clock on the mantelpiece of his study – a quarter past one in the morning. Bazhukov hovered apprehensively in front of him.

'Who was it?'

'Erik Fyodorvich Harkov.'

Konstantin shrugged; he didn't recognise the name.

'He's not one of our crew, hangs out with Stef. A break-in merchant... I thought this was going to be straightforward.'

Konstantin let out a guffaw. 'We have a dead prostitute, a man assaulted, a flat trashed and the police involved. It's hard to see how it could be more complicated. You will have to deal with Harkov. We can't have Mikhail Dimitrivich, the police, or anyone else tracing him back to us.'

Bazhukov nodded.

Why couldn't the KGB take care of its own affairs? Why involve him? He wondered why with all their resources they had never managed to find these photos before.

'Where did he find them?'

'Inside the base lining of the sofa.'

Konstantin wondered if Mikhail knew why these photos were so important.

There was a knock. Viktoriya appeared in the doorway, her hair dishevelled from being in bed.

'I heard voices,' said Viktoriya, her voice throaty from sleep. Her eyes went to the photographs in his hands. He replaced them on his desk, face downward.

'Misha is being questioned at the police station on Liteyny Prospect. Apparently some scuffle at his apartment, and that girl we saw with him is dead... He's fine, apparently a little concussed... I would have told you later.'

Viktoriya frowned uncomprehendingly, shaking off her slumber.

'Misha wouldn't have *anything* to do with that.'

Konstantin felt a stab of jealousy. Why did she *always* defend him?

'I'm sure it's just a formality. His apartment was turned over...'

He could see her hesitating, undecided as to what to do. 'Call him tomorrow from here or your apartment. I'll have one of my men drop you off early if that's what you want. Let's go back to bed. I'm sure Mikhail will not be up to much tonight.'

She relaxed a little. 'You're probably right. Yes, if someone could drop me back early that would be good.'

Konstantin gave a silent gesture of dismissal to Bazhukov. Konstantin slid his hands inside her silk robe and followed the curve of her stomach. She moved closer to him and kissed him on the mouth.

Konstantin looked into her eyes and not for the first time that night felt himself aroused.

CHAPTER 16

'Erik Harkov.' Ivan said when Misha finally emerged from the police station.

'Who?'

'The man who did this… How's the head?'

Misha reached up and touched the clean dressing; his head still throbbed.

'Fine… How do you know it's him?'

'I had you followed. Rodion recognised him leaving your building. He's a petty criminal, used to hang out on the islands.'

'I thought I said I didn't want any protection.'

'*God keeps them safe who keep themselves safe*. Besides, anything happens to you and we are *all* in trouble.'

Misha looked at his watch – two fifteen in the morning. He had been questioned for over two hours. The police had emptied the entire contents of Sveta's handbag on the table in front of him and rummaged through its contents: two hundred dollars, three condoms, a make-up bag, fifty roubles and a business card for the Angels escort agency. It was clear what she did. *Had there been some dispute over money, a service he had demanded that she hadn't been prepared to provide? What and trash his apartment into the bargain?* he had replied. He'd been attacked and had no idea why. At least, not one he would share with them.

'Where does this Harkov live now?' asked Misha.

'Fifteen Sovetskaya.'

'That was quick.'

'Friends in high places…'

He pointed at the Lada parked on the corner. Misha could see Nestor at the wheel and Rodion sat beside him gesturing with a lighted cigarette. Life going on, he thought. Anger welled up in him for the girl who had been killed. She was no innocent but she hadn't deserved such a fate.

★

Sovetskaya was a sixties' concrete apartment block in the east of the city. Misha climbed out the rear of the car and took the beany out of his coat pocket and pulled it down gently over his bruised ear and dressing. Nearby a dog nosed rubbish by an open bin. It stopped and watched a man enter the building opposite before resuming its business. The dull thud of a door closing echoed down the street.

'This is it,' said Ivan pointing at a building with an outsized '15' painted above the main entrance.

Here and there, lights burned in windows; an old lady on the second floor looked down at them.

'Nestor, you take the rear,' ordered Ivan.

The stench of urine overwhelmed them when they entered by the main entrance.

'Rodion, you wait here,' said Ivan. Rodion held up a scarf to his face.

'Thanks, boss.'

Misha followed Ivan up the concrete stairwell, suddenly conscious that the shoulder of his jacket was covered in dried blood. They stopped for a moment before moving on to the next floor. A black shape scurried by, glancing his foot. Involuntarily, Misha kicked out and caught the tip of its thin tail with his boot.

On the fourth floor a flickering fluorescent light illuminated the plastic number '25'. Ivan pressed the doorbell. A grinding sound escaped from the mechanism. A door opened three doors down. A woman peered out before closing it again quickly.

Misha put his eye to the small square frosted-glass door panel of number twenty-five and banged the door loudly.

'Who is it?' It was a woman's voice, high and anxious.

'Ivan Antonovich Pralnikov and Mikhail Dimitrivich Revnik,' Misha said, trying to reassure her. 'We've come to ask you some questions about Erik Fyodorvich.'

'I've already spoken with the police,' she answered, making no move to let them in. Misha looked at Ivan. There was no way the police could have found out about Harkov.

'I doubt they were the police...' There was no response. Misha sensed her thinking on the other side of the door, her hand resting on the catch, trying to decide. 'Look, if those people get to your partner first... well, I wouldn't want to be in his shoes.'

For a moment Misha thought they might have to put their shoulders to the door and force it open, but the rattle of a security chain being unhooked and bolts being slid back signalled otherwise. The door swung open and a short young woman with mousy hair in her early thirties stepped back to allow them in. She directed them into a small living room furnished with a fading brown tweed sofa, a coffee table and small plastic-topped dining table with two pine chairs. The three of them pretty much filled the space.

'Thank you,' said Misha, appreciating that the presence of two men in such close quarters must be intimidating. 'We are trying to locate Erik,' he went on. 'This is his address?'

She nodded.

'I don't know where he is though,' she said. 'I've only known him a few months.'

'Is he from Leningrad?' asked Misha.

'Kalinin, I think, although he never calls or has any calls from family there... I shouldn't be talking to you really.'

'Have you any idea where he might be?' said Ivan.

'No, he pretty much keeps himself to himself,' she said, pulling her dressing gown tight around her. She looked exhausted.

'Where did you meet?' Misha asked.

'At the Imperial on Kirpichny. It's a nightclub. He promised we would be moving to a new apartment...

That doesn't look like it will be happening any time soon now.'

Misha felt sorry for her. He guessed she had no part in this but had been caught up in it anyway.

They fell silent. Misha looked around the room. On the coffee table, next to a half-empty cup of cold tea, stood a photograph in a metal frame of three people standing in front of a fountain smiling broadly at the camera. Ivan recognised the girlfriend immediately, looking a lot happier than she did at that moment, with two men standing either side of her. The girlfriend caught him looking at the photo and picked it up.

'This is Erik,' she said, pointing at the man on the right.

'And who is this?' said Ivan, indicating the other man.

'Stef Baturin, a friend of his, someone he used to work with years ago. We met him one Sunday afternoon for coffee. He lives somewhere in Oktabrsky... more than that I don't know. Wait a minute. I might have his telephone number, I wrote it down... in my diary I think. He had just moved, and I was the only one with pen and paper at the time.'

The young woman rearranged her dressing gown.

'Wait here,' she said, and disappeared from the living room. She returned a few moments later with her handbag. From inside she pulled out a small diary and began leafing through it; recognising an entry, she paused.

'Here you are. This is him, the man in the photo.'

She read out his telephone number. Ivan took it down.

'And you think he lives in Oktabrsky district?' he asked her again for confirmation. She nodded.

'Look, here is my number. If you think of anything else, let me know... and thank you,' Misha said sympathetically. For a moment he thought she might cry.

'We need to find a phone box,' Ivan said once back in the car. They found one after a couple of blocks. Ivan jumped out of the car. Misha checked his watch – three fifteen in the morning. Rodion lit another cigarette and took a long drag. Misha's head had at last stopped throbbing. What he really needed now was a strong black coffee – not the best for concussion, he knew. Ivan climbed back into the car.

'Thirty-three Fonarny pereulok, flat seventeen. It's registered to a Stef Baturin, mechanic... no previous record for subversive activity,' Ivan informed him for good measure.

They crossed the frozen Fontanka and followed the embankment. Five minutes later, they pulled up a couple of blocks down from Baturin's apartment building.

Ignoring the lift, Misha took the stairwell with Ivan. At the third floor, bent over with his hands resting on his knees, Misha signalled Ivan to stop while he caught his breath. Seventeen was only two doors from the stairwell. This time they were going to be less polite.

Ivan handed Misha an automatic and released the safety catch on his own.

'You remember how to use this?' said Ivan, a faint smile on his lips.

Misha nodded. After two years in Afghanistan it felt almost second nature. He put his ear to the solid door. Inside he could hear muffled voices arguing in a panicky staccato. Ivan nodded at him. In unison they took one step back and rammed the door with their shoulders. Three hundred and eighty pounds of bone, flesh and muscle tore the inside lock from its fixture, snapping the door chain in two.

The two of them all but fell into the unlit apartment. Ivan found the light switch first as Misha darted into the living room... nothing. By the time he turned around, Ivan was already pushing a man, dressed in a scruffy T-shirt and boxer shorts, into the living room. He was Harkov's friend from the photo.

'So where's your friend? We haven't time to be nice,' Ivan said threateningly.

'I don't know what you're talking about? Who sent you?' he said breathlessly.

'The good guys.' Ivan slapped him hard around the face. 'Where is Harkov?' Before he had time to respond, Baturin's eyes gave the answer away.

'The fire escape!' shouted Ivan. 'Move from here or make a call, you're dead, is that clear?' Ivan swept the side of his Markov across the top of Baturin's head, knocking him to the floor.

The door to the fire escape from the living room was unlocked. Harkov could have only gone two ways: up or down. Misha shouted down to Rodion, and with Ivan right behind him he took the fire escape to the roof, covering the three short flights in less than twenty seconds. Unexpectedly, Misha discovered his second wind.

At first they didn't see him. Misha and Ivan stood stock-still searching among the TV aerials and electrical service boxes that peppered the flat roof. Ivan waved his gun in the direction of a large water tank. Misha went one way and Ivan another. The sudden crunching of shoes on asphalt alerted them that Harkov had broken cover. He dashed from behind the tank and sprinted across the rooftop to a doorway giving onto the internal stairwell. Barely missing a step, Harkov disappeared into the building. He was faster than they would have credited and kept just one flight ahead as they hurtled towards the downstairs lobby.

At the third floor a figure stepped forward from an apartment doorway. A gun exploded. Misha dropped to one knee and shot Baturin in the chest. Ivan was already past him. He could hear him pounding down the stairs.

Jumping over Baturin's lifeless body, Misha raced after Ivan and the echo of descending footsteps. The thud of a heavy door being shoved open and then a second told him he had escaped onto the street. Misha skidded into the entrance hall, ran past a dazed Rodion, prostrate on the hallway floor, and punched open the half-open plate glass door. East down Fonarny, Misha spotted Ivan in close pursuit of a clearly flagging Harkov.

Misha saw the flash of the car's headlights first. A

black Volga, its windows down, lurched from the kerb, U-turned and, fighting to find traction, slewed past him in the direction of the two runners. Ivan turned at the sound of spinning tyres and threw himself to the ground as the flash of two AK47s ruptured the night in an ear-splitting staccato. Harkov's last expression was one of terror and disbelief. The gunfire stopped as abruptly as it had started. Misha stood there, frozen, staring at the receding taillights as they faded into the night.

'Who was that?' asked Ivan as Misha helped him to his feet. He looked over at the lifeless body of Harkov.

'I'm not sure. Looked like one of Kostya's cars. It was a private Leningrad plate. Can't be many of those. I've memorised the number.'

CHAPTER 17

Two security guards watched Misha's car draw up outside Konstantin's club. It had just turned two in the afternoon. Misha had managed to get a few hours' sleep at Malaya Morskaya while one of Ivan's men traced down the car registration plate.

'Are you sure this is a good idea?' said Ivan. 'You know what he is like.'

Misha had to agree that turning up unannounced on Kostya's doorstep was not necessarily the best plan, but he was not about to duck the fact that Ivan had tied the Harkov murder to one of Kostya's cars and, by implication, to Sveta's murder.

'Just pretend we are at high school… with guns,' he answered, climbing out.

'Boris, Pyotr,' Ivan addressed the guards as they pulled open the door for them and pointed to the back stairs.

Inside, more men, all armed, sat at empty tables; the club did not open for a few hours. One of them stepped in Misha's way and told Ivan to wait before escorting Misha down the back stairs.

Konstantin was sitting on a sofa at the far end of the room. A dark-haired girl got up and walked past him and out of the door, her deep brown eyes momentarily holding his as she passed him.

'Misha, you've not been here before,' he said, gesturing him over.

Misha took in the oak-panelled basement room, the large mahogany desk, green leather armchair, the sofa and coffee table, and the wall of books. He was struck by the lack of natural light; only a single ceiling lamp suspended over Kostya's desk and a table lamp by the sofa provided any illumination.

Konstantin flicked his head in the direction of the man who had escorted him down. The door closed behind him leaving Misha and Kostya alone.

Misha took Konstantin's desk chair and swivelled it around to face him.

'With your capacity for maths,' Misha said, eyeing the books behind Kontantin, 'I don't know why you didn't do something more worthwhile.'

'Like rocket scientist?'

'Precisely.'

'You and I know there is not enough money in it… So what do I owe the honour of this unexpected visit?' Konstantin was staring at his matted head wound. "A coffee if you want it, but I don't think that would be very good for concussion."

"Harkov," Misha said.

Kostya gave him a blank stare and shrugged his shoulders.

'Am I supposed to know him?'

'I was there when your men took him out.' Misha recited the registration number of the vehicle.

'Do you think I memorise every registration plate?'

'Well, take it from me, it's one of yours.'

'And if it is, so what? Wasn't he the guy that killed that hooker-date of yours? Wasn't that justice?'

'I've never thought of you as big in the justice department… looks more like a failed cover-up and a botched burglary. Harkov worked for you.'

He could see Konstantin struggling to control himself.

'You really don't know how lucky you are,' he spat out. 'If it wasn't for me…' but he didn't finish.

'So *you* stole the photos?'

'Such as they are. I don't know what all the fuss is about… but you have rubbed some important people up the wrong way. I wouldn't want to be in your shoes.'

'Who?'

Konstantin shrugged again and rose to his feet.

'That's for you to find out. Interview over. And don't let me find these ugly rumours on the street… or these other people, they will be the *least* of your problems.'

CHAPTER 18

The temperature had dropped to minus twenty. Two men seated at the far end of the café, a bottle of vodka between them, watched Viktoriya as she pushed the door shut behind her. Towards the front, a pensioner dressed in a shabby brown coat, still wearing his sable ushanka, its flaps hanging limply round his ears, chatted to an elderly woman.

Viktoriya walked over to the food counter and examined the paltry selection: three unappetising pastries on a chipped green plate, a small stack of hazelnut teacakes dusted in sugar, and a tureen of thin cabbage soup. The serving woman behind the counter, her hair tied up roughly in a bun, wiped her hands down the front of a grimy apron and waited for her to speak.

'Tea, please.'

Silently, the woman selected a mug and held it under the samovar until it was full.

'Sugar is extra,' she said bluntly.

Viktoriya declined, paid her twenty kopeks, and carried it over to a table facing the front window. She took off her fur hat and padded coat and placed them on an empty chair where she could see them.

A solitary photograph of the previous general secretary, a stern looking Chernenko sporting thick snow-white hair, a blue jacket and a medal pinned to his chest, stared down at her. The glass sparkled in its glossy black frame and round it hung a red-and-silver garland. Viktoriya studied the woman behind the counter again and tried to guess her age: late fifties, early sixties, born in the twenties, old enough to have experienced the siege as a young girl. How different their lives had been. All that sacrifice, and what had it brought her... communist Utopia? She thought of her last visit to Milan. Maybe ignorance was bliss... or at least less bewildering. The portrait seemed ridiculous to her now.

She looked at the wall clock, its second hand frozen at thirty-two; the effort of its upward journey had clearly proved too much: three forty, ten minutes late. Suddenly anxious that this should be over, she fought the desire to get up and walk out. She had no desire to meet her father, even after so many years. His drunken binges had made her and her mother's existence a living nightmare. She remembered the feeling of coming home from school on an afternoon when he wasn't working and the feeling of apprehension as she turned the key in the door. How often had she invited herself round to Agnessa or Misha to put off that moment? Agnessa knew about her father – they lived on each other's doorsteps – but she had never told Misha, she was not sure why, but thinking on it now she was certain he had known or suspected... the absence of return invites, his mother always so welcoming, always asking after her mother, never her father. It wasn't such a big neighbourhood… and that final night, when he had taken the poker to her mother in one of his blind rages. She had fought it from him and cracked him over the skull. That had been the last time she had seen him. He was gone when she had returned from Agnessa's the next morning.

The sound of the café door opening made her turn. A tall figure, a scarf wrapped tightly across his face, stepped into the café and quickly closed the door behind him. He turned looking for someone. His eyes settled on her. Still standing by the door, he pulled off his beanie and scarf and shot her a tight-lipped smile. The serving woman attempted to tidy her hair and poured her father a steaming hot mug of tea without him having to ask. How many years had it been since she had last seen him? Nine, ten, more…?

From where she was sitting he didn't seem to have changed. He still had the same thick thatch of fair hair swept back off his forehead and was as lean and sinewy as he had always been. He sat down opposite her. She was glad he didn't attempt to touch her.

'Been waiting long?' he asked, clearly not intent on making an apology.

'Fifteen minutes.'

'You were always one for being on time, the reliable one.'

He raised the mug of tea to his lips and fixed his icy-blue eyes on her as he took a sip and blew the steam in her direction. 'You've turned into a real beauty. I always thought you would, just like your mother.'

Growing up, most people had commented on how she looked like him, not her mother. She didn't think that had changed. Close up now, she could see the signs of ageing, weathered skin from working years outdoors and the all too familiar signs of too much vodka: thread veins and reddened skin.

'How *is* your mother?'

'She is fine,' she said – *all the better for not seeing you*, she wanted to say.

'Leningrad Freight? Hear you're quite the director's pet... big operation.'

She felt herself blush.

'I'm not here to talk about work.' From her handbag she extracted a small unsealed brown envelope and slid it across the table to him. 'Five hundred roubles – that's what you asked for. You don't have to pay me back; just don't bother my mother – or me – again.'

He flicked through the notes without taking them out and, satisfied, tucked the envelope into the inside pocket of his coat.

'From what I hear, you're doing pretty well there, got a good little business running on the side with that old school friend of yours – what's his name... Konstantin Ivanivich. He was always a nasty piece of work.'

Unlike you, she didn't say.

She could sense where this one-sided conversation was going. 'You'd be best not to start bandying his name around,' she darted back coldly.

'*Pouf...* I'm not worried about that young man.'

He was silent for a moment. 'I've got a job back down at the docks... stopped drinking, you know.'

How many times had she heard that in the past?

'So I heard.'

'The place I'm staying at is pretty crappy though. It's not like the place you have. It's over on Trefoleva, I share it with a family of four... pretty wife though.'

How did he know where she lived? Had he been following her around? She pushed back the chair to leave.

'One minute,' he said, gesturing her to sit. He reached into his pocket and pulled out an official-looking document. It was an old internal passport, badly frayed at the edges. She frowned uncomprehendingly. He flipped open the photo page. It took a second for her to register. Staring up at her was the face of a man she would never forget: Pavel Pytorvich Antyuhin.

'How did you get this?' she hissed angrily. She reached out to grab it but his hand got there first. He slipped it back safely into his pocket.

'Wouldn't be good for this to fall into the wrong hands, have people asking questions... they never did find the killer – nasty business.'

Outraged, she started to say something and stopped herself. She wasn't about to confirm what he did or didn't know.

'What is it you want?' she said coldly.

'More of what you just gave me... somewhere acceptable to stay. I know you can afford it. It doesn't have to be as nice as your place, one bedroom would do fine... after all, I *am* your father.'

CHAPTER 19

MILAN

Misha handed Ilaria a small key he'd taped under the filing cabinet in her office. She looked surprised.

'Put this somewhere safe. Maybe give it to a friend.'

Misha wondered whether he should be giving it her at all. Hadn't somebody already died in search of what the safe deposit box contained? But this was Italy, not Russia, he reminded himself. Yesterday, locked in Ilaria's office, he had pored over four blow-up black-and-white photos with renewed interest: two men – he guessed early forties, similar height, five foot ten, maybe eleven, dark raincoats, one with thick dark spectacles – half turned towards the Neva. The man on the left – the one without glasses – had extended his arm just past his bodyline, his palm open as if denying some point the other was making. Was it 'I don't know' or 'I don't care'? The last shot was of them facing the camera and the man with the spectacles pointing a finger at him. He was shouting: '*Get him!*' Misha could still hear his voice.

He thought back to that April morning ten years ago. It had been raining, he remembered. Cloud had malingered heavily over the city for days, casting a grey oppressive pall over the Neva, turning it a deep black. He had just crossed the Lomonosova Bridge on his way to Apraksin Market, when a man blocked his way. He was taller than Misha's then five foot ten, wiry, intense. He had flashed him some official-looking ID but it was too quick for him to take in beyond a photograph, the hammer and sickle. He waved him towards a café only a few metres away. Misha had held his ground at first as people streamed past them on either side.

'Just a coffee and a chat. I have something that might interest you.'

Curiosity had eventually got the better of him. It didn't look as though whoever-he-was would take no for an answer either.

'What would you like?' the man had asked once inside the café. Misha could remember precisely what he had chosen: sweet tea and honey cake. The waitress had somehow divined his new benefactor's status – perhaps it was the highly polished black shoes or a raincoat that fitted him better than the average raincoat fitted an average citizen, or was it simply his air of confidence or sense of underlying menace? '*Yes comrade*,' was all she said after scribbling down their order and hurrying back to the serving counter. They had sat there in silence and waited. The waitress returned shortly, deposited the contents of her tray and retired safely out of earshot.

'I am told that you are a bit of a chancer around here, up for things?'

Misha shrugged noncommittally, wondering who he was and how he had come by that information.

'If you are interested, I might have a small job for you, something suited to your talents.'

Misha had remained silent.

'There's a meeting taking place, Saturday morning, eleven o'clock, two men... Can you use a camera?'

Misha had nodded. Back home he had an album packed with photos, mostly friends larking around. A third-hand Zenith had been a present from his mother for his fifteenth name day.

'I need someone to get close, close enough to get a clear shot, and you fit the bill.'

Misha had asked if he was to do it how he would identify them, and he had been shown a photograph of a man wearing heavily rimmed spectacles and a fedora hat. He had known better than to ask who he was or why he wanted a photo of him.

'Fifty roubles, take it or leave it,' the man had said bluntly.

Misha stared again at the photo until his anonymous host had leaned across the table and plucked it out of his hand.

'Eighty,' Misha had countered, as the man placed it back in his wallet.

'Seventy.'

He had nodded his assent, not quite believing his luck. It was more than his mother earned in a month. Misha remembered the man pulling a small camera out of his raincoat pocket and handing it to him.

'Just point and shoot. And don't worry about finding me. I'll find you.'

But, of course, ten years later he still hadn't. Things had not gone as intended, but at least he had had the foresight to put a backup plan in place; when his pursuers had searched him they had come away empty-handed.

'Can I ask whose those men are?' said Ilaria, staring over his shoulder.

He had asked himself the same question for years. 'I wish I knew.'

'Why have you held onto them?'

Because someone wants them badly enough, he thought, enough to have ransacked his place, enough to kill for. Months before, Misha had had Ilaria's photographer friend blur a set of prints to abstraction. Whoever had them now, he hoped, would assume he had nothing of value and leave him alone.

'You never know when something might be useful,' he said, 'particularly in Russia.'

From the look on her face he sensed she was disappointed he had not told her more.

'Look, Ilaria, I'm sorry, but I suspect the less you know about these photos the better. The fact is I don't really know any more than you do. You've looked at them – two men standing by the Neva on a wet April morning... period. But whoever they are, or whoever they are involved with, ten years later they are suddenly important again.'

'What's changed?' she said, softening.

'That's it… I can't figure it out… the Soviet Union, Russia, everything is changing, falling apart… why now… the renewed interest… how valuable can a ten-year-old photo be?'

She stared at him for a moment.

'Don't worry. I'll take care of it,' she said, rolling the key between her fingers.

'I think we should go back to work. Can you ask one of the girls to go to Carlo's and fetch me a cappuccino? I want to talk with you about the oil business.'

CHAPTER 20

LENINGRAD

Viktoriya ran a finger over the faint scar under her right eye and searched for her reflection in the steamed-up bathroom mirror. She reached forward and with the palm of her hand cleared a small patch. She stood there for a moment just staring into her own eyes, her father's eyes, trying in some way to see into herself, beyond the superficial exterior. She knew she was beautiful, but that same beauty had got her into trouble, had drawn her attacker too. Maybe it was impossible to see oneself as someone else might. She wondered how Kostya viewed her; time had not made him any more transparent. Was she just the trophy girlfriend – replaceable, expendable? He never shared his fears with her or discussed his business interests... not in any meaningful way. They might spend a night together and the next day she would receive a call from him; he would be in Moscow, Yekaterinburg, Novgorod, or some other place, and would not have mentioned anything about it to her the night before. She had given up asking why. She did not want some veiled excuse, or, worse, be lied to. Was there another woman? She never had a sense of that. Did he have sex with other women? It was hard to believe he didn't. In the sort of places he frequented, he had only to point. Misha was right, of course. You didn't acquire the cars, the property and the standard of living Konstantin enjoyed just from owning nightclubs. Her life felt in limbo, unresolved, uncertain.

Through the half-closed door, Viktoriya heard the phone ringing in her bedroom. It was Misha.

'I thought you were in Milan,' she said, pleased to hear his voice.

'I was. I'm at Pulkova. I landed fifteen minutes ago.'

She looked at her bedside clock; it read 8:10 a.m.

'How about I pick you up in an hour? I need to talk to you about something.'

Fifty minutes later, the concierge called, a Mikhail Dimitrivich was waiting for her in the lobby. He looked a lot better than the last time she had seen him. The bandage was gone and he was bubbling with supressed energy. Outside, three cars lay parked up against the kerb. Ivan and four men with Kalashnikovs covered the space between the lobby entrance and the street.

'Vika!' Misha kissed her on both cheeks, holding her by the shoulders. He looked at her intently, as though he hadn't seen her in years. Did he see something in her that she had been unable to find earlier?

'You look great, Vika.'

He kissed her again and took a deep breath.

'Givenchy,' she said, amused, before he asked. 'You gave it to me. You had a consignment of it delivered to the warehouse, I seem to remember.'

Misha raised his eyebrows. 'Well, it was a good choice.'

As they drove across the city to Malaya Morskaya, chelnoki traders standing alone or in small groups plied their wares on street corners. Here and there, queues were forming; on the Moika embankment, Viktoriya saw women and men stoically wait their turn at a vegetable stall. She thought back to the last time she and her director had visited the central food distribution centre in Leningrad – an oxymoron in itself – how long ago could it have been? A month, six weeks? She remembered the smell of rotting food and rats the size of cats.

'Any more on your break-in and that unfortunate girl?'

Misha shook his head, but she sensed he was not telling her everything; Ivan had been much the same, despite her prodding. And why had Misha flown to Italy so soon after the incident? She didn't believe it was all about business.

They pulled up at the solid steel gate that separated the street from the rear of the building. An armed guard turned to a speakerphone and the heavy doors moved back electronically. Three cars lay on the far side of the oval courtyard, a truck parked at the warehouse entrance. Viktoriya had not been to his office for several weeks; each time she visited it had morphed into something different.

On the first floor a young model showed off a new collection to a group of buyers. In an adjacent room three men sat at desks busily engrossed in telephone conversation. The older of them waved at Misha and replaced his receiver.

'Grigory Vasiliev,' he said, introducing himself. Viktoriya took in the heavily set man, his jowly face and alert eyes.

'Meet our new currency and – soon to be – commodity trading floor,' said Misha. She looked at him quizzically.

'Roubles for US dollars, yen, Deutschmarks… it's just another trade when it comes to it.'

'Perhaps a bit more complicated than that,' countered Grigory, clearly not wanting to be downgraded.

Misha ushered her to a meeting room on the first floor overlooking the courtyard to the rear. A van that hadn't been there when they arrived had pulled in close by the warehouse door. The movement of an armed man on the rooftop caught her attention. She counted at least ten men in the yard. What had happened to the man who never bothered with security? Two men were busy hauling boxes from the rear of the vehicle into the warehouse. The driver skirted round the side of the vehicle trying to get a look in. A security guard blocked his way and pushed him back with the barrel of his gun. She wondered what the van contained that was so valuable. When she turned around she found Misha quietly studying her, a look of faint amusement on his face.

'So what is this *new* idea?' she said, trying to sound enthusiastic. He was clearly inured of her cynicism.

'It's not so new. I've been thinking about it for a while… well, a couple of weeks at least. It was you who planted the seed.'

'Well it can't be all bad then,' she said, sitting up straighter.

'I'm going to register one of these new *cooperatives* tomorrow – you know, private companies by another name. The city gorkom have been pushing me to do something; those communists are not so dumb that they can't smell an opportunity. It's the *how* that baffles them. Nothing is for free; they'll want their cut, of course.'

'To do what precisely,' she asked, intrigued.

'Trade in diesel to start… you've told me Leningrad Freight runs half-empty trucks all over the country to meet some ridiculous quota that has nothing to do with efficiency. Am I right?'

'Yes.' She had been complaining about it since she joined.

'Well *no one* cares about quotas anymore. Tell your director boss that you are going on a maximum economy drive. I want Leningrad Freight to transfer its surplus diesel to our new cooperative enterprise… at cost.'

Viktoriya could see where this was going.

'At the state subsidised price, which is nowhere near the market price?' she filled in.

'Precisely, and we ship it over the border at Smolensk where we sell it for quadruple what we pay for it… in hard currency, US dollars. No loss to Leningrad Freight – they charge us what it cost them. We repay them in six months, a year with depreciating roubles. And the second phase… you start requisitioning fuel in much greater quantity than you use now and pass it through.'

'And if the director won't cooperate…?'

'…the gorkom will lean on him. He'll have nothing to complain about anyway. He'll be looked after, as he always has been. And before you say anything, I'm going to make you a significant shareholder in the new cooperative… I couldn't do this without you, Vika.'

Misha got up from the table and walked over to the window. From where she was sitting she could see another van had taken the place of the previous one, and the same unloading process was underway.

'Come,' he said firmly as if he had suddenly made up his mind about something.

Misha led her downstairs to the ground floor. For an instant she thought he was going to give her another guided tour of the warehouse and show her his latest favourite thing, but instead he pointed to another flight of stairs she hadn't noticed before. She followed him down.

Misha had not said a word since leaving the meeting room. As they stepped around the last curve of the newly constructed concrete stairwell, she was totally unprepared for what she saw next. She let out a gasp. A large open vault door, perhaps six feet in diameter, set in the middle of a recently cast grey concrete wall, stretched floor to ceiling, from one side of the building to the other.

'A *Mosler*,' Misha said proudly, pointing at the name engraved on the vault door. 'One of these even survived the blast at Hiroshima.'

A man pushing a trolley with two of the boxes she had seen being taken out of the van exited the service lift and steered past them and the two armed guards at the strong room door.

'After you.' Misha gestured with his hand, a huge grin on his face.

She stepped inside the steel and concrete sarcophagus; it was a step up from the old lock-up she remembered on the English Embankment. The intensity of the light inside was almost painful. It took a moment for her eyes to adjust. She blinked hard, not believing what she was seeing. In a space as large as the warehouse above, piles of dollars lay on open shelves wrapped tightly in clear polythene. The man with the trolley emptied a box of dollars onto a large counting table, where two men sorted through mixed denominations.

Misha took one of the packets off a shelf and threw it to her. She caught it.

'Ten thousand US dollars. Hold on to that; it will help oil the wheels of our new venture.'

She was dumbfounded.

'It's not all mine... I hold some for other people. I'm officially a bank now – Moika Bank... Grigory's idea.'

She looked around the room again, trying to calculate how much might be sitting there.

'There must be what… fifty million here?' she guessed wildly.

'Not even close! Let's walk over here.'

Misha led her to the back of the vault and a small safe embedded in the concrete wall. Misha spun the dial lock with his fingers.

'Russian dolls,' she said.

'Yes, a safe within a safe. Ivan, Grigory and I have the code for the main vault but this one is just you and me, Vika.'

She stood there about to ask what it contained and the combination number, but he had already turned his back on her and was halfway back to the steel door.

CHAPTER 21

SMOLENSK

Misha rose from the table. He was freezing. A lone paraffin heater struggled vainly to cast off the winter chill gripping the small barrack meeting room and the Arctic air that forced its way past the newspaper stuffed into the gap between the rusting metal window frame and the sill itself. The state of decay only seemed to reinforce the low mood that had set in when he and Viktoriya had landed at Smolensk an hour earlier. Like some ghostly armada, row upon row of rotting aircraft fuselages lined the taxiways and airfield, engines stripped and cavities boarded over, standing there useless, abandoned and desolate, somehow a symbol of what the Soviet Union was or had become. Misha wondered how long it would be before the whole edifice collapsed and whether he would be dragged down with it.

Outside, a soldier shouted something towards the sentry box. In the near distance, snow-capped domes cast themselves against a deepening grey sky and blue and brown high rises. The Dnieper eased its way lugubriously towards them.

'I think I'm going to die of cold,' Viktoriya said, hugging herself for warmth. 'How long do you think he will keep us waiting?'

'We're early,' he reminded her.

Outside, the crunching of tyres alerted them to a jeep pulling up in front of their hut. A young man in his early thirties wearing a padded khaki winter Afghanka and a grey fish fur ushanka climbed out and bounded up the narrow cindered path towards their hut. Misha wondered if he had been sent by the colonel to collect them.

'I see they've put you in the warmest room,' he said with a wide grin on his face. He was tall, perhaps six foot two, broad-shouldered with thick dark eyebrows and close-cropped black hair. His blue eyes darted between him and Viktoriya. The two red stripes and three gold stars on his chest gave him away.

'Colonel Marov?' Misha said, extending his hand.

The young colonel pulled off his gloves and shook hands.

'I think we should go somewhere a bit more comfortable, certainly somewhere warmer. The city is only a few minutes away. I know a restaurant; the food's passable, not great… if you haven't eaten lunch yet?'

'That would be fantastic,' said Viktoriya with obvious relief. The colonel's natural exuberance had already begun to snap them out of their low mood.

The restaurant was warm, hot even. They peeled off their winter coats and hung them over their chairs. A young waitress, recognising the colonel, made a beeline for them.

'Sausage and cabbage with rye bread or hot cheese pasties today, Colonel.'

'Like the rest of the week, Alisochka.'

'The sausage is new, sir.'

Misha noticed that the colonel had used her diminutive name. Alisochka's eyes hardly left Marov's.

'Have you seen the freighter cab yet?' the colonel asked once they had made their choice. 'Not that there is much that can be done with it... spare parts, perhaps.'

On arrival they had been directed to the burnt and bullet-ridden Kamaz in the military vehicle park close to the gate. It was a wonder anyone had survived, Misha thought.

Viktoriya shook her head. 'I doubt even that. Can you dispose of it?'

He nodded.

'You were in the forces?' he said, turning to Misha.

'Conscript, rose to the rank of corporal, two years in Afghanistan, 1981 to 1983, more of a *fixer* than a *fighter.*' Misha reflected on how he had become a sort of unofficial quartermaster with generally more success than the official version at procuring anything from cigarettes to mortars.

'Well, fixing is often a lot more useful, and now... still the fixer?'

'Colonel, you probably have a better idea about what I do than I do.'

There seemed little point in beating about the bush. After all, how many Leningrad freighters had the colonel seen carrying merchandise across the border from Western Europe?

'The last time I looked at a manifest it was computers, fashion, perfume, CDs, players, TVs... and oh, brandy,' he added, almost as an afterthought, a faint crease of amusement on his face.

The door opened, and a man walked in and took a table in the far corner of the room.

'How many men under your command, Colonel?' Viktoriya asked. 'You have quite a border to patrol.'

'Twenty thousand regulars and conscripts,' he replied, as though it were nothing in itself. The colonel turned and looked at the man who had just walked in. He was reading a newspaper, a steaming hot cup of tea in front of him.

He turned back to address Viktoriya.

'And you are a friend of Konstantin Ivanivich Stolin?'

Viktoriya blushed, taken by surprise, not knowing quite how to respond. He had clearly done his homework.

'The three of us all went to school together,' Misha cut in. 'He's the main reason I ship my stuff through Smolensk. He and the local military have Leningrad pretty much under siege when it comes to freight: land, sea or air. You, on the other hand, seem more reasonable, Colonel.'

Misha noticed that the man in the corner had not turned the page of his newspaper.

'KGB...' said the colonel. 'Old habits die hard... at least it keeps them out of trouble.'

'Are you a security risk?' Viktoriya half joked.

'We all are… the question is to whom? There are so many opposing views and factions.'

'And which side of the debate are you on?' Viktoriya asked, trying to regain the initiative.

'Progress…'

The colonel looked at his watch. Misha decided it was time to come to the point. He wished he had more time to get to know him but his gut feeling told him that the colonel was someone they could trust. He hadn't robbed them thus far.

'I think we are on the same side, Colonel. Progress comes in many forms. I provide people what they want… and make a profit – still a dirty word in Russia – doing it. And there are, of course, plenty of people who try and stand in my way. I am sure this is not foreign to you.'

The colonel did not reply but continued listening.

'I am starting a new venture. It has some small but important political backing in Leningrad, buying diesel and oil from state companies and shipping it across the border.'

'At Smolensk.'

'Exactly.'

'And you want my support.'

'Yes.'

'And for me?'

'A stake in the business, a significant stake. I need partners, long-term partners with the same interests. There are going to be plenty of opportunities out there. It strikes me that you are just the sort of person we need… progressive, by your own admission –

not like Vdovin in Leningrad – of a similar age to us, plenty of contacts, and you can organise... like Viktoriya here. I could go on. Weren't you strategic command in Afghanistan?'

'Yes.'

'Graduated top at the General Staff Academy, a rising star until your reformist views had you consigned here. Somehow I don't think you are the sort of person who will be held back long, and in the meantime... this is an opportunity – dare I say *historic* – to make serious money. The smart communists already have a sniff of it, but years of doing what they are told has deadened their senses. The world belongs to our generation now, at least Russia...'

The colonel nodded, stood up abruptly and held out his hand. 'Let me think on it. I have to take my minder for a walk now. It's been a pleasure meeting you both.'

And with that, he and the man in the corner were gone.

JANUARY 1988

CHAPTER 22

LENINGRAD NIGHTCLUB

General Vdovin leaned forward and helped himself to a *Cohiba* from the lacquered box sitting on Konstantin's desk. Dance music interspersed with loud cheering and clapping filtered from the club floor above. Someone wolf-whistled, joined by several others.

'Busy night?' he asked in between puffs of the aged cigar. 'This is very good.' He helped himself to another and put it in his jacket pocket.

'Help yourself,' Konstantin said sarcastically.

Despite the millions he had placed in the general's Zurich bank account, Vdovin still clung to the old dress code: an ill-fitting dark grey double-breasted suit. Konstantin could even picture the store he purchased it from in the GUM arcade opposite the Kremlin, one of those outlets exclusively reserved for party members. It was a joke, ridiculous, that such things were still regarded as a sign of privilege. He wondered which bright bureaucrat years ago had come up with the original design and how many committee meetings he had had to endure while the lapel size and number of cuff buttons were finally determined. Konstantin reached for a cigar himself, and, without lighting it, put it in his mouth.

'There's talk of a pull-out,' said Vdovin.

'We've been here before.'

'*Serious* talk… it's an unpopular war and the new general secretary wants an accord with the Americans. The arms race is beyond the country's means, *he* says… not that it has ever bothered any other general secretary that I have known.'

'And does he have the support to do it.'

'At the moment… but there is increasing internal opposition… not just with his policy towards the *imperialists*.'

Imperialists, thought Konstantin, hadn't the Soviet Union donned that epithet when it invaded Afghanistan? How long ago? Christmas Eve, 1979… at least, the Catholic Christmas Eve when the so-called *imperialists* were waiting for Santa. Brezhnev should have left well alone, but then again he would have missed a huge business opportunity. The drugs business was booming.

'And will they continue to support Najibullah?'

The general shrugged.

'I don't know, perhaps, but I doubt it will be decisive. The Americans have created a monster in the mujahideen. They will tear the country apart.'

And the price of opium sky will rocket, he thought. If Vdovin was right, the general secretary would indeed prove to be a sore in his side. He would have to renegotiate his supply routes and make friends with a whole new circle of tribal leaders, who might not be quite so well disposed to a Russian.

Above, someone had turned up the music. Konstantin looked at his watch – eleven o'clock. He wondered whether the new girl Bazhukov had hired would be on the floor yet. She had been sitting at the bar when he had entered earlier that evening before the club had opened. For some reason he had found it hard to concentrate on Bazhukov's daily update and had found himself staring at her across the room. Wearing a T-shirt and stretch jeans, she was tall with alabaster white skin, jet-black hair, and a wide, sensuous mouth. At first she had ignored him, intent on the men checking out the stage floor lighting. Perhaps she had thought him a punter. It was Bazhukov, sensing his distraction, who had finally waved her over.

'Adriana… meet the boss.'

'Where are you from?' he'd asked.

'Horlivka,' she had replied in a deep, throaty voice. He didn't know the place but recognised her Ukrainian accent. She was older than most of the girls at the club; he guessed late twenties, sexier, more mature-looking.

'First time in Leningrad?'

'She knows Cezanne' said Bazhukov, interrupting. She was another Ukrainian, with a reputation for doing a lot of coke.

Half an hour later she had been ushered down to his office by one of the guards. Wordlessly, he had unbuttoned her blouse and slid his hands under her bra, cupping her breasts. She had stood motionless and looked unflinchingly into his eyes as he had caressed her nipples and then pinched them hard. Her eyes had only closed when he found the moist space between her legs and forced her back on the sofa, roughly pulling down on her jeans and taking her.

'I need a meeting with the KGB chief,' Konstantin said, snapping back to the present. 'In fact, the defence minister *and* KGB.'

Vdovin looked surprised.

'Isn't it best to go through me?' Vdovin said defensively.

'Here in Leningrad or in Moscow, it doesn't matter, just fix it up,' he said, ignoring him. He needed a face-to-face meeting. Go-betweens could only accomplish so much. 'And what about those photographs, thinking about the KGB?'

'*Bah*... much ado about nothing! They're just a blur. You have to wonder why Revnik kept them at all. My KGB contact seemed satisfied, so you are... we are, off the hook.'

Konstantin felt relieved. It had been more problematic than it should have been but the KGB was off his back and Harkov taken care of.

'They wanted Revnik dealt with,' Vdovin added. Konstantin sat up. 'I told them they were misguided; there was no advantage in it. He's become too well connected; it would just stir up a hornet's nest for no good reason. I think they've backed off. I told them you wouldn't have anything to do with it.'

He certainly wasn't in the mood for bumping off

his girlfriend's best friend – anyway, not before he had a foothold in his flourishing business interest. The rest he would pick up for free, or rather, after a few well-placed inducements.

Vdovin rose heavily from his chair. Stolin pushed a button under his desk. Two girls appeared in the doorway: Adriana, changed into a short black tube dress, and a skinny brunette with flushed cheeks and heavily made-up eyes. They stood there waiting his instructions.

'Look after the general, make sure he has whatever he wants,' Konstantin said, addressing the two of them. He was *still* procuring girls for him, he thought, years later.

'I'll be back to you shortly on the other matter… the meeting.'

Bazhukov entered the moment the general left.

'We may have a problem, boss.'

'Sit.' Konstantin pointed at the chair the general had just vacated.

'There's a man, claims to be Viktoriya Nikolaevna's father. One of our men overheard him bragging in a bar. He's a drunk, hangs around there a lot, and doesn't seem to work. Has a nice apartment, though, off Makarova, across on Vasilyevsky Island, by all accounts.'

'And?'

'Says he has the goods on a mafia boss.'

'Have you seen him?'

'No.'

Konstantin shook his head, wondering if indeed it

was Viktoriya's father and what it was he could have on him. What teenage misdemeanour that could be so terrible? He laughed dismissively. His recollection of her father was at best vague. But it was odd, if he was who he claimed to be, that Viktoriya had not mentioned him. He remembered the neatly stitched cut she had turned up with that morning at school. She had told the class that she had caught her face on an open cupboard door, but he had guessed there was an alternate explanation.

'And he hasn't said anything specific?' Konstantin prompted.

'No. He hangs out with the guy that used to work for you years ago – they are drinking partners. I fired him a year or two back.'

'What was his name,' Konstantin asked, suddenly alarmed.

'Just trying to remember… Lev, that was his name… Lev.'

CHAPTER 23

LENINGRAD

Viktoriya turned the key in the lock and tentatively gave the door a push. It swung inward into the small hallway. Apprehensive, she stood there steeling the courage to go in.

'Father,' she called. There was no response. Her father had telephoned her making one of his usual demands for more money and then not turned up at the café, their usual meeting place. At first she had put it down to his general unreliability; perhaps he had been lying drunk somewhere or had forgotten. But that was two days ago, and she had not heard from him. The woman at the café had not seen him either. If he was ill or in hospital she was sure he would have managed to make a call or had someone do it for him. It was unlike him to drop off the radar quite as he had.

From where she stood on the threshold of the tiny hallway, everything had the appearance of normality. She had only once visited her father's apartment, and that was the day he moved in; for the most part she had succeeded in keeping her distance.

The door to the living room was closed. Instinctively she sniffed the air – musty, but no obvious smell of rotting food or worse. Bracing herself, fighting the desire to turn and run, she stepped into the hallway and closed the front door quietly behind her. Warily, she opened the living room door. Mayhem confronted her: table and chairs turned over, the sofa and armchair slashed, books strewn across the floor. In the bathroom the panel under the bath had been torn out and the drugs cupboard emptied into the bath. She walked into the bedroom. The bed had been shoved off its base and clothes from a small wooden chest of drawers thrown all about the room. There was no sign of her father. She looked out of the window, trying to gather her thoughts.

Five floors below, cars and bicycles hugged the embankment, an endless stream of traffic making its way homeward. She wondered what had befallen him. Had he got himself into more debt? But then he would have come to her as he was planning to do. Or was this some random burglar chancing his luck at one of the better apartments in town? Her thoughts were interrupted by the click of the front door and someone being shoved roughly into the living room. Quickly, she slid back the mirrored wardrobe door and squatted down inside, leaving it a quarter open. Outside, she could hear whoever it was moving around the apartment. She caught the exasperated sigh of a man. He entered the bedroom breathing heavily. She imagined him looking around the room, at the chaos. At any moment she expected to be discovered, for him to slide open the wardrobe door.

'So where is it?' a voice said. 'Your twenty-four hours is up.'

'You've made a mess of my place. My daughter won't be best pleased.' It was her father's voice, slurred from alcohol.

'Wasn't us, it was your mate, Lev; he couldn't help us either. But he won't be bothering anyone anymore.'

Viktoriya's blood ran cold.

'Where's the passport,' asked another familiar voice she could not place.

'I don't know. I sold it,' her father said belligerently.

'You've got five minutes,' sneered the second man.

Viktoriya knew she would only have seconds before she was discovered. She slid back the wardrobe door and pulled up the sash window a few more inches. Below, perhaps only three feet down, stood a wide ornate plinth stretching right and left to the building's edge. It looked solid enough. She had no time to weigh up her situation; it just seemed a lot more dangerous inside than out. Easing herself over the windowsill, Viktoriya dropped onto the stone shelf and shuffled sideways away from the window. As long as they didn't look out, she thought to herself. Heart racing, she edged along the stone ledge towards the neighbouring apartment, leaning in against the wall, her hands flat against the stone, her feet gingerly trying to find a secure purchase. Two feet from the next apartment window, her right foot slipped on loose plaster. Struggling to find her balance, she lunged for the wooden frame and grabbed it. She took two deep breaths, trying not to panic, and looked back at the window she had exited, half expecting a head to appear and spot her. She needed to get off this cliff face and call for help. Edging her way level with the window, with the sill at waist height, Viktoriya looked in on an empty kitchen. There was no way of knowing whether the occupant was in, but staying out here, five floors up, about to be discovered, was not an option either. The window was firmly shut and locked from the inside. Carefully, she tugged off her short leather jacket and placed it against the window. When the next car horn sounded, she drove the jacket through the glass with her elbow. The glass shattered inward. Expecting someone to come rushing in at any moment, she quickly released the inside latch and pulled up the sash window. Fortunately, it gave easily. She slipped in and landed on the kitchen floor feet first and stood stock-still, expecting the door to burst open at any second. She tried to picture the layout of the apartment. If it was the same as her father's it would give onto a small hall off which the bedroom and living room extended. Carefully opening the kitchen door, she peered out. The flicker and booming sound of a television reached her from the living room. She edged out into the hall and peered through the crack of the door jamb. An old lady with a rug over her legs sat in an old leather armchair staring at a TV screen, a smile on her face. Relieved, Viktoriya opened the apartment door. The corridor was empty. She stepped out, closed the door and rang the bell. There was a pause. She wondered whether the old lady would actually hear it with the TV turned up so loud, but the next second it opened.

'I'm from the floor above,' Viktoriya announced. 'I've just moved in. I was having a window frame repaired and the workman managed to knock his bucket of tools off the ledge. It was on a rope. He heard breaking glass; I think it may have been your window.' It sounded improbably true, she thought.

The old woman looked momentarily confused.

'Would you mind if I checked; I am very happy to pick up the bill and get a glazier over here straight away? Can I use your phone to call him? Mine's not working.'

'I thought it was Mr Ikanov that lived upstairs,' she said suspiciously, not opening the door further than six inches.

'He moved out,' said Viktoriya. She reached into her handbag and handed the woman a business card. Time was running out. This seemed to reassure her.

'You best come in then,' she said finally, and opened the door onto the kitchen. The old lady looked through the gaping hole that was once the window.

'Something seems to have happened,' she said, pointing outside and at the street below.

'Let me see,' said Viktoriya. The old lady pulled back. A small crowd had gathered on the pavement around a motionless body. One or two faces looked upward. Across the street she caught sight of Bazhukov climbing into a car with another man. Bazhukov, why hadn't she thought of it before – it was *his* voice. She looked back at the inert crumpled figure and at the familiar dark blue coat that was her father's. It was all too much to take in. How did Konstantin *know* about Antyuhin's passport, if that was indeed what they were looking for? It would only be minutes before the police arrived and worked out from which window her father had fallen. She had to find that ID before they did.

'I have to be going,' she announced suddenly, her voice trembling. 'You have my card. I'm going to send someone round.'

The door to her father's apartment was closed. She opened it and quickly slipped in. The flat was in even more of a mess than when she had entered only half an hour ago. Bazhukov and his companion had ransacked the place a second time. Maybe he had found what they were after? Where would her father have hid it if it were here? Her eyes darted round the room at the turned-up furniture, broken crockery and ripped-open cushions. Her eyes alighted on an old photo of her mother in a new frame. It struck her as odd, out of keeping. He rarely mentioned her mother. She picked it up and turned it over. The cardboard backing was fixed by three small hinged fasteners. She flipped them sideways and pulled off the cardboard back. The ID card her father had shown her in the café fell to the floor. She picked it up. Why had he not given it to them? But then it was her father she was thinking about, not anybody… maybe he had simply calculated it would end badly either way and decided not to give them the satisfaction – he was bloody-minded enough. Anyway, this was not the time to speculate, she chided herself. She stuffed the card into her pocket and dashed out of the apartment to the lift.

As she stepped out on the ground floor, two stern-faced policemen walked in past her. Viktoriya flagged down a taxi and ordered him to take her to Pravdy. She guessed Kostya would be at his club now.

The taxi driver ogled her in the rear-view mirror.

'Keep your eyes on the road,' she snapped.

'No problem!' he said gruffly, as though she had misunderstood his prurient attention.

By the time she arrived at his club on Nevsky Prospect it had begun raining. The club doorman rushed towards her with an umbrella and sheltered her inside.

'Thank you, Erik.'

'I'll tell the boss you're here.'

'No need.'

The bar was already busy with punters chatting up girls. On a circular stage two girls gyrated to the throb of beat music while men, both single and in small groups, looked on, beer in hand. A third dancer peeled off her top to catcalls from the male audience.

A man stepped in her way. He was a good four inches shorter than her. 'When are *you* on?' he said, raising his voice above the din. A wave of beer breath rolled over her.

'In your dreams,' she answered, stepping around him.

Viktoriya headed to the stairwell at the back of the room leading to the basement, brushed the bodyguard aside, and made for Konstantin's office. Unsure what she was going to say to him, she knew he had to be confronted. He had killed her father... or had his men do it.

She wasn't sure how she felt... confused... conflicted... guilty... she had told her mother she would handle her father and she hadn't.

'You can't go in, Viktoriya Nikolaevna.'

'Get out of my way, Boris,' she said, and bowled past him, seizing the handle of the double door and pushing it wide open.

Konstantin was already standing up, adjusting his shirt. A tall dark-haired girl with crimson lipstick pulled down the hem of her skirt but made no move to raise herself from the sofa. To her surprise, Viktoriya felt no pang of jealousy or sudden rage.

'Get her out of here, Kostya,' she ordered him. The girl stood up, readjusted her skirt and stared insolently at Viktoriya, who turned her back on her.

'Leave us, Adriana,' said Konstantin. There was a pause before she heard the door close.

Viktoriya reached into her handbag and threw the ID card on his desk.

'Is *this* what you are looking for?'

Konstantin picked it up and opened the passport at the photo page. 'He got what he deserved,' he said. She was unsure whether he was referring to her assailant or her father.

'Why didn't you discuss it with me? I could have handled it.'

'But you hadn't.'

'I'm sorry that I didn't tell you,' she said. 'That was my mistake, but I didn't want you taking things into your own hands, not like before, not with my father, as despicable as he was… I had it under control.'

'He was blackmailing you… threatening to tell everyone… how could you trust him?'

She thought of the young girl in the room a few minutes before.

'And what about me? Am I to be trusted? Am I a threat too?'

She realised, of course, that that was the reason he never shared anything with her, certainly not his business interests. The girl who had just exited the room was a fool if she thought she meant anything to Kostya. He would have no compunction in getting rid of her or anyone if they became a danger.

'Look, Kostya, I'm no angel… I certainly don't want to be judgemental, but I don't want this either, living life in the shadows…'

'…but it's over… is that what you are saying? It's that small-time hustler,' Konstantin almost spat at her.

'If it's Misha you are referring to, it has nothing to do with him, nothing. I just don't want to live like this.'

'Well, it's a rough world out there,' he said coldly, 'and your friend is not up to it.'

'If killing all the opposition means *up to it* – no, I don't think he is.'

Konstantin raised his fist and dropped it back to his side.

'Boris!' he barked. 'See Viktoriya Nikolaevna off the premises.'

APRIL 1988

CHAPTER 24

LENINGRAD

Across the cobbled square of the Leningrad Freight yard by Pulkovo airport, lorries and delivery vans pulled in and out of cargo bays as armed security guards paced the yard and manned exit and entry points. Viktoriya sheltered from the rain that was falling steadily. In the fifteen minutes she had been standing there, she had witnessed four diesel tankers exit the depot bound for Smolensk and Eastern Europe.

Yuri had not been long in giving his answer and for over six months now had been a joint shareholder of Leningrad 176, unofficially dubbed Russian United Industries. But something was up. Yuri had been summoned to Moscow. He had downplayed it and rarely discussed the military but this time she sensed it was different. She hoped it wasn't curtains for Yuri or Smolensk.

Besides, she had a new problem. Leningrad Freight seemed to have reached a ceiling on requisitioning more fuel. Perhaps someone in Moscow had done their sums and calculated that it was impossible for

Leningrad Freight to consume so much, or maybe her director's contact was not lying and supply shortages were real.

A truck started to reverse into the bay she was standing in, forcing her to step down into the yard.

She looked at her watch as Misha, in a convoy of three cars, pulled into the depot. Ivan was first out and Misha last. How things had changed, she thought, from that time not so long ago when he drove around so proudly in his red Zhiguli. She wondered affectionately what had happened to it.

'Vika,' he said, grabbing her by the hands, kissing her on both cheeks. 'Where is our comrade director?'

The comrade director appeared in the doorway to the main building and forced a nervous smile.

'Maxim,' Misha almost shouted. She saw him flinch as Misha gave him a hug. 'Relax… we are going to work this out.'

They walked to his office and seated themselves around a table.

'So what are we up to at the moment… diesel… deliveries?' Misha asked.

'Eight tankers per day, six days a week, thirty-two thousand litres per tanker,' said Viktoriya reeling off familiar numbers.

'A million and a half litres a week,' threw in the director.

'And no let-up in demand?' said Viktoriya.

'None. Ilaria could place three times that with Eastern European customers. We are only scratching the surface.'

Viktoriya thought about the millions of US dollars pouring into the company's Swiss bank account. It was hard to get over how simple an operation it was. Buy at the domestic price and sell for four times as much on the international market.

'So supply…?' Misha continued.

'Moscow can't supply us any more fuel, more than we have at the moment, that is,' replied the director. 'They are having their own delivery problems. I offered him more money, as you suggested, but my contact says it is out of his hands. When I pressed him, he suggested I take it higher.'

'Namely?'

'The Ministry of Oil and Gas.'

'Do you have any connections there?'

'No… not my area – transport, yes,' said Maxim.

'Well, where there is a will, and a dollar to be made, there's a way. Let's all think on it. We need to get this right.'

CHAPTER 25

MOSCOW

A tired-looking General Ghukov entered the general staff meeting room. Yuri snapped to attention and was bid to take a seat by the colonel general, who placed a wad of papers wearily on the table. Yuri had seen the colonel general six months before, when he had visited his command, but he seemed to have aged ten years in the intervening period. His normally round face looked gaunt, and there were dark bags under his eyes. Yuri speculated on the pressure he must be under.

That morning, Yuri had boarded the military flight to Moscow with some apprehension. His orders had not come via his own commanding officer but directly from the chief of staff, Colonel General Andrei Ghukov. He had summoned him to general staff headquarters on Znamenka Street in the Arbat district. There had been no hint of its significance, only a brief order to report.

Yuri had wracked his brain for possible explanations. Were the army suspicious of his connections with

Misha Revnik? Did they judge his loyalties divided? Or was it his radical views on reorganising the Soviet Army into a smaller, better-equipped regular force?

The gulags may have disappeared, but there was always some forlorn military outpost as an alternative. It would be a disgrace, money or no money, if he were reassigned to some backwater.

'Colonel Marov,' the colonel general began, 'how aware are you of the talks going on in Geneva?'

Yuri felt a wave of relief and hoped it didn't show.

'Very little, sir... bilateral talks between Afghanistan and Pakistan with the United States and us present... to end the conflict... and that the mujahideen will not take part.'

'Well summed up, Colonel. The pace has of late been glacial, but there seems to be a thaw underway. What I am about to discuss, Colonel, you will appreciate is top secret and not to be discussed with other staff. Do I make myself clear?'

'Yes, sir.'

'Your views on the reorganisation of Soviet forces are well known. I reread your *subversive* academy paper on this recently to refresh my memory. You are to be complimented, Colonel. As you know, these ideas are not welcome in many quarters but the fact of the matter is that *virtue has become a necessity* in our present economic predicament.

'It is likely that a Russian pull-out of Afghanistan will be announced shortly, maybe within days, of uniformed troops anyway, but in parallel, and to come to the point, we have been quietly sounding out the

Americans on a withdrawal of Soviet troops from Eastern Europe. Our retired generals have been in discussion with theirs… all hypothetical of course. Privately, the general secretary has made it abundantly clear to me that he will not have Soviet troops suppress an East European uprising, not like in Hungary.'

The colonel general turned over the top page of the pile on the table and handed it to Yuri.

'Read, Colonel, Eastern European military dispositions.'

Yuri was finding it hard to take in. It was not what he had been expecting; the end of his career it wasn't. He began to read. Twenty-four divisions, forty-seven airfields, four thousand tanks, six hundred and ninety aircraft, six hundred and eighty helicopters… he continued down the page… in total just under three hundred and sixty thousand soldiers and two hundred and eight thousand civilians, relatives and employees, in three hundred locations.

'I can also tell you we have one hundred and eight thousand military personnel in Afghanistan,' Ghukov added when Yuri had put down the sheet.

'I see,' said Yuri, dropping the *sir*, stunned.

'A reorganisational nightmare.'

'Or opportunity, sir,' followed Yuri, finding his second wind.

'I thought you of all people might see it like that, Colonel. This will be a pull-out on a different scale, perhaps the largest anywhere in peacetime history. The general secretary is looking for a half-million troop reduction. I need someone to chair the committee of district generals and evolve a plan. Someone who is not part of the current group… I think that person is you, Colonel Marov.'

For a moment Yuri was speechless. Each district general commanded several armies. This was not just about downsizing, it would be about generals unwilling to surrender their fiefdoms – their parallel economic and political interests.

Yuri thought of the main military groupings and what he knew of their district commanders. The North-West under Vdovin would oppose, as would Volkov of the Western Group of Forces in Germany; the same went for Southern; the others – Central – he didn't know.

'Thoughts, Colonel?'

He was being placed directly in the firing line. If he succeeded, all well and good; if he failed or the government faltered or failed to gain sufficient support, he would be the first to go.

'What can I say, sir, that it would be an honour.'

'That's what I hoped you would say and no more, Colonel… Major *General* now.'

JULY 1989

CHAPTER 26

MOSCOW, LUBYANKA, KGB HEADQUARTERS

'I'll give you Afghan economics,' said Konstantin coldly; he had been trying to get his point over for the past half-hour. 'This is how it works: 5,000 tons of opium, 500 tons of heroin, $250 billion dollars street value. It doesn't come much bigger.'

The KGB chair, Karzhov, nodded. General Vdovin sat silent next to him.

'Occupation or no occupation, Najibullah needs arms and the Soviet Union wants to supply him arms; well, I can do that… Geneva Accord or no Geneva Accord,' he said, trying to not to raise his voice. While the KGB were past masters at espionage, frustratingly, their apparent grasp of markets was less secure.

In fact, forget Najibullah, he thought, they were all at it – more factions and tribes than he could name – they all wanted to get their hands on more weaponry to kill each other.

'Look, you sell me arms, I pay you in dollars, they pay me in opium and it costs this country nothing in

Russian lives. The Americans were at it before, and now it is our turn.'

The KGB chairman stared at him a moment. 'And where do you make opium into heroin?'

'Along the border with Pakistan. I just need the political cover to operate – like before – and an arms licence, that's the new bit. The KGB receives a share and you get a slice into your Swiss account. You don't have to worry about the transactions in between, delivery... nothing... that's my responsibility.'

'But you want support – my support?'

'Yes. I don't want the military breathing down my neck... that new guy, General what's his name... their rising star?

'General Marov?' said Karzhov.

'Yes, General Yuri Marov... Well, when they brought him back from wherever he was and put him in charge of the Afghan pull-out, he gave me a lot of grief. Grounded aircraft, delayed shipments to my suppliers, questions, questions. He never caught us out; we were always a step ahead, well informed, thanks to you.'

'He's nobody's fool. He complained to the Defence Ministry. Fortunately, they see things the same way we do,' said Karzhov.

Konstantin remembered bumping into Marov in Kabul at a late-night bar only the month before. He was with a beautiful Persian woman. It was the general who had approached him.

'I don't want you fuelling this conflict while I am reducing the garrison,' he had warned him. 'I have one hundred thousand men to get out of here as safely as I can.'

Thirty minutes later the bar had been abandoned in the face of a rocket attack from outside the city.

'I find a rocket with a *Made in Russia* sign on it, I'll make it my personal business to make sure the person who put it in their hands pays,' was the general's parting shot.

He was a cut above most Russians, Konstantin thought, and had money too, that was the rumour. Marov was not someone he could buy, that was clear. And wasn't he thick with Revnik and his old flame?

'What precisely is the general up to now?' asked Konstantin.

Vdovin, who had remained mostly silent until then, spoke.

'Apart from the pull-out... reorganisation of the military.'

The KGB chairman shook his head. 'God knows where it will end. The *general secretary*,' he said in a mocking tone, 'is discussing a troop withdrawal from Eastern Europe. Our enemies must be rubbing their hands with glee.'

'And where does the Politburo sit in all of this?' asked Konstantin. It was hard to keep track of events, they were unfolding so fast.

Karzhov shrugged. 'They're all clowns,' he jeered, 'there's even talk of devolving more powers to the republics.'

The Soviet Union seemed to be teetering towards collapse.

Karzhov threw a glance at General Vdovin, who nodded back.

'The general says you are to be trusted?'

'We've worked well together so far; our interests are not dissimilar,' Konstantin replied.

'There is a group of us, a small group, but I am sure with wide general support, who are committed to ensuring that the Soviet Union does not disintegrate, that all that has been achieved through decades of sacrifice is not lost.'

'That we do not wake up one morning with the Americans and NATO parked on our borders,' interjected Vdovin.

'Quite...' continued Karzhov, 'we do not intend to dismantle our general forces or lower our strategic guard.'

Nuclear capability by another name, thought Konstantin.

'And how do you intend to prevent that?' Konstantin asked. A revived Soviet Union would make his life a lot simpler.

'By any means,' the KGB chairman said, looking at him directly.

There had been countless talk of coups. Something had to give, Konstantin thought. Back in Leningrad it had become so bad that the newly elected mayor was doling out Western food relief. And here he was with arguably the most powerful man in Russia talking about any *means* – that old communist epithet.

'And in what way do you want my help?' said Konstantin before the chairman asked him.

'You have your network, not unlike our own, covert... global... sworn to secrecy? You understand the meaning of betrayal,' Karzhov continued.

'We don't have defectors... not live ones, if that's what you mean.'

'You have political and business affiliations, money and... what shall we call it, your own security force? When the time comes... when our plans are further advanced, I might call on you for support... to neutralise, shall we say, anti-Soviet elements... Do we have an understanding?'

'Of course, Comrade Chairman... and the arms licence?'

The chairman nodded. 'You'll have that by the end of today.'

CHAPTER 27

MOSCOW

For a split second, Yuri struggled to remember her name, distracted by the twin sensation of her finger, as it traced the long shrapnel scar on his left side, and her tongue, that flicked over his lips… Natasha.

'General *Yarouchka*,' she whispered, using the diminutive. 'Surely a general can make his men wait.'

General Yuri Marov moved back a few inches to take her in. Her auburn hair fell straight to her shoulders. She was still wearing the blouse she wore the previous evening hung open and off one shoulder.

'What meeting is more important than *me*?' She lunged forward with bared teeth to bite his lower lip as he snapped back out of range, grabbed her by the shoulder and overbalanced her onto the bed, pushing her face into the pillow. His hand traced the inside of her leg.

'I *knew* you were KGB when I first laid eyes on you!' he said, laughing. He had met Natasha two nights before at a high-level Moscow party. She was a cut above many of the women he had dated, an ex-model turned businesswoman. She ran her own Moscow agency specialising in exporting models to Western Europe.

'I have to be going...' He let go of her and jumped off the bed like a trapper releasing a wild animal. She rolled over.

'You have a beautiful apartment.'

He guessed what she was thinking, *how this on a general's pay?*

His apartment on the Arbat had indeed cost him a great deal of money; army pay would hardly have covered a studio rental within the Sadovaya Koltso – the Garden Ring – around Moscow.

'Thank you,' is all he said, without elucidating.

Forty minutes until his car arrived. He looked at his uniform and pressed shirt hanging on the wardrobe door and then at the woman on the bed looking up at him with those smokey eyes, her lips distractingly parted.

'Ten minutes... ten minutes!' he heard himself say.

Five minutes later than he normally would have been comfortable with, Yuri took the lift to the ground floor. He passed the concierge seated behind an expensive-looking reception desk, more sculpture than furniture, and took the revolving door onto the street. His staff car was directly outside. The driver, a young dark-haired Chechen, jumped out of the vehicle and rushed round to open the rear passenger door. As Yuri bent down to get in, he noticed a man standing on the other side of the road, ten feet from a parked Lada. He wasn't sure why he noticed him that morning. Maybe it was a gap in the traffic that was normally bumper to bumper. But his brain had registered something. Without giving the Lada or the man a second glance, he climbed in and settled back into his seat as his driver pulled away from the kerb.

Yuri shifted his position so that he now had clear sight of the wing mirror. The man he had spotted opposite was climbing hurriedly into the Lada, which had pulled up swiftly beside him. A second later, the man and the car disappeared from view.

Had he been imagining things? Could it have been a simple coincidence, he thought? He went through a mental list of likely suspects: CIA, MI6, and MSS. One was almost as likely as another. But this was Russia, he reminded himself, where not even generals were to be trusted.

CHAPTER 28

'Viktoriya Nikolaevna Kayakova. I have a ten thirty appointment with the minister of oil and gas.'

As the receptionist checked the minister's calendar, Viktoriya looked across the entrance hall towards the front door where Yuri stood making sure that everything went smoothly.

An hour earlier, the two of them had had coffee together to discuss strategy in a café close by the GUM. Yuri had seemed distracted, directing her to a corner table out of earshot of other patrons and telling her to keep her voice down. He was clearly wary of something. She wondered what he did now that he was back in Moscow. It was not something he ever raised or discussed; she knew better than to broach it with him. All she knew was that he worked at general staff headquarters. Misha guessed it was all to do with the Afghan pull-out, which according to official media was nearly complete. But whatever his role, where her director had failed, Yuri had succeeded. There had been no hesitation from the minister in meeting them once there had been a call from his office.

'ID?' said the receptionist, a dowdy-looking

woman in a grey uniform. Viktoriya wondered if she was always as rude or had just taken an exception to her. There was a tap on her shoulder.

'I have to be going,' said Yuri as he kissed her on both cheeks. 'You'll have to give me a full report later.'

Viktoriya held his arms for a moment.

'Everything all right, General,' she said, using his title affectionately. Outside, it had begun to rain heavily. A passing truck hit a pothole in the road, sending a sheet of water over the pavement.

'Yes, absolutely,' he said, his normal smile returning. 'A lot going on, that's all.'

A young man interrupted them and motioned for her to follow. Viktoriya watched as Yuri ran out into the street and jumped into his staff car. Despite his protest, she couldn't banish her sense of unease.

'Please wait here,' said the young man. He parked her in a bare-looking meeting room, all wood and frosted glass, and pointed to a pot of coffee brewing on the table.

Before she had time to pour herself a cup, an older man – she guessed late fifties, in a regulation Soviet double-breasted grey suit – stepped into the room and introduced himself as Stephan Federov.

Viktoriya wondered if Federov had any real sense of the power he wielded, his fiat over every well, refinery, and fuel distribution centre. Most state-level bureaucrats she had met simply had no understanding of how the *real* system worked.

'Viktoriya Nikolaevna, a pleasure to meet you,' he said, self-consciously tidying his hair. 'What can I do for you? General Marov made the introduction, I gather? Can I ask what your relationship is with him?'

Viktoriya explained that Leningrad Freight had dealt with him on customs and security issues when he was a colonel in charge of Smolensk and he had been kind enough to recommend her. It was halfway to the truth.

'I also have a letter of introduction from the Leningrad gorkom and my director at Leningrad Freight.'

'You do indeed come highly recommended,' said Federov, glancing at the documents before returning them. He took off his glasses and placed them on the table.

'So, Miss Kayakova... back to the beginning. It says in my notes that you wish to discuss fuel supply problems for... Leningrad Freight. Normally I would not get involved in such matters but, as I said, you come highly recommended, not least by General Marov, who tells me you are trustworthy and discrete.'

Viktoriya had the impression Federov was beginning to talk in code.

'Leningrad Freight is the second largest shipping company in Russia,' he continued. 'You have done well to rise so fast. You must only be...'

'Twenty-eight.'

'Yes, I have that here too,' he said, referring to his notes, 'first-class honours in Economics at Leningrad State.'

Viktoriya felt this was turning into an interview.

'You will appreciate I like to know who I am dealing with.'

He turned a page. It was a list of diesel supplies to Leningrad Freight over the past four months.

'I am a petrochemical engineer,' he added apropos of nothing. 'Your requisitions have increased substantially. It's good to know that at least someone is moving goods around Russia,' he said with a deadpan face and shut the folder.

'May I suggest we continue at a café close by? They do much better coffee and it has stopped raining now.'

The café was indeed close, a few doors down from the ministry. It was spacious with a freshly painted vaulted ceiling and newly installed red velour booth seating.

'I think this will be more private, Miss Kayakova.'

Coffee arrived almost instantly.

'I'll come to the point. You have a supply contract with Mikhail Revnik's cooperative to supply him diesel, in which... how shall I put it, the gorkom also have an interest?'

The minister for oil and gas was not a simple state-level bureaucrat, after all, she thought.

'Yes, fuel surplus to Leningrad Freight requirements.'

'Quite, sound economics... Tell me, do you know of the oil refinery at Roslavi?'

Viktoriya said she did. Leningrad Freight had made sporadic deliveries for it going back years. It was south of Smolensk, halfway to Bryansk.

'General Marov, I am sure, is very familiar with it from his previous command,' added Federov. He paused, and she wondered for a moment whether he would continue.

'It will not come as a surprise to you that perestroika has turned everything on its head. First there were rules, and now there are none. Many of our industries, and that includes oil refineries, are plagued by criminal gangs. In our motor industry there is wholesale theft from the production line of spare parts, even cars. No one dares challenge them, not if you value your life. Mikhail Dimitrivich has his bank – Moika – and accounts in Switzerland?' he continued.

She nodded.

'Do you think that between yourselves and General Marov you can secure Roslavi?'

Secure Roslavi? Occupy it, militarily? That was a tall order, she thought.

'And if I could?'

'I grant your new cooperative a distribution agreement with the refinery, all you can manage.'

'At the domestic price, in roubles?'

'Naturally… and 15 per cent of the market price, US dollars, into a Swiss bank account, which your friend will set up for me.'

What he was proposing was on an entirely different scale. The current offtake would seem like petty cash to this. The revenues would be enormous.

'Comrade Minister, let me speak with my principals. I'll come back to you shortly.'

'Well don't wait too long… *carpe diem*.'

CHAPTER 29

The aircraft taxied to the edge of the runway. Out of her window, Viktoriya glimpsed the aeroplane in front lift from view, its wheels already retracting, as it rose into an unblemished morning sky. On cue, the giant Ilyushin made a slow turn to face down the runway, square onto the flight strip. It rolled forward a few metres and stopped.

'Prepare for take-off,' said the address system.

Viktoriya looked at the second hand of her watch as the engine noise swelled to deafening pitch and she resisted the temptation to cover her ears. Like a dog anxious to be unleashed, the aircraft struggled against its master, shaking and shuddering. Surely now, she thought. There was an almost imperceptible change in gravity, the infinitely small gap between stillness and kinesis, a stasis, where opposing forces cancel each other out. The sudden, precipitous, forward movement of the aircraft forced her, almost threw her, back in her seat. She looked again at her watch as the behemoth gathered momentum and lift with every inch. Thirty, thirty-five, she had guessed fifty seconds, forty, forty-five; the Ilyushin slipped the lead and clawed its way skyward before turning north to Leningrad.

She reached for the briefcase stowed under her seat and pulled out the latest shipping figures. Blankly, she stared at the numbers, unable to concentrate on the neat schedule of rows and columns. Her mind drifted to the meeting she had just finished with Yuri, who had delivered her to the airport that morning. They had sat in the busy concourse watching the early morning bustle while she recounted her conversation with Federov.

Yuri had sat quietly thinking it through. It was entirely within his power whether they went ahead or walked away.

'I know what you are thinking, but there is no honour in penury, not unless you're a religious obsessive, and we've surely had enough of them,' she had thrown in. 'And if it is not us, it will be someone else.'

'Not always the best way to justify one's actions.'

'Maybe not, but you can *see* the state things are in... One day soon the ordinary Russian is going to wake up and discover that the money in his bank account is worth nothing, zero, the government have spent it all. I don't want to be that *ordinary* Russian. You don't either.'

He had stared at her for a moment. His expression changed. It was as though he were seeing her for the first time.

'*Carpe diem*,' he had said with the hint of a smile on his face.

'*Carpe diem.*'

'Look, I can't commit the military, not to secure the refinery, but there is a way. It's no secret that we are decommissioning whole regiments with the Afghan pull-out. There are a lot of soldiers looking for work – officers and men. I know a few from my old regiment. We build our own security force.'

'A private army.'

'Four hundred men… to start, one battalion. The way things are going we'll need more, a lot more. Tell your minister we'll take care of Roslavi.'

She closed her eyes.

'Coffee, madam,' asked the hostess. She looked up and placed her cup on the small tray held out to her.

Yuri – he was his own enigma, she thought. What did he ultimately want? She didn't believe it was *all* about money… but didn't wealth and power go together, and was he not quietly accumulating both.

AUGUST 1989

CHAPTER 30

MOSCOW, THE ARBAT

'So we are agreed on the preliminary timetable?' Yuri heard himself say. He looked around the long table at the district generals and their delegates. Here and there was the nodding of heads, none spoke. It had been another exhausting and frustrating meeting trying to tie down a phased time for the evacuation of the Western Forces Group from East Germany… should negotiations get that far. He thought, at last, after months of meetings, they were finally there. On an easel at the far end of the meeting room stood a flip chart listing a dozen or more military groups with dates scribbled out and reinserted. 'We evacuate through Rostock and Reugen.'

'You are good at *retreats*, General,' said General Vdovin, breaking the silence.

Yuri counted to ten; losing his temper was just what Vdovin and his supporters wanted.

'We have been over this, General. This is a political decision. At the moment it's still a *what if*. Last time I looked, the Berlin Wall was still standing.'

'We were never interested in Eastern European government support before,' scoffed Volkov. He was shorter than Yuri, eagle-eyed and driven. As commander of the Western Group he was the most immediately affected. 'It is the general secretary who is out of step. He needs to be better advised.' Volkov meant that he should better advise him, or better still somebody else entirely.

'I would remind you, General, that the economy is on the brink of collapse. Your soldiers have not even been paid for months.'

'And whose fault is that?' added Vdovin.

'We start with the 2nd Guards Tank Army, followed by the 2nd and 8th Shock Armies,' continued Yuri, ignoring Vdovin's remark. He went round the table, eying each general in turn, not breaking contact until they said yes or grunted their assent. Volkov was last. He looked across the table at Vdovin, who had already signalled his agreement.

'Agreed,' he said finally. Volkov stood up abruptly and everyone clambered to their feet. The meeting broke up. Two minutes later, only Volkov and Yuri remained in the room.

'Does it make you *proud* presiding over the collapse of an empire?' Volkov said bitterly.

'General, I don't see it like that.'

'Clearly not.'

Volkov opened the door and was gone.

Yuri sat down at his desk and rubbed his temples. The colonel general had told him it would be hard going; he wasn't wrong. He was taking the lion's share of the flak for both the general secretary and the general staff. He sensed Volkov and Vdovin were not about to give up that easily, despite their verbal assurances.

He stood up and walked over to the window. Drizzle lightly wetted rooftops and street lanterns. Five floors below, on Arbatskaya Square, next to a canvas-covered stall, a group of hippies tendered Afghan coats and roughly made leather bags to passers-by. Yuri laughed to himself – weren't they twenty years too late? A seventies song he knew but couldn't identify drifted upward, piecemeal and incomplete. He felt the sudden need for fresh air, to get out of the defence building he had been cooped up in for most of the day.

He lifted the papers off his desk, placed them in the drawer, locked it, and buzzed through to the outer office.

'Olga, can you please call my car.'

He stood up, walked over to the coat stand and unhooked his raincoat. His hands went instinctively into his pockets to check for the apartment keys. They were where they should be. But there was something else too, something he had not expected. He pulled out a small folded piece of paper and studied it in the palm of his hand. He had no recollection of putting anything in his pocket. Maybe it was Natasha? She had put a love note in his pocket when he was in the shower. It brought back memories of the previous night. He must give her a call. Yuri walked over to the window and idly unfolded what he assumed must be a message.

In neat handwriting it read: *TONIGHT 8.00 P.M. BARFLY, PUSHKINSKAYA PLOSHCHAD.* There was no signature, nothing that would indicate who might have written it.

He wracked his brains. Who could have put it there and when? To have put it in his coat pocket inside the defence headquarters, they would have had to run the gauntlet of security and Olga, who was herself not to be underestimated in this. She had successfully guarded him from a myriad of unwelcome callers. It had to be someone with easy access to his office. He stood there a minute wondering whether to respond. He reckoned that rubbing a three-star general up the wrong way by inviting him on a pointless clandestine meeting was unlikely to improve their position in life. It could, of course, be some sort of trap. He looked at his watch. It was only seven fifteen and he could make it easily, but he would need to throw off whoever had been following him… if indeed he was being followed.

'Tervaskaya,' was all Yuri said to his driver. Ten minutes later they had slogged their way through heavy traffic to the front entrance of his apartment building. Acting as he did every day, he checked for messages before taking the lift to the seventh floor and his apartment. Quickly changing out of uniform, he donned jeans, an everyday jacket and silk scarf, which he wrapped loosely around his lower face, covering his mouth.

Ignoring the lift, he descended the emergency stairwell to the first floor and exited onto the landing. The corridor was empty. He followed it round to the rear of the building and an unmarked door, used in Stalinist times as a bolthole, and took a narrow staircase down to the ground. A janitor shifted bins ready for the morning collection.

Yuri walked up the long incline to the main street and continued for a couple of blocks before stepping off the kerb and holding out his hand. A car pulled up, a government employee out to make some extra money on his way home.

'Pushkinskaya metro.'

The driver named a price. Yuri nodded and climbed in, ignoring attempts to engage him in small talk. The drizzle had thankfully stopped. Residents swept clean the entrance to their buildings as a construction brigade attended a burst water main.

'Here's Pushkinskaya.' The driver pointed to a sign two hundred metres ahead. 'Where do you want to be dropped?'

Yuri recognised Barfly on the opposite side less than one hundred metres away.

'This will do fine.'

Outside, a photograph pinned to a cracked and broken glass frame displayed a poorly lit, smoke-filled interior. A girl, sidestepping puddles in her high heels, passed him and gingerly took the steps down to the basement entrance. He looked at his watch: five minutes before eight. He followed her down. A flat-nosed, shaven-headed bouncer blocked Yuri's way.

'I have to search you,' he said bluntly. Yuri noticed he was wearing an old military jacket and heavy army boots. The tattoo of a claw crawled up his neck.

Yuri stood still while the bouncer patted him from head to foot. At least this way, Yuri thought, it would only be the bar staff that carried guns. The bouncer nodded; he was free to go.

A heavily made-up girl in a small cloakroom cubicle took his coat and handed him a ticket. He pocketed it, drew back the curtain and stepped into the bar. The photo outside did not do it a disservice. Cigarette smoke hung thick and pungent, draining what small light and oxygen there was in the room.

Negotiating low tables, Yuri made his way over to the bar, grabbed a stool and ordered a beer. It took a minute for his eyes to adjust. A woman, sitting at the far end of the bar, caught his eye, held it and smiled an invitation; around the room, men and women, both single or together, sat at small circular tables under outsized revolutionary posters that decorated the red-painted brick walls: a virile-looking man driving a sparkling new tractor in a sun-filled scape, his adoring wife looking on; a woman with her index finger at her zipped mouth; a man at dinner, his hand up, refusing a proffered glass of vodka. Yuri smiled; if only life were like art.

He looked at his watch again and wondered who he should be looking for: a man, a woman, someone he would recognise? He looked again at the woman at the bar. What was it that was so important that he be dragged out here? The bartender caught his eye and cast a look to the back of the room. A woman was signalling to him. Picking up his beer, he carried it back to her table.

'May I join you,' he said, standing over her. She was dyed blonde with thick smokey eye shadow and dark red lipstick. He didn't recognise her at first. It took a few seconds for his brain to process her image, strip away her make-up. She was Volkov's adjutant. Not unexpectedly, she looked entirely different out of uniform.

'Another drink?' he said, and she caught the bartender's attention and pointed at her near empty glass.

'Galina,' she said, introducing herself – Lieutenant Galina Biryukova, he remembered. He had caught her studying him across the table during the day's negotiation. He put her in her early thirties.

'Please call me Yuri.'

Galina cast her eyes nervously around the room.

'Just to reassure you… Yuri… I don't normally go out looking like this. I had to pay the doorman five dollars to come in… I assume that's the going door rate for sex workers.'

'Well I *do* look like this when I go to hockey matches,' he countered, and smiled, trying to put her at ease. She was certainly more provocative than in uniform.

Her drink arrived. Yuri waited for the waitress to move out of earshot.

'Does General Volkov know you are meeting me?'

Galina shook her head.

'So what is it that is so important?'

'I am not sure.'

'Not sure?' Yuri started to wonder whether the lieutenant was wasting his time.

'General,' she slipped into army mode, 'Yuri…
I trust I can rely on your discretion. From what I've
seen and heard, I believe I can.'

'I think you need to spit it out,' Yuri said, without
giving her any guarantee.

She nodded and seemed to relax, almost
anticipating the relief of telling him what was troubling
her.

'Look, I may be *way off* beam but something
is going on which I can't explain. You know I am
General Volkov's adjutant; I've been working
for him just under three years. I organise, attend
and take minutes of all his meetings. There's not
much I don't know. But a month ago he attended
a meeting at the Ministry of Defence. It was only
by coincidence I found out. I was delivering some
papers to the ministry and spotted him coming out.'
She hesitated.

'Go on,' Yuri encouraged her.

'Well, it was who he was with.' She paused, almost
frightened to say their names.

'And… they were?' Yuri prompted her.

'Gerashchenko, Karzhov, Dubnikov and Vetrov.'

Yuri frowned, puzzled. The deputy general
secretary, KGB chairman, Soviet defence minister
and the interior minister. There might be a hundred
reasons why such a meeting might take place, but he
couldn't think of one offhand.

'Did General Volkov see you?'

'Yes… I could see he was startled at first… he could
see that I thought it odd. He just said, "*An emergency*

security meeting". It just didn't ring true. I know him. There isn't a meeting in three years that I have not known about, not until that day, at least. When I got back to Berlin, I checked his desk diary. Under July 5 he had written in faint pencil the letters *EC...* I am not in the habit of checking on my commanding officers...'

'No, I understand... please continue.'

'Well, I flipped back through the diary and found two other *EC*s, a week or two apart and coinciding with his visits to general staff in Moscow. It's just he's never mentioned them...' her voice trailed off. 'And that's it really. I'm sure there is a perfectly good reason...'

'But you can't think of one... and nor can I at this moment.' Not one that sounded innocent at least. He could understand now the risk she was taking by seeing him. 'And why did you bring this to my attention and not someone else.'

'I'm not entirely sure myself... you seem to be doing the right thing... we do need to move on... and General Ghukov trusts you, and the general secretary.'

Yuri was silent for a minute. He needed time to think on what she had said. Maybe there was an alternative explanation, a legitimate reason, but then why the secrecy and why the deputy secretary general and all those people in the same room? Yuri took a gulp of beer as the lieutenant waited patiently for him to respond.

'Does General Volkov have any idea of your suspicions?'

'I'm not sure. Clearly he knows I saw everyone at the Defence Ministry.'

Volkov was no fool, though, thought Yuri. If there was something going on he would not want it leaking out. He wouldn't want loose ends.

'Have you noticed any sort of surveillance?'

'No... I'm not sure... maybe, maybe it's just paranoia creeping in.' She smiled for the first time.

'Well, you did the right thing, raising this with me. The safest course of action for you now is to carry on normally. Doing anything else is going to set alarm bells ringing... if something is going on.'

CHAPTER 31

LENINGRAD

Misha looked down on the dark waters of the Bolshaya Neva as his small cavalcade crossed the Dvortsovy bridge and headed south onto Vasilyevsky Island in light traffic. Reflexively, he pulled the collar of his coat tight around his neck. Soon the islands would weld together in a vast seamless plane of white and grey. Ivan turned and looked at him and then glanced at the black Volgas tucked in close behind; the one to their front was already beginning to make a left turn.

'I'm not expecting any trouble,' said Ivan. He extracted his automatic and distractedly examined it before returning it to his shoulder holster.

Misha thought back to the days of the red Zhiguli not that long ago, when he hadn't bothered with protection. Life had been a lot simpler then, freer. He was a target now to kidnappers and criminal syndicates, not to mention the more straightforward entrepreneur who saw an opportunity to accelerate market share by bumping off the competition.

A grand plan there had never been. He would have

laughed at anyone who would have mentioned the *strategy* word. It was just an opportunistic progression and *money* made *money*. In the Soviet Union, he reflected, nothing belonged to anybody, not until now, and those that controlled enterprises and contracts had little compunction in virtually signing anything away, as long, of course, as there was something in it for them.

The car in front dipped as it ran over a pothole, and they swerved slightly to avoid it. The cavalcade had picked up speed now, and there was no stopping for red lights. They ran two, horns blaring and headlights full beam, and took another sharp left and stopped. Four identical cars sat on the cobbled forecourt of the Academy Café; their occupants seemed barely to give them a second glance. Misha recognised Bazhukov in the nearest car.

He climbed out of the car and looked across the water and to the Admiralty to the east. A gust of wind caught him.

'You wait by the car,' he told Ivan. 'You can keep an eye on these guys.'

The café was a large conservatory-like structure moored against the Neva's edge, all glass and heavy metal beams. He pushed open the door and took the wrought-iron staircase to the first floor. Misha spotted Konstantin at a table set back from the bar, sipping a cup of something, enjoying a view of the river and the left bank.

'I always like the view from here. Dramatic, don't you think?' Konstantin said when Misha sat down opposite. There was no shaking of hands or warm smiles. Misha thought back to when he had spoken to him last – a year ago, maybe longer? Konstantin looked slightly heavier than he remembered him but not necessarily the worse for it; traces of premature grey peppered his jet-black hair.

'Thank you for coming.' Konstantin waved at the barista standing at the bar well out of earshot. Misha wondered how many scenes like this the waiter had witnessed. A normal morning turns into a gangland meet.

The barista took Misha's order for a cappuccino, brought it to him and retreated out of range.

'We can't go on meeting like this,' Misha said with an over-serious face and laughed.

'Always the joker...' Konstantin retorted nonplussed. 'And how is Vika? She has moved into your offices on Morskaya.'

'Well... makes more sense than her being stuck out by the airport.'

'You impress me. I underestimated you... and Vika and your general friend, of course. You have not let the grass grow under your feet: fashion, freight, oil, and currency dealing... whatever next? Your success has far exceeded my initial expectations... Russian United Industries... R... U... I,' he said slowly and deliberately.

There was silence for a moment. Misha took a sip of his coffee.

'You wanted to meet,' he said, wondering where this conversation was going.

'*You* are expanding and *I* am expanding. You move money; I need to move money... into offshore accounts. I understand you can do that.'

'Getting nervous?'

'Things might get a whole lot worse before they get better... or they might just get a whole lot worse.'

'How much are we talking about?'

'One hundred and twenty-five million dollars US to start... Grand Cayman, BVI, Jersey, Cyprus.'

It didn't appear that the drugs business was suffering.

'One per cent,' Misha said.

'That's *outrageous!*' flared Konstantin.

'I'm quoting you an old-school discount; ask around, if you find someone who can do it for less, be my guest. I'm sure you've done your homework.' Misha thought of the commissions and backhanders that Moika would have to pay; Russia was not a cheap place to do business. 'You can always set up your own bank.'

'I've got enough on my plate,' he said coolly.

Misha wrote down Grigory's number on a napkin and handed it to him.

'I'd also like to invest money here... in RUI.'

It was Misha's turn to be surprised; having one of Russia's largest mafia bosses as a shareholder was unlikely to improve his corporate credentials either in the Soviet Union or abroad.

'A small percentage to start... through an offshore holding, so you are not embarrassed.'

'And why would *I* want to do that, or my co-shareholders.'

'Peace of mind, a good price. You know what it's like out there – a jungle.'

'And you're "King of the Jungle".'

'Something like that.'

'I'm sure you can guess my answer.'

'Why don't you think about it? I wouldn't want you rushing into any sudden decision... but don't delay too long. Life's too short.'

Misha pushed back his chair and stood up to go. From his back pocket he peeled off a twenty dollar bill and threw it on the table. Konstantin remained seated and signalled the barista for another coffee.

'It's been good talking with you, Mikhail Dimitrivich.'

CHAPTER 32

MOSCOW

Yuri didn't go directly home after his staff meeting. He needed something to eat. Having dismissed his driver, Yuri flagged a lift from a passing motorist and gave him the route. As he sat there in the front seat, he contemplated his meeting with Lieutenant Biryukova the night before. She had taken a considerable risk in seeing him; he could have denounced her or even been part of the conspiracy himself – that is… if there were a conspiracy.

The question was what to do? He could hardly blurt out his suspicions to Ghukov. He had no evidence, only the suspicions of a young woman. Volkov would just laugh it off, tell him he was being paranoid; weren't their constant rumours of dissatisfaction in the army, possible coups? And even if he didn't mention his source, Volkov was smart enough to figure it out. He didn't fancy her chances if that were the case. Yuri needed someone he could bounce his thoughts off. The car turned off Dmitrovka onto Nastasyinskiy; a thought percolated up from his subconscious.

'Stop here, please,' he said.

Yuri backtracked to Malaya Dmitrovka, took a left and walked up to the next main junction, before taking a right onto Degtyarny. He stopped outside an apartment building built seamlessly into a row of neoclassical nineteenth-century houses. Typed on a yellowing piece of card next to flat number five was the name Terentev. Yuri pressed the button. There was no response. Maybe Ilya was out. He turned up the collar of his coat against the sudden cold and peered into the small dimly lit lobby through a side window. The lift was directly ahead, three metres away, the floor indicator stuck on four. He looked at his watch: eight thirty; it was still relatively early. The indicator blinked.

A young woman exited the lift and opened the door onto the street. She was smartly dressed and wore a neat red beret over shoulder-length hair. Yuri stood to one side, reached up and held the door open for her. She looked at him briefly and from her expression decided he was clearly not a vagabond.

'Good evening,' he said. 'I have been trying to buzz a friend but there is no answer,' he continued, trying to reassure her as she ducked under his arm.

'It hasn't been working for weeks,' she replied, holding his eyes a little longer than necessary. If it had been another evening he might have even enquired her name or given her his card.

'I'll just go up,' he said, and slipped past her as she turned onto the street.

Yuri took the lift to the second floor and walked

along the corridor until he found the number he was looking for. From inside Terentev's apartment Shostakovich drifted onto the landing. Yuri knocked on the door. There was a pause. The visible light on the magic eye on the door went dark and the door swung open. Ilya Terentev stood there in an apron, a cooking spoon in his hand.

'Like something to eat?' he said, as though he had expected him. 'I'm about ready to serve.'

'As long as I'm not eating your rations.'

The flat was small: a living room just large enough for a sofa, armchair and the dining room table. It was very different to his own apartment in the Arbat.

Ilya shook his head. 'Help yourself to a beer from the fridge.'

'Water will be fine.' He needed to keep a straight head.

'What brings you here?' asked Ilya, coming straight to the point. 'One of your girlfriends giving you grief?'

'No, just passing.'

His friend looked at him. How long had he known Ilya? Ten years? More? They had met when they were both junior officers, and then again in Kabul. An easy friendship had developed, with serious conversation invariably gravitating towards women and ice hockey.

'*Passing Degtyarny?*' he said, raising his eyebrows.

'Almost… anyway.'

Ilya didn't push him further. He sat down and Ilya served him fish with potato and cabbage and black bread on the side.

'Tuck in!'

Yuri was more ravenous than he thought.

'This is good, Ilya. Where is Anna tonight?'

'Out at a friend's. I've been left to my own devices.'

Yuri looked at a photo of Ilya and his wife Anna on the dresser looking radiantly happy. He stared at it for a few seconds, gathering his thoughts, thinking how to approach the subject he wanted to discuss without endangering either his friend or informant.

It was Ilya who provided the cue.

'How's the reorganisation going?' Ilya was used to him letting off steam over his frustrations with the district generals.

Yuri nodded and took a bite of black bread.

'Volkov… he's not a happy man. He's against us pulling out of Eastern Europe, even discussing it with the Americans.'

'There are plenty of people I'm sure would support him if it were common knowledge. The general secretary *is* taking a risk.'

Yuri nodded, wiping the bread around his plate, mopping up the fish broth.

'Volkov has backed down for now, but I don't know for how long… maybe he is just biding his time.'

'For what?'

'I don't know… a *new* general secretary?'

'You mean a coup?' It was more a rhetorical statement than a question. Yuri shrugged. His friend continued. 'Personally I think all this rumour-mongering is just the same old state paranoia that not so long ago led to purges and arrests. Look… the KGB would be the first to pick up on anything.'

'You may be right. It's just there have been some high-level meetings taking place between the military, KGB and senior government figures.'

Ilya didn't respond.

'And Karzhov?' Yuri said, leaving his name hanging in the air. It was Ilya's time to shrug.

'Our new chief? Not much to say… met him at a directorate meeting. Old KGB, bit of a closed book, as you might expect.'

'This is good, Ilya,' he said, downing his last piece of bread.

'I don't suppose you get much home cooking.'

Yuri laughed and shook his head.

'I also think I'm being followed.'

His friend's face took on a serious expression. He was silent for a moment.

'I'll tell you what. I'll make some discrete enquires, see if I can come up with anything.'

Yuri took his leave just after ten and caught a lift back to within a couple of blocks of his apartment. Making a wide circle around his building, he came out on the street in front of the main entrance, on the pavement opposite, a hundred or so metres down, and stopped. His eyes searched for the tail he'd had this morning. The street was empty. Reassured but still cautious, he made his way round to the secret exit he had left by and took the emergency stairwell back to the first floor and the lift to the seventh.

He entered his apartment and switched on the

light. There was a sound from down the hallway. Yuri reached for his automatic hanging discretely behind his coats on the wall rack. Silently, he slid back the safety catch and rebalanced the grip in his hand.

The door giving onto the living room was open, the room in darkness. His free hand reached for the switch and rotated the dimmer switch. There was a sudden movement from the sofa. He swung round to meet it as his finger took first pressure, ready to loose two rounds. Svetlana lay there in a short dress and heels.

'Don't shoot!' she said, over-dramatically raising her hands above her head in mock surrender.

'*Fuck*, Svetlana... I could have killed you...'

SEPTEMBER 1989

CHAPTER 33

LENINGRAD

Misha looked around the vault. Viktoriya stood next to Grigory, who was idly weighing up wads of dollar bills in his hands before placing them back where he had found them.

'Did we get the last of Kostya's money,' Misha asked Grigory.

'Over two hundred million US. He seems in a hell of a hurry.'

'That's way up on what he told me,' Misha said, frowning.

Misha cast a glance in Viktoriya's direction as if she might be able to throw some light on Kostya's extra millions. It was odd. She guessed Moika was not the only bank Kostya was pushing his money through and Misha would definitely not have been his first choice. Why the rush now? There was less chance of it being noticed by the authorities if it were drip fed.

The wall phone rang and Grigory picked it up.

'Ivan on the phone.'

They had been waiting for news on Roslavi. Ivan

had joined Major Gaidar's brigade and entered the plant at first light. They had little idea what to expect, only Federov's hazy report.

'Put him on speaker,' said Misha.

'We have the plant under control, but they were waiting for us, someone must have tipped them off... a heavily armed local gang, maybe fifty, ex-army I suspect, ten dead, four of ours.'

It was almost useless speculating who had leaked their arrival, thought Viktoriya, but they did need to improve their own intelligence about such matters.

'And the plant director?'

'Not very cooperative, at first... he's onside now. If he gives us any trouble he'll be *out* and he knows it. Vika, you can send in your tankers in forty-eight hours, but it'll take time to get back to half-decent production levels. The place is a mess.'

The Soviet Union writ large, thought Viktoriya. No wonder Federov was so keen to secure the place, and thank God for Yuri. Between him and Ivan it had taken less than ten days to assemble a small army, kit them out and put them in position.

'Comrade director says that requisitioning spare parts is futile; he's been doing so for months. The only thing it generates is more paperwork – not what he needs.'

'Ivan, just tell him to give you the list,' said Misha. 'We'll sort it out, bring in the parts from Europe. It'll be much quicker, and tell him to get hold of some contract engineers. Put them on our payroll. Let's get this refinery up and running. Who knows how long we'll have to benefit.'

The sums they were looking at on the trading side were enormous if they could get back to anything like the capacity levels Federov had told them had been achieved two years before; sinking some of their profit into improving their return would be a small price to pay. Besides, Federov had even hinted that he might get the ministry to cover the cost ultimately, but first things first, thought Viktoriya.

'I've LF setting up the transport depot as we speak,' said Viktoriya, 'on the outskirts of Smolensk, courtesy of Federov. I'll fax you the details. I'm positioning the first five freighters there this week, more next. They'll need security.'

Smolensk was no safer than any other city.

OCTOBER 1989

CHAPTER 34

SMOLENSK

Yuri sat enjoying a drink at his favourite bar in Smolensk with Viktoriya sitting on the bar stool opposite. Combining a visit to the Western District with Viktoriya's visit to the Leningrad Freight depot seemed like a good plan.

'Bring back memories, General?' she said smiling. Two girls at the far end of the bar had been making eyes at him for the past ten minutes.

'Not much changes round here… fortunately.'

'I'm sure. How long were you stationed here?'

'Eighteen months.' *Eighteen months*, it had seemed more like a lifetime immediately after Afghanistan.

'So…?' she said, interrupting his train of thought.

'I was thinking how *beautiful* you are.'

'You'll have to do better than that, General. I'm not one of *those* girls,' she said, casting a glance down the bar. But he could see she was not offended.

'Old habits die hard.'

Sitting there only inches from her, Yuri wondered if she were seeing anyone. He knew that she and Stolin were no longer, only from what Misha had said, but that was as far as his knowledge went.

'Do you mind if I ask you a question?' he asked.

'Depends.'

'You and Konstantin Ivanivich... no, it's none of my business,' he said, suddenly getting cold feet.

'We're not seeing each other, if that's the question.'

'Not quite, more why, really, or a how.'

'You mean how a nice girl like me gets involved with someone like him... maybe I'm not so nice.'

'That I can't believe.'

'It's complicated. I've asked myself the same question... often. He's smart... good-looking... I always used to feel I could rely on him... he came to my rescue once.' She looked down at the floor, and Yuri could see she was struggling with her emotions and wished he hadn't pursued the conversation. She looked back up at him with watery eyes.

'I'm sorry,' Yuri heard himself say. 'I didn't mean to upset you.'

'No, that's fine,' she said, wiping her eyes and giving him a broad smile. 'Kostya and I go back a long way... we were at Ten Year School together, along with Misha and Ivan. You know, I can't say I had a perfect home life, far from it, but Kostya's was chaotic. His mother had a series of affairs that his father turned a blind eye to... neither of them were ever at home. It was his older sister, Zoya, who mostly looked after him.'

'How did... do... those two get on together – Misha and Kostya?' he said, attempting to shift the conversation.

'They don't, but over the years they've learned to maintain a respectful distance... after a few run-ins. I was the common factor, a sort of go-between, keeping the peace.' She smiled. 'They are very different. Misha flits from one idea to the next. You've met him... a human dynamo... Kostya is much more self-contained; in fact, the most single-minded person I have ever met... and when he focuses on you, he focuses on you. He can be very charming. I was younger then, when I first became involved with him... he was very glamorous... but the one thing I have learned is that Kostya has only really been interested in satisfying one thing.'

'And what is that?'

'Himself. We are all means to his ends.'

They fell silent.

'Enough about me... what about you,' Viktoriya said with a wry smile.

'Not much to say... men don't come more superficial than me, I'm afraid... or so I've been told... many times.'

She laughed. He resisted the temptation to reach out his hand and touch her.

'I'm sure... parents, brothers, sisters?'

'Father, retired colonel; mother a teacher – a devoted couple; and younger brother an Aeroflot engineer, married, a son, lives in Moscow... great kid.'

'And you decided to follow in your father's footsteps?'

He nodded.

'Always seemed like a good idea. I can't remember when I didn't want to be a soldier.'

'And has it lived up to expectations?'

'It has its frustrating moments... but yes, I can honestly say I feel born to it.'

'And have you ever been frightened?'

'Sure...' Yuri remembered Afghanistan and the first time he experienced incoming, halfway up a mountain pass when mortars rained in without warning. The soldier next to him had been ripped to shreds by scrap metal that had miraculously left him unscathed.

'But you get used to it... most of it... otherwise you couldn't function.'

He took a swig of beer.

'You seem very distracted of late. I'm sure you have a lot going on.'

'You could say that,' said Yuri, and laughed. He hesitated, deciding whether to share his suspicions. 'I think we are reaching some sort of tipping point.'

'Go on.'

'You saw Roslavi yesterday. Just another example... perestroika isn't working, not yet... On top of that we have democracy breaking out in Eastern Europe, a new government elected in Poland, anti-communist and anti-Soviet, and now Hungary. If there is an uprising, the general secretary is not going to be the man to put it down...'

'But someone else might, you think?'

'I've been wracking my brains on that one. You and Misha will have to watch out. We all will. We'll be right in the firing line, literally, if someone tries to turn the clock back.'

'In the meantime?'

'Soldier on, that's what a soldier does.'

It was as he drew back that Yuri clocked the two men sitting at a table towards the back of the bar observing him. He had subconsciously noticed them before, but it was only now that he became alert to them studying him across the room.

'Excuse me, Vika.'

He walked over to their table.

'Can I help you?' asked Yuri. 'You seem overly interested in either me or my friend.'

'Good evening, General,' said the taller of the seated men. Yuri was not in military uniform. 'How does it feel to be back in your old hunting ground?'

'What's that to you?'

'You've certainly moved up in the world, General, fame and fortune, not to mention a beautiful... and rich woman, it would be a shame to see that all come to an end because you backed the wrong people.'

'And who precisely are the wrong people,' said Yuri, feeling his anger rise.

'Anti-Soviet, of course.'

They had to be KGB, Yuri thought.

'You know what, whoever you are, life is full of threats and opportunities,' said Yuri. 'I'll take my chances. You can tell your boss, from whatever directorate you are from, I won't be so polite next time I find someone trailing me. Now, I don't want you spoiling my favourite bar or evening so I suggest you leave quietly or I can always have those soldiers over there assist.'

The two men got up. The taller of the two took a step forward towards Yuri.

'Let's go,' said the other man, placing a restraining hand on his colleague's arm.

Yuri watched the two of them cross the bar and exit onto the street. When he turned to find Viktoriya, he discovered her studying him from across the room, a concerned look on her face.

'Well they clearly liked you,' Viktoriya said when he made it back to the bar.

Maybe they were closer to that tipping point than he had at first thought. When the KGB started threatening the military, things were indeed coming to a head.

'Dinner?' he said. 'They haven't put me off my food. But not here.'

Snow had already begun to fall when they headed out, lightly at first but within minutes heavily, covering domes, buildings, streets and the frozen Dnieper itself in a thick white blanket. As it swirled in flurries and eddies around them, Yuri put his arm around Viktoriya in a protective manner, engulfing her in his long great coat. When they finally arrived at the restaurant, Yuri gave her a gentle tug. Wordlessly, they agreed to continue to explore this new wonderland… until the cold finally drove them back inside.

CHAPTER 35

Early morning, two men trudged out from the city centre towards the suburbs along still and mostly deserted snow-covered streets. Others shuffled by, pulling small sledges, embarked on some essential errand, wrapped in padded coats, hoods up, heads down, faces masked by woollen scarves against the sub-zero temperature. Single white flakes drifted slowly past, threatening another major early snow. Snowploughs would eventually do their work but probably not until the next day or the day after that, after the main roads were cleared. Until then, the roads would remain impassable to ordinary traffic.

The shorter of the two men gripped a small but heavy bag. They had taken turns carrying it, switching it from arm to arm as they crunched along the narrow lanes. Up ahead, they could make out the snow-covered outline of the Leningrad Freight warehouse on the edge of the deserted industrial estate, its east face rising above an adjacent open storage lot. In the snow it looked different to the yard they had reconnoitred the day before, prior to their unfruitful encounter with the general.

They paused for a moment under the canopy of a snow-covered tree. The small man put down the bag to catch his breath. They stood there, silent, hidden from view for some minutes, looking and listening for sounds of life and security patrols. Only their breath, visible in the freezing air, gave them away. A stray dog appeared, sniffed around their feet and wandered off disinterested.

'What do you think?' said the shorter one.

'Looks perfect, the place is deserted,' he replied, looking beyond the warehouse and lot to the derelict windowless building behind.

Staying close to the building line, they walked the final hundred metres to the entrance of the storage lot. It was secured by a flimsy metal gate tied shut with a padlock and chain.

'Pass me the wire cutters,' said the taller of the two. He cut a vertical opening in the chain-link wire mesh fence, peeled it back, and, after one final look around, slipped through, his partner close behind. Making their way past building materials and construction equipment in varying states of disrepair, they arrived at a mountain of empty wooden pallets, stacked five metres high, close against the wall of the neighbouring Leningrad Freight warehouse and wooden rafters above.

'Made for the job, I would say,' said the taller man, looking up at the dry inner layers of timber.

They wandered around the yard collecting sacking, old paint and fuel cans – anything they thought might burn – and stuffed them roughly between the stack of pallets.

'This'll teach that general to watch his mouth.'

'I hope they've got insurance,' the smaller man joked as he stepped back a few feet. From the carrier bag he removed a large can of petrol. The taller man, the one who had spoken to Yuri in the bar, extracted a lighter from his pocket and ran his thumb over the wheel. He adjusted the flame till it leapt several inches into the air.

'Okay, we don't want to waste this, so make sure you give the dry wood a good soak,' instructed the taller man. Petrol fumes tainted the crisp winter air as his partner emptied the can, shaking it vigorously to extract every last drop.

'That'll do!' said the man with the lighter. 'Best move right back now, well away from this lot.'

The shorter man threw the now empty can into the pallet shelving and stepped back a good twenty feet, close to where his partner stood waiting.

'Here goes then.'

He hit the flint again. The flame spurted upwards.

'Enjoy the fireworks!' he said, and took a step towards the tinderbox of pallets.

Blood and brain splattered the ground as a single rifle shot echoed off the buildings and walls. The lighter flame traced the arsonists fall to the ground, finally extinguishing itself in the snow.

In an upper window of the derelict building his companion caught the glint of a telescopic sight.

'Don't shoot!' he yelled. 'Don't shoot!' He threw his hands up into the air and fell onto his knees.

'Stay where you are! Don't move!' shouted back

the marksman. 'Or you'll be as dead as your friend.'

'I'm not moving!' the arsonist shouted back.

Kneeling in the snow, his face turned towards the pallets and wall, he heard the crunch of footsteps making their way towards him from the gate. He made to turn around, but a powerful kick to his back sent him sprawling, face forward, into the snow.

'I thought my comrade told you not to move. Isn't that right?'

'Yes! Yes!' he shouted, as a boot applied pressure to the knuckles of his right hand.

'Put your other hand up where I can see it!'

From the corner of his eye, the prone man noticed another standing next to the man that kicked him, a man in a military coat. He caught the faint citrus scent of his aftershave.

'You were right, General. You thought they might try something,' said Ivan.

Ivan waved at the sniper in the upper window.

Yuri bent down and turned the dead man over. The bullet had exited through his nose, shattering most of his cheekbone and eye socket, but he was clearly recognisable as the man in the bar.

'Get him up,' said Yuri, indicating the man slowly freezing in the snow.

Ivan grabbed the would-be arsonist by the scruff of the neck and dragged him to his feet.

'I won't insult my intelligence or yours by asking who sent you. As you see, I'm not entirely surprised to see you.'

'We all take orders, General, although this little bonfire was a bit of unplanned arson'

Yuri raised his pistol and shot him in the forehead. 'There's no doubting his boss will get the message now.'

CHAPTER 36

LENINGRAD

'Good evening, Viktoriya Nikolaevna,' greeted the concierge as Viktoriya walked into the lobby of her apartment building.

The journey back from the airport had taken well over an hour, and she was looking forward to a glass of wine and running a hot bath. Standing in front of the lift door she absentmindedly watched the indicator light describe its downward journey.

'Your electrician called in earlier.'

At first she thought the concierge was talking to someone else.

'What electrician?' Viktoriya said, jolted out of her thoughts.

'He said you had some urgent electrical work needing doing,' the concierge replied. He looked uncomfortable. 'When I queried him, he showed me a typed order with your name and address on it.'

'Shouldn't you have checked the log? I hadn't informed you of any such call,' Viktoriya said angrily, doubly irritated by the concierge talking to her legs.

'When he showed me the order I thought you had just forgotten. I'm sorry. He left a few hours ago.'

Viktoriya headed back out through the revolving door onto the street and waved at her security detail parked across the street. Two men jumped out and jogged over to where she was standing.

'We'll go up and check,' said one of the men when she had explained what had happened.

'Why don't you wait down here in reception?' said Vladimir, one of her more permanent bodyguards.

'I'm coming with you,' she said firmly.

'Misha wouldn't be very happy if he found out.'

'Are you more frightened of Misha or *me*?'

The two men looked at each other and shrugged. 'Okay, but you stay behind us.'

The two extracted their automatics from under their black leather jackets.

'I hope there isn't going to be any shooting,' said the concierge somewhat bravely when she reappeared in the lobby, this time with two armed men.

'I hope so too,' said Viktoriya.

Her apartment was on the fourth floor. Rather than take the lift, they climbed the staircase that wound its way around the lift shaft to her landing. She fished out the front door key from her bag and handed it to Vladimir while the other man checked for obvious signs of wires or booby-traps. He shook his head signalling the all-clear and released the safety catch of his gun, ready to cover his partner. Vladimir inserted the key, turned, and pushed the door wide.

Burglaries were becoming a common occurrence,

and Viktoriya expected to find her apartment ransacked. To her surprise, everything looked in perfect order. The coffee table with photos of her and her parents, and one of her and Misha taken as teenage school friends, found recently, were undisturbed, as was an expensive wristwatch she had left there in full view that morning. Viktoriya wondered if the concierge had somehow got it wrong, mixed up her apartment with someone else's. She looked at her two bodyguards and shrugged.

'Let's check the other rooms,' she said, and explained the layout of the apartment.

Leaving Viktoriya in the living room, the two men moved down the corridor. There were two doors to the right – her bedroom and a spare room – and her bathroom and one for storage on the left.

The doors were all closed except the one to her bedroom, which was slightly ajar.

'Do you remember how you left these?' asked the bodyguard facing the first door on the right.

'No,' said Viktoriya. 'The cleaner was in this morning.'

As the door was already slightly ajar, they decided on the bedroom first. Vladimir extracted a small torch from his jacket and, with his fingers, slowly and carefully began to explore the door frame for wires or triggers. He moved down the door and architrave, waving the torch beam back and forth for any filament reflection.

'Where's the light switch,' the first bodyguard said, looking back at Viktoriya, who was now at the sitting room end of the corridor.

'On the left as you go in.'

He nodded, and pushing the door open a fraction more, he reached in with his hand and switched on the light.

The bedroom was as Viktoriya remembered it, except, of course, for the now made-up bed. She slid open the mirrored wardrobe that ran along one wall of the bedroom. Dozens of dresses and outfits, neatly arranged, hung from the wardrobe rail, and below them pairs of shoes and boots stretched from one end to the other. Viktoriya shrugged, baffled.

They repeated the same procedure for the spare room – again nothing. They returned to the bathroom door where they had almost begun. Maybe the whole thing was some sort of prank, or the concierge really had got it wrong. Viktoriya thought of calling the front desk, asking the concierge to come up to the apartment and confirm that this was the one he had let the electrician into, but her two security service men were concentrating on the bathroom door and she decided not to disturb them. Vladimir tensed to push it open.

'Stop!' she shouted. An alarm rang in Viktoriya's head; some instinct or ghost of intuition screamed at her that something was wrong.

Startled, the two men stepped back. The bathroom door was always left ajar to ensure it was properly aired, so that damp did not build up. Her cleaner, an elderly woman, had told her in a motherly way not to close it. She always left the door and the outside bathroom window open a crack.

'I may be overreacting, but that door is normally left open,' she explained.

From the corridor there was no way they could see into the bathroom.

Vladimir opened the storage room door, pulled up the sash window and leaned out. It was a short distance, six feet, from the corner of the storage room window sill to that of the bathroom, a stretch and a bit. He looked down four floors to the street below; a wide shelf ran around the outside of the building, four or five feet directly below the window.

'Are you sure you are up for this?' said Viktoriya, genuinely concerned.

'The alternative is to go through the door. No, this is a piece of cake.' He didn't sound so confident.

As he flattened himself against the wall, with his partner firmly gripping his left hand, Viktoriya watched Vladimir edge his way along the shelf, testing it gingerly with his foot as he went. He stopped when his hand made contact with the end of the bathroom sill.

'Right,' he said out loud to himself. He took a deep breath, let go of his friend's hand and shuffled directly under the bathroom window. With his left hand firmly grabbing the sill, he forced the sash window up with his right and hauled himself through the gap.

'I am in!' he shouted, not without some considerable relief in his voice.

'Can you see anything Vlad?' Viktoriya asked.

Underneath the door she saw the beam of his torch moving back and forth and then the door open inward.

'All-clear,' he said brushing ice off the front of his jeans.

The *electrician* or the cleaner must have closed the bathroom door, she thought.

Going back into the living room, Viktoriya flopped down on the sofa.

'I want the concierge gone by tomorrow.'

Neither of them commented.

It was then she noticed something she hadn't picked up on before. The phone on the small coffee table by the sofa normally faced away from the sofa but now faced towards it. The cleaner might have moved it but she invariably replaced it where she found it. Viktoriya put one finger to her lips and caught the eyes of the two men. Inspecting the outer casing first, she gently unscrewed the mouthpiece. Inside was a tiny electronic listening device. She had seen something similar before at a friend of her father's, who worked for the Peasants' Union. Viktoriya pointed the device out to Vladimir and the other guard, and then carefully reassembled the receiver and replaced the handset back on the glass tabletop. She stepped back into the centre of the room away from the sofa.

'I said I'd call in on Misha this evening. Let me get my coat.'

Viktoriya spoke to them again when they were all out in the corridor.

'I want you to go over my apartment with a bug detector, every centimetre... but do not disturb anything... you never know, it might come in useful.'

11 OCTOBER 1989

CHAPTER 37

MOSCOW

'Come in, General Marov. Thank you for coming to see me so promptly.'

Yuri heard the door click shut behind him.

Colonel General Andrei Ghukov stood next to a wall map of Europe. A line traced the Iron Curtain dividing East from West and coloured pins the disposition of allied and enemy forces – red for Soviet, black for local and blue for NATO.

'I've just met with the general secretary... I suppose you have been following the reports.'

'Yes, sir,' was all he said. What had started a month ago, with Hungary opening its borders with Austria and letting thousands of East Germans use it as an escape route to the West, had escalated into mass protest against the East German government. The general secretary's recent visit had only increased tensions.

'Honecker is a fool if he thinks he can keep a lid on this,' Ghukov continued. 'The general secretary has signalled change and all his government have done is stonewall. He is losing control. He's been there too long.'

Eighteen years, thought Yuri. Honecker and the Communist East German government had seen three general secretaries come and go.

'We are putting pressure on him to resign, as are his colleagues. I don't think it will be long in coming. But the long and short of it is that the general secretary will not intervene. He has assurances from the Americans that they will not take advantage of the situation if we allow Eastern Europe to break free.'

'You trust them, sir?'

'I don't think we have a choice, not if we want to avoid a lot of bloodshed.'

'And General Volkov?' asked Yuri. Volkov had enough hardware and manpower to steamroller Western Europe.

'Volkov called and recommended I persuade the general secretary to intervene before it's *"too late"*, to use his actual words.'

They were both silent for a minute.

'And your view, sir?' asked Yuri.

'We shouldn't intervene. I am with the general secretary for all the reasons we have discussed. It's time we stepped back.

'General, you are close to the district generals. How do you think they will react?'

Yuri shrugged. 'I don't know sir, they are hard to read… with the exception, of course, of generals Volkov and Vdovin… I can't say there is much enthusiasm around the table for Soviet troop reductions.'

Yuri wondered whether the colonel general, having come so far, might backtrack. He and the general secretary were clearly under pressure.

Ghukov fell silent and contemplated the map as though the answer he was looking for might be there.

'Where are you going to be for the next few days, General?'

'Archangel, sir... a new weapons trial. I can reschedule if you'd rather I stayed in Moscow.'

'No, General, you go. It would send the wrong signal not to.'

As Yuri's staff car drove him back to his apartment building, Yuri reflected on the conversation he had just had with the chief of staff and earlier that morning with Terentev. His KGB friend had drawn a blank; there was no record of *any* meetings, which only deepened his suspicions. He knew from the lieutenant that that wasn't the case, and he didn't think she was lying.

As he passed reception, the concierge handed him an envelope. Yuri waited until he was in his apartment before opening it. Inside, a card read:

Dear General, Further to your enquiry, I can confirm your suit will be ready on October 13.

It was a message from Biryukova. So there was to be another meeting. He must get a message to Ilya. If Ilya could have some of his men trail the committee members the lieutenant had identified, maybe he could take his suspicions to Ghukov with some hard facts. He called a driver and scribbled a note.

Thank you for dinner the other evening and sorry I will miss your celebration on October 13. See you when I return from Archangel.

He was sure Ilya would get the point.

CHAPTER 38

LENINGRAD

Adriana rolled a dollar bill, inserted it into her left nostril and snorted the line of white powder Konstantin had neatly cut her and left on the low table. She closed her eyes and fell back into the sofa. When would Konstantin be back? She couldn't remember what he had said now. Her heart was pounding in her ears so loudly that she thought it might burst. He had only left a few minutes before, but she wasn't certain now. The sound of catcalls and music filtered down from the bar. For the first time that evening she was alone, away from lecherous looks and pawing hands.

How many lines of coke had she snorted that night? She tried to remember. Evenings had begun to blur since she had begun to work at Pravdy. Konstantin seemed to take a special pleasure in summoning her when she had been on the floor a few hours. He would pump her with coke before fucking her on the sofa or presenting her to one of his political cronies or that disgusting General Vdovin, tipping her with extra coke if she performed well. She *hated* all of them.

There was a bang on the door, and a male voice shouted '*On in ten minutes!*'

'*Okay!*' she shouted back. Re-energised, Adriana stood up and loosened her short pink satin kimono; she was boiling. Catching sight of herself in the mirror, she eased it off her shoulders and gyrated to the dull beat of the music. She looked *great*, better than great. Thank God for coke, she thought. Had she had one or two lines before sex with Konstantin? She lost her balance, nearly fell over and grabbed the edge of the desk. He had to keep the stuff somewhere in his office, the way he dished it out.

She kicked off her high heels, walked round to the other side of the desk and pulled open the main drawer: Cuban cigars, a guillotine cigar cutter, condoms, a vibrator, a Markov automatic with its safety catch off, a photograph of Viktoriya. She held it up and studied it. She was finding it hard to focus and wondered if she would be able to make it back on stage. Maybe she could persuade Irina to take her place. Studying the image of her former competition, she wondered what was so special about her. She was good-looking, but then weren't all the girls in Konstantin's clubs? She knew that they had had an almighty row some time ago and he had thrown her out, but according to the other girls he had never roughed her up, ever, but how did *they* know. She put back the photo and picked up an old ID card. A man in his fifties with Brezhnev eyebrows stared up at her. She read his name out loud, 'Pavel Pytorvich Antyuhin.' She thought it looked like the same card

Konstantin had been holding in his hand when she had re-entered the room after his old flame had been shown out. Maybe it had been her who had given it to him. Buried under a small notebook Adriana found what she was looking for, a small bag of white powder. Using the ID, she marshalled two lines on the desk and snorted them back in quick succession.

Recharged, she stood up and wiggled back on her shoes. The face of Antyuhin stared up at her from the desk. She picked it up again, puzzled. Who was he? *Trouble*, no doubt, for that too good whore ex of Konstantin.

CHAPTER 39

'These are the *proscribed*, the supposed enemies of the state.' Konstantin looked down the list. Someone had taken the trouble to put it into alphabetical order and head it *Leningrad*. On it were seven names: Gavrilov from the gorkom was there, marked with a tick, Artem, a deputy, a tick, the list went on with ticks and crosses… and Mikhail Dimitrivich Revnik, a cross.

'They…' said Vdovin. The famous *they*, thought Konstantin, '…want you to detain the ticks and eliminate the crosses.'

Vdovin gawped at him across his desk.

'*You* signed up to it,' Vdovin reminded him when Konstantin said nothing. 'They can revoke that arms licence just as easily as they issued it.'

Vdovin was right in more ways than one. He could hardly back out now, not unless he wanted his own name added to the list. He would just have to make sure he covered his tracks.

'For the record, I tried to change that cross to a tick. He wouldn't wear it. He's adamant, made a big point about it. He also said you can sequestrate his business and take over control of Leningrad Freight for good measure.'

Mikhail Revnik. It was an irony that that one-time-nothing had become public enemy number one. And over what... some fogged photographs? Before, keeping him alive might have mattered, but not now; he didn't owe him or his ex-girlfriend anything. Hadn't he even offered him a partnership and been laughed off? Konstantin took a lighter from his pocket, lit the list and watched it turn to ash.

'And when does this all kick off?'

'Imminently... East Germany is not going to be allowed to collapse.'

'And how will I know?' For the first time in years, Konstantin felt he was back taking orders from his old colonel again.

'When I give you the code word.'

'Which is?'

'Stroika.'

12 OCTOBER 1989

CHAPTER 40

Viktoriya answered the phone.

'I hope I haven't caught you at an awkward time.' It was Yuri. She had not heard his voice since the evening in Smolensk.

'No, it's fine.' She looked at her watch: eight thirty in the morning.

'I just wanted to say how much I enjoyed our evening and I hope we can do it again.'

'Yes, that would be lovely.'

Indeed, she had thought of that evening a great deal. Not much had happened. They had kicked the snow, walked and talked and talked. She had hardly noticed the freezing temperature buried inside his coat. But back in Leningrad she had felt different, more settled, centred. It was hard to define, but she was sure it was to do with that evening.

'Maybe when I'm back from Archangel.'

She hadn't had the opportunity to tell him about her eavesdropper and was beginning to regret not having it removed. 'I leave Moscow tomorrow for a few days; we can sort something out when I get back, maybe even go to Europe, if I can pull some leave.

Yes,' she found herself saying. 'I could give you the grand tour.'

There was a pause as if he were weighing something up, trying to be careful with words. It occurred to her then that he might well suspect her phone being bugged; he couldn't take the chance that it wasn't.

'Okay, I'll let you plan it. It's like what we were saying at the bar, *now or never*. Take care, Vika.'

She replaced the receiver and stood staring blankly at the wall going over his words. She should have felt delighted but somehow it did not ring true... *now or never*. They hadn't talked about *now or never*. They'd talked about a potential coup and a tipping point. But, of course, that's what he *did* mean. He must know or suspect *something*, and weren't there all sorts of rumours flying around about what was going on in Eastern Europe?

A loud bang on her apartment door made Viktoriya jump. She switched on the security camera. Outside in the corridor three uniformed police stared up at her while another argued with her two bodyguards, waving a piece of official-looking paper at them.

Viktoriya pulled open the door.

'Viktoriya Nikolaevna Kayakova?' asked the one with the official-looking paper in his hand.

'Yes.'

'We have a warrant for your arrest in connection with the death of Pavel Pytorvich Antyuhin.' The officer showed her the warrant and his badge.

'I don't know what you are talking about,' she lied.

How did they know? *What* could they know? Kostya wouldn't have betrayed her, not when he was directly involved. 'You've made some mistake.'

'You'll have to come with us, madam, I'm afraid. You can either do it peaceably or not.'

He stood there and stared at her, calmly, daring her to disobey him.

Vladimir stepped in between her and the police officer.

'You're not taking her anywhere.'

The last thing she wanted was a fight.

'Vlad, it'll be all right. I'll sort this out; there's clearly been some mistake. You can follow me to the police station. I was meant to meet Misha and Konstantin Ivanivich later. Will you please tell them straightaway what has happened?' Indeed, she had no plan to meet Kostya that day, but maybe he could figure out what was going on.

CHAPTER 41

'So where is she being held?' asked Konstantin. He'd arrived unannounced five minutes before at Malaya Morskaya and been quickly ushered in to Misha's office.

'Leningrad Oblast Main Internal Affairs Directorate, GUVD,' replied Ivan. Vladimir had just radioed through that they had moved her to police headquarters on Suvorovskiy Prospect.

'That's a shithole of a place,' said Misha. 'People go in there and never come out, not in one piece anyway.'

'Why was she arrested?' said Konstantin.

'I've sent a lawyer over there to find out. It's something to do with the murder of that Khozraschet director who got washed up on the Neva years ago. It doesn't make any sense... what would she have to do with that? She was only a student at the time.'

Konstantin rubbed his chin. What could they have on her after all this time? How many years had it been? Only five people had known, if he included Viktoriya's father, and he was clearly no longer a witness.

'Any ideas?' prompted Misha.

'Nope,' he said, genuinely at a loss. And if they had something on her, did they have something on him? The police weren't knocking on his door, not yet. He had to trust she would keep her cool and deny everything, but the GUVD were hardly famous for their record on human rights. They had broken stronger people than Viktoriya.

'Let me dig around, see what I can come up with. Let me know what your lawyer says.'

For once, thought Konstantin, not without some irony, they were on the same side.

*

Viktoriya waited for what seemed hours. The room was airless, lit by two recessed lights protected by a metal mesh. Her jewellery and watch had been removed when she had arrived and there was no way she could measure passing time. A policeman entered and took down her personal details: date of birth, address, place of work, marital status. When she had asked for a glass of water she was simply ignored.

A few minutes later the interview room door swung open. Two police officers walked in and took the chairs opposite her: one a woman – a sergeant by her stripes – and the other, the man who had served the arrest warrant at her apartment.

'So tell me, where were you on the night of December 11, 1982?' asked the man.

'I've no idea; you can hardly expect me to

remember so far back. Can you remember what you were doing that night?'

The sergeant leaned forward threateningly. 'You may have money and a fancy apartment, but in here they are worth nothing… don't be smart.'

The man extracted a photograph from a file.

'Do you recognise this man?'

It was Antyuhin. She felt her heart quicken and her face go red.

'No,' she said, looking him directly in the eye with a confidence she did not feel.

'The night before he disappeared it says in the file he drank at the Muzey bar. You worked there as a student – it says so here in your file.' He referred to a second file with her name on it. It was at least three centimetres thick.

'Yes, that's true, I waitressed there as a student… but I served *hundreds* of customers. I don't keep a mental log of each of them. Do you remember *everyone* you interview?'

'Absolutely.'

He picked up the other file again. 'It goes on to say that a young girl, of your description, was spotted outside the Palace Bar the following night, the night he disappeared and was probably murdered.

'*Murdered?*' She acted astonished. 'And you think I had something to do with it?'

'There are witnesses that say he drank at the Palace that evening.'

'I did meet my boyfriend that night outside the Palace Bar. I remember the policemen. I never saw

256

this man though,' she said, tapping the photograph.

The captain reached into the file again and tossed an ID card onto the table.

'And you haven't seen this before?'

It was Antyuhin's ID card. How had it got into their hands? Had Kostya betrayed her? But that didn't make sense either; he would only be incriminating himself if he had.

'It came with this note.'

He showed her a piece of paper with her name on it, nothing else.

'An *anonymous* note, it's all circumstantial. You should be trying to find the person who sent you this. I want to see my lawyer.'

The captain picked up the papers he had spread on the table and carefully put them back in their folder.

'We are trying to locate your previous flatmate, Agnessa; maybe she can throw some light on this.'

CHAPTER 42

Konstantin sat in his armchair, staring at his desk, going over that night nearly seven years before. Ilia, who, with his friend Lev, had been with them on that night long ago, had been as surprised as he when confronted with Viktoriya's arrest. What possible motive would he have anyway? And Ilia knew the price of disloyalty.

He reached into his desk drawer and felt for Antyuhin's ID card, as if by looking at his photo it might tell him more… nothing. He scrambled around, unpacked it; the ID was nowhere to be found. For a moment he wondered whether it had fallen down the back of the drawer, but then he noticed the bag of coke. He held it up to the light. It was a good deal emptier than when he last looked at it. He picked up the telephone and dialled the bar upstairs. A minute later Dimitri Bazhukov appeared in the doorway.

Konstantin looked at his watch: eight o'clock.

'Where is Adriana?'

'Upstairs, getting ready to go on?'

'Get someone else to cover for her and send her down. In fact, accompany her down. I don't want her doing a runner.'

Alone again, Konstantin wondered what was happening at the GUVD. He knew Viktoriya; she was smart, but she wasn't indestructible.

Adriana walked into the room and sauntered over to his desk. She was wearing jeans and a T-shirt, her hair was pulled back tightly from her face and held in place by a headband.

'Early for you, Kostya. As you see, I'm not properly dressed yet,' she said sarcastically.

Konstantin picked up the small polythene bag containing the cocaine and waved it in front of her.

'I reckoned you owed me after last time,' she pouted defiantly.

'Anything else you removed from my desk?' he said casually. She shifted onto her other foot.

'No, just some coke,' she replied, shaking her head.

Konstantin got up, walked round the desk, grabbed her by the hair and banged the side of her face down hard on the desk. Doubled over and clearly in pain, she squinted up at him sideways.

'All I took was the coke,' she whimpered.

He lifted her head up from the table and this time banged her face down on the table. Blood gushed from her broken nose. He gave her her due; she did not give in easily. She was moaning now. Her legs gave in and collapsed. Konstantin dragged her by the hair to the coffee table, flicked on the cigar lighter and moved it close to her hair.

'No, no, stop!' she stammered. 'All right, yes, I took the ID card. That *bitch*, she deserves it, with her airs and graces.' Konstantin moved the flame closer and wondered if her hair would just singe or go up in a whoosh with all the product she had in it. 'I posted it to the police with her name on a note – that's all, nothing else. I didn't mention you or anything.'

So they hadn't got anything concrete *yet*, Konstantin thought, it would all be circumstantial. Maybe they could place Antyuhin at the Muzey the night before he disappeared but then *so what... what else?*

'Dimitri, find Agnessa Raskolnikova Agapova. She works at Technopromexport. Keep her out of sight; send her on holiday... anything, while I sort this out. And you,' he said to Adriana, 'you are going to write a confession, fiction of course, that a punter gave you the ID and that in a fit of jealous rage you tried to incriminate Viktoriya Nikolaevna. Igor is then going to take you down to Suvorovskiy and you are going to hand it in personally to the police and take the consequences. Do I make myself clear?'

She nodded.

'And clean yourself up, you're a mess.' Konstantin let go of her hair and pulled her to her feet.

Bazhukov waited until Igor had led Adriana out of the room.

Konstantin looked up at him, wondering why he was still hanging around.

'There was a message from the general, boss. He said to make sure you got it, he was in a hurry.'

'What did he say?'

'*Stroika...* just *Stroika...* he said you'd understand.'

13 OCTOBER 1989

CHAPTER 43

MOSCOW

Yuri boarded the military transport by the cargo ramp and made his way up to the cockpit. Four faces looked up at him as he entered.

'General,' said the captain. He introduced himself as Captain Yevgeny Derevenko. 'We'll be pushing off in fifteen minutes, now that you are on board. There's a seat up here in the cockpit, if you'd prefer.'

Yuri nodded and buckled himself in in the seat behind the co-pilot. Opening his attaché case, he pulled out his brief for the weapon's test scheduled for that afternoon in Archangel – a new anti-aircraft shoulder missile – and sat there staring at it, struggling to concentrate. Misha had assured him Viktoriya would soon be released and that Konstantin had it all in hand, but the fact was that she hadn't been, not yet. His first instinct, when Misha had told him, was to hop on a plane to Leningrad, but Misha had convinced him against it and persuaded him he would be more use to her in Moscow with his contacts there if there was no progress. He had reassured himself he could be back in Moscow that evening if necessary but still a big part of him felt he was deserting her.

'Coffee, General?' The engineer handed him a welcome shot of caffeine. He looked at his watch: seven thirty.

Ten minutes later they were airborne. Yuri marked familiar landmarks as they cleared Moscow on a perfect October morning. There was nothing he could do now. He would ring Misha when he landed at Archangel and decide whether to return that afternoon.

Yuri looked around the crew, each intent on some task or other. Hardly anyone spoke. He wondered if they would be more talkative if he weren't riding up front but was grateful for the quiet after everything that had been going on. He picked up his brief again, ready to read, when a loud thud reverberated down the fuselage. The aircraft shuddered like a fatally wounded bird.

'We've lost all fuel pressure on the port engine,' said the co-pilot, reading off the control panel. The aircraft lurched to the left. Derevenko threw his coffee into the bin, reached forward and switched off the autopilot.

Warning lights flashed red. An alarm sounded. Yuri leaned forward and looked back at the high octane fuel that trailed the aircraft.

'Pyotr,' said the captain to the flight engineer, 'cut the fuel supply to the port engine.'

Derevenko took a firm hold of the stick to correct the yaw. The aircraft steadied momentarily.

'Send out a Mayday, Anatoly,' the captain said calmly. 'Let's do a position check.'

The navigator checked the computer navigation system and a foldout map indicating surrounding airfields.

'The nearest airport is Cherepovets, 100 kilometres to the south-east' said the navigator, reading out the bearing. He handed the map to the captain.

'Anatoly, give them our position and airspeed.'

'We don't want to bring her in over the city,' he said, studying the map. 'We need to swing in over the mountains to the north.'

'We can jettison fuel here,' said the navigator. He indicated a position twenty kilometres south of Cherepovets.

Anatoly switched to Mayday frequency.

'Air traffic control Cherepovets, this is Flight 236, we have an emergency… do you read?'

There was a pause and then the reply: 'We read you, Flight 236. We have you on radar.'

Yuri looked over Derevenko's shoulder at the map; a mountain still stood between them and the runway… if they made it that far. It was hardly the easiest approach, even on full power. Yuri guessed their chances at less than even.

Derevenko tacked the aircraft through a slow turn eastwards. The co-pilot looked rattled but busy, checking instruments and gauges. The flight engineer and navigator had their heads down concentrating on the flight displays and mapping systems.

'We just follow the book, all of us. It's not going to

be easy but we can bring her in. Is there any coffee left in the thermos, Anatoly?' asked the captain, trying to bring some normalcy to the situation.

Anatoly reached for the thermos and poured his friend a cup of hot strong coffee, his hand shaking.

'General?'

Yuri held out his cup for a top-up.

Cloud had settled in over the mountains ahead. If there was any error they would have little or no time to adjust their inbound course. With only one engine and no fuel they would have insufficient lift or time to circle the airport a second time and the descent from the mountain to the forest canopy in front of the runway would be almost vertical.

The minutes ticked by painfully slowly.

'We'll only have one chance at this, boys,' said Derevenko.

'This is air traffic, Flight 236 adjust your bearing five degrees to south. This will put you into the wind when you approach the mountain.'

'Roger that, control tower. That will help' said Derevenko, turning around to face Yuri. 'It will give us some natural lift.'

The mountain loomed on the radar. It would not be long now, just minutes. The captain banked the plane using the rudder to counteract the effect of the dead engine and began a one hundred and fifty knot turn before tipping the yoke forward to begin their descent.

The aircraft yawed as the plane picked up speed and the flight engineer started to dump fuel. The captain stared alternately at the radar and out the cockpit window. They were descending rapidly now through thick cloud. Air traffic had told them this would break at about five thousand feet, which was no great height above the mountain top. Eight thousand feet... seven thousand feet... Yuri watched the LED clock their descent. Derevenko had already switched the warning systems to silent. Every one would be flashing or buzzing right now.

The cloud broke. They had come in too low. The mountain rose up in front of them, a flat wall of stone. Derevenko reached for the throttle. He had only seconds to correct the Antonov's height before they flew into the cliff face. Pulling back on the yoke, he throttled the engine to full power and applied left rudder with his foot to prevent the aircraft turning round on itself. A fraction's delay and the engine kicked in. The nose of the aircraft lifted, hauling its load upwards, the noise deafening. Loose objects clattered to the deck. Slowly at first, but with gathering momentum, the aircraft began to rise.

Too slow... too slow! thought Yuri. Like a siren, the mountain beckoned them forward.

Seconds later, it was upon them. The screeching and rending of metal seemed to go on forever. Yuri imagined rock ripping undercarriage panels and lights.

'Air traffic control,' said the captain, 'we're over. We've incurred damage. We are beginning our final descent.'

Final descent, Yuri said to himself.

Derevenko made one final check. 'Everyone strapped in? General?'

Yuri fastened his seat belt as tight as it would go.

'Flaps half down, Anatoly.'

Derevenko tipped the controls forward and throttled back. The aircraft nosed down towards the forest that stretched for a mile directly in front of the runway.

'Eighty-five knots,' Derevenko read from the airspeed dial. 'Wheels down,' he said calmly.

Anatoly pulled the lever to lower the landing gear, but nothing happened – the undercarriage display flashed *fault*. It must have been damaged in the scrape.

'Air traffic control, we have no landing gear. I'm going to crash-land. Brace to my order.'

Nineteen kilotons of metal hurtled earthward. Yuri could see the forest immediately below and then, in front, the runway welcoming the Antonov to her final resting place.

Derevenko lifted her nose a fraction. She was parallel with the surface now. Eighty-five knots and they crossed the runway's edge.

'Brace!' he shouted, and plunged the controls forward. Anatoly, on cue, cut all power to the engine.

All that was aeronautical flight vanished in that instant. The stricken aircraft lost all lift and collapsed onto the runway. Torn by gravitational force and mortally wounded, she began to disintegrate as she hurtled, sparks flying, along the landing strip, a half-dozen emergency vehicles in pursuit. There was nothing they could do now until the aircraft came to a halt, exploded, or both... except pray.

Finally unable to bear the stresses pulling her in

every direction, the Antonov snapped. The starboard wing tore free of the fuselage as the Antonov abandoned its preordained route and ploughed off the runway into the mud and quite suddenly stopped.

Silence replaced the ear-splitting sound of rending metal. Frozen for seconds that seemed like minutes, Yuri's hearing adjusted to the sound of burning and fire engines. The engineer was only semi-conscious and bleeding from a cut to the face. Yuri hit the release of his safety belt and wrestled him from his seat. How long they had before the whole aircraft went up could only be seconds. The captain and co-pilot opened the emergency exit and helped lower the engineer to the ground, Yuri followed, and the captain jumped last. Four firemen rushed up and pointed towards the fire trucks. They staggered thirty feet before the fuel tank ruptured and the explosion blew them off their feet. A hand pounding his back told Yuri he was still alive. He looked up at Derevenko's mud-covered face.

'Still with us, General,' he said, laughing and crying at the same time, no doubt in disbelief that they were here, alive, in one piece.

CHAPTER 44

LENINGRAD

Viktoriya sat on the edge of her bed in the windowless cell. She had slept fitfully on the hard horsehair mattress, randomly disturbed by cell checks and the incomprehensible shouts of inmates.

The noise of door hatches being opened and shut again and the rumbling of a trolley alerted her to the sound of breakfast. She had not had anything to eat since the night before and realised now how hungry she was. Her hatch slid open and a steaming bowl and a mug of something were placed wordlessly on the inside shelf. Viktoriya picked them up and carried them to a narrow shelf table. She was surprised how good oatmeal porridge and stewed tea could taste.

A half-hour later, the sound of the lock turning in the door brought her to her feet. The sergeant from the previous afternoon led her back to the interview room where the other officer sat with his now familiar brown file.

This time he produced a police photograph of the girl she had seen that last time in Kostya's office.

'Do you know this woman?' he asked.

'*Know* is probably not the operative word. I have seen her once or twice at a friend's club. I have never spoken with her.'

'And is this friend Konstantin Stolin?'

Viktoriya couldn't see how she could avoid a straightforward answer and told him that was the case.

'This woman has confessed to falsely implicating you in the murder of Pavel Antyuhin... All the same I find it all very convenient, as is the disappearance of your old flatmate.'

The sergeant sniffed, wiped her nose with the back of her hand and looked at her belligerently.

'If it wasn't for pressure from on high, I wouldn't be releasing you.'

'So you are letting me go?'

'Yes, you are free to go, once you have signed your release papers.'

He got up and left the room.

'You'd better watch out if you don't want to land up back here,' the sergeant whispered, clearly aggrieved that she would not be staying longer.

'I don't like being intimidated,' said Viktoriya, 'Sergeant...?'

'Sergeant Bobrika,' she replied looking slightly rattled.

The sergeant led her resentfully up to the reception hall. On the other side of the glass partition she saw Misha talking with Ivan. He caught sight of her and signalled.

'Just sign here,' said the sergeant aggressively.

Viktoriya gave the form a cursory review and added her signature.

Misha greeted her with a much-needed hug.

'Everything okay?' he asked.

'I certainly don't want to be visiting here again anytime soon,' Viktoriya replied, staring at the sergeant through the glass.

'I had a call from Kostya, an hour ago. Some girl that works for him fitted you up. She's been taken into custody.'

'I've been told.' Viktoriya wondered what Kostya had done to force a confession. 'Can you please take me home? I need a shower and a change of clothes. Have you heard from Yuri?' she asked, half expecting him to be there.

'*Constantly*, it took all my persuasion to stop him getting on a plane to Leningrad. I told him he would be more use in Moscow if we could not secure your release. He's on some mission out east, top secret and all that. He's been calling me every few hours asking about you, although he seems to have gone silent this morning. Maybe he's lost interest… you two clearly hit it off in Smolensk,' Misha said, smirking.

Viktoriya felt unexpectedly relieved, as if a niggling doubt she had been unaware of until then had been suddenly exorcised.

Outside, Ivan waited with the security detail. Viktoriya took in the scene: two men at the bottom of the steps; a half-dozen more across the street, their backs to the iron railings of the square, Kalashnikovs idled at waist height, three cars, engines running, tight against the kerb. A guard threw away his cigarette while another pushed himself off the railings. Eyes turned in every direction. A passing motorist slowed, curious, and was waved quickly on.

'Twitchy?' said Viktoriya.

'I've capital flight, you, and Yuri sending up distress flares. Yes, you could say so.'

She knew he was right; hadn't she been telling him for weeks to up his protection?

Ivan kissed her on both cheeks without taking his eyes off the road and indicated the middle car, flanked by four security men, parked only a few feet away. Viktoriya slid in first, Misha next.

The first and last cars filled quickly. Waved on by a bodyguard, the convoy pulled out into the road, crossed Suvorovskiy and ran a red light into Rozhdestvenskiy Square.

Viktoriya reached for Misha's hand and squeezed it, nuzzling her face against his black leather jacket, pleased to be free and in the company of her best friend.

He turned to say something, when the car in front disintegrated in a ball of fire. Deafened by the explosion, Viktoriya instinctively covered her ears. Wreckage fell like rain, heavily at first and then light, drifting in the smoke that pushed its way past them. There could be no survivors. The blazing carcass of the stricken Volga blocked the north exit.

'South exit! Flat down! South exit!' Ivan bellowed to the driver, who was already flooring the accelerator.

Black smoke rose from the spinning tyres

and the car lurched forward, dodging debris. The windscreen shattered. Splintered glass stung her face as bullets thudded into the car. Twenty metres on, the fusillade stopped as suddenly as it had begun. The car behind moved into a blocking space. Ivan leant forward and smashed out what remained of the front windscreen.

Misha slumped forward in his seat, unconscious. Viktoriya grabbed him. Her hands came away wet and sticky with blood.

'He's been shot!' she shouted, but where? It was then, in all the chaos, she saw the bullet wound to his head. She felt for his pulse. He was still alive.

'Hospital!' she shouted. Ivan nodded, but they had to survive the square first.

Intuition comes sometimes with divine clarity. Viktoriya knew beyond any doubt that the southern exit to the square was a death sentence. Whoever had planned this attack would expect them to take it.

'Hard left!' she screamed over the pounding of the car engine. 'Hard left, into the square!' They had to regain the initiative if they were to come out alive.

The driver swung the car through ninety degrees up onto the kerb. Wrenching the gateposts free of their moorings, the half-ton battering ram careered down a wide footpath to the small mountain of boulders that excused itself for a decorative feature. Once covered in alpine flowers, it was now a canvas for anti-police graffiti.

'Behind that!' she shouted. 'We can take cover here. Ivan, the south exit, they're going to be waiting there.' She knew they only had seconds before their attackers figured out they had turned off the square.

★

Ivan jumped out of the car and signalled two men – Iosif and Vladek – from the car behind to follow as Vladimir and Roman shinnied up the rock, Kalashnikovs strapped to their back.

The three ran full tilt out of the square towards the south exit. A grenade whooshed passed Ivan to his left and exploded against the railings as he dived for cover behind a line of parked cars. Iosif ran in behind him, quickly followed by Vladek.

'Did you see how many?'

Both of them shook their heads.

Ivan counted to three. Vlad and Iosif leapt to their feet and fired of a clip of shells. Ivan clocked the muzzle flash from two guns and a third man on the corner holding a GP-25 grenade launcher.

Using parked cars for cover, Ivan quickly worked his way to within twenty feet of his attackers. He shot the first as he swung an AK towards him, Vladek killed the second. Ivan watched the man with the grenade launcher raise it to his shoulder and Iosif run forward from behind, raise his gun and fire. The rocket grenade man froze and slowly toppled forward onto the pavement. Whether it was the force of the fall or the dead man's final twitch on the trigger, the percussion cap detonated, sending shards of shrapnel in every direction. Iosif took a chunk in his shoulder and fell to the ground as a fourth man emerged from nowhere. Vladek took advantage of his blind side and loosed a burst from his Kalashnikov. The perpetrator, dead on his feet, smashed into a gate behind him and slid to the pavement.

Iosif stood up, clutching his shoulder, and gave the thumbs-up.

'Vladek, let's go… the square… we'll be back for Iosif.'

Ivan paused at the mangled entrance to the square. Fifty metres to his front he caught sight of the limp figure of Roman dangling precariously from a high boulder he had seen him climb only minutes before. His Kalashnikov hung around his neck like a tourniquet pulling him downward. Blood trickled from his open mouth and his eyes stared unblinking.

Vladek touched Ivan on the shoulder and pointed at the dead body of one of their assailants, lying in the open to the side of a tree. Two others, using the same trees for cover, worked their way forward trying to get behind Vladimir, who was crouched behind a rock only a couple of metres from the dead Roman.

Ivan and Vladek were directly behind them. Neither of the two antagonists noticed their approach. When they were less than ten metres distant, Ivan and Vladek opened up with their automatics and kept firing until the two lay still on the wet grass.

Ivan looked up to the sound of spinning tyres. Two Volgas broke cover from behind the rock and raced forward. Ivan jumped into the first and Iosif and Vladek the second.

'Vladimir… the Mariinsky!' Ivan shouted at the second car, as his, with its critically wounded passenger, pulled forward and exited the killing field.

CHAPTER 45

CHEREPOVETS

A blanket over his shoulders, wet through and covered in mud, Yuri sat with a mug of hot coffee squeezed between his palms in the officers' mess at Cherepovets airport. Derevenko sat across the table, making notes while the crash was fresh in his mind.

'What do you think happened?' asked Yuri.

'Fuel line, I guess, never happened before… ruptured, loose? Odd, though, it was inspected this morning. I saw the mechanic on the wing, making an inspection.' The captain frowned.

'And…?'

'He wasn't one of the usual ground crew. I know them all pretty well, see them every day. This guy was new.'

The double door swung open and a major marched into the room with two soldiers and snapped to attention.

'General, Captain,' he addressed the two seated officers.

'General,' the major looked awkward, 'I have a

warrant for your detention.' The two soldiers stepped forward, fingers resting on the trigger guard and safety catch in the *fire* position. 'Please hand over your firearm and come with me.'

Yuri rose to his feet, furious.

'On what charge, Major?'

'It doesn't say, General.'

'This is ridiculous!' exploded Yuri. 'Who is it signed by?'

'Comrade Dubnikov, the minister of defence.'

Yuri inspected the fax now held out to him by the major.

'Military police are flying out from Moscow later this afternoon to take you back to Moscow.'

'I want to speak directly to the colonel general, General Ghukov, at the GSHQ.' He would surely sort this out.

'General, I have been trying to reach his office for confirmation but he is unavailable. I'm sorry.'

Yuri looked from the major to the two soldiers and shook his head.

'Give me the fax again.' He looked at the date and time of the warrant and up at the clock. It had only been issued half an hour ago, a good hour after the crash. Was this their fallback position?

'Please, this way. I have prepared an office for you, General, rather than the detention cells. You will be under guard, but I hope your stay will be as comfortable as possible given the circumstances.'

The major led him across an expanse of tarmac to the edge of the airfield where a small group of buildings hugged the main gate. The office was on the second floor, thirty feet above ground, its window facing inward to the runway. In the corner a gas heater glowed next to a low armchair, opposite a desk and chair on which was perched a neat pile of clothes: jeans, T-shirt and a heavy sweater.

'General, I took the liberty of organising you some clean clothes. I think we are pretty much the same size. If you hand your uniform to my men I will have it bagged and returned with you.'

'Thank you, Major… don't I recognise you from the military academy… 1986?'

'Yes, sir, we were on the same course, *Organisational Theory and the Army*. I remember how your views used to wind up the senior officers.'

'They still do, Major. I suspect that is why I am here.'

The major looked embarrassed and took his leave, promising to return in an hour or so to check on him. Two soldiers were posted guard in the outside corridor.

Yuri stripped off and changed into dry clothes. They were a good fit. He could almost have been off duty at home. He slumped down in the armchair and rotated his left arm above his head: whiplash, he was beginning to ache, he rubbed his neck. What was going on? he asked himself for the tenth time. And why was Ghukov unresponsive? None of it made sense. There was a knock on the door and the major entered. He looked perplexed. Yuri wondered what had brought him back so quickly; he had been gone for less than half an hour.

'Have you managed to get hold of the GSHQ, and spoke with General Ghukov?'

'General Marov… Colonel General Ghukov has been replaced.'

'By whom?'

'… General Volkov.'

'Volkov!' Yuri was stunned. He could see the major had something further to say. 'And…?

'The general secretary has been taken ill in his dacha outside Moscow and the deputy general secretary has temporarily assumed his responsibility… and there's more, sir… the Western Army has been put on combat-ready alert.'

'Major, if this is not a coup, I'm my uncle's aunt. The air crash and now my arrest are just part of this. God knows what has befallen Ghukov. I'll warrant there are detentions going on all over the Soviet Union as we speak. If the Western Army starts putting down the uprising in East Germany, I don't think NATO or the Americans will stand by this time… Major, do you want to be on the *wrong* or *right* side of history?'

CHAPTER 46

LENINGRAD

Viktoriya felt completely numb. Seconds before, the medical team had rushed Misha into the operating theatre, and only the gently flapping doors marked his departure. In the faces around her she read failure and defeat: five men dead, one injured and the man they were paid to protect critical. They had been exposed as weak and unprepared. She had no doubt about who was responsible; it had Kostya's hallmark. A liability inside a police cell, she was a target outside. And hadn't he already threatened Misha? Besides, nothing happened in Leningrad without Kostya's sanction.

Ivan reappeared, white and shaken. Viktoriya wiped the tears off her face.

'I need to get a grip,' she said to Ivan but really to herself. She had to bottle up her desperation and the feeling of helplessness. This was not the time nor place for either, not here.

'How many men can you call on?'

'Twenty, at most. Most of our men are covering

Roslavi and the route to the border, and we have to cover the vault.'

'Well I suggest you call them in now. We need to secure this hospital.' A hundred would hardly do it, she thought. The Mariinsky was one gigantic warren of doors and corridors.

'I blame myself for this. We should *never* have been so exposed,' Ivan said, his voice cracking.

'Misha knew the risks too. We all did. We all do.'

'Still, it was my job…'

'It still is, and Misha is still with us. You can't turn back the clock, but you can stop them finishing the job.'

Ivan looked at her more calmly. 'You know whose work this is?'

'I do and he is going to pay for it… now go!'

A cough made her turn. A uniformed police officer introduced himself as Lieutenant Lagunov.

'I'm sorry,' he started, 'this must be very difficult.' He was mid-forties, with greying brown hair and a neat moustache. 'Was Mikhail Dimitrivich your partner?'

'Friend and *business* partner, yes.'

'I need to take your statement and then I will leave you in peace.'

The fact that she was surrounded by armed bodyguards did not seem to concern him at all. Shootings had become commonplace. The last place law enforcement officers wanted to be was between two rival factions, particularly if Konstantin were involved. As far as they were concerned, money bought protection and the more money you had, the more protection you needed, which was why she was doubly surprised when he offered to leave two of his men on guard outside his wardroom.

Physically and emotionally exhausted and suffering from lack of sleep, Viktoriya lifted two metal tubular chairs from a stack she found in the waiting room, put her feet up and closed her eyes, opening them occasionally to check on the clock. As hard as she might she found it impossible to nod off; her mind would not stop racing. A gentle hand on her shoulder made her sit up. The surgeon stood over her, his mask pushed down around his neck and his blue theatre gown spotted with blood.

'He's still with us,' the doctor smiled weakly. 'He took a bullet to the lung and there has been trauma to the brain. We've removed all the shrapnel and stopped the bleeding. I've given a dose of barbiturates to reduce the intracranial pressure; he'll be unconscious for some time. We're just going to have to wait now.'

'What are his chances, doctor?' Viktoriya said, almost too afraid to ask.

'Hard to say. He's young. The body is a marvellous thing.'

There was a pause.

'We are not mafia, doctor, if that's what you're thinking. The mafia is the reason my friend is here.'

'I see this every day. Our new-found freedom comes at a price.' The doctor wrote down his number on a pad he pulled from his white coat. 'This is my telephone number. If you need to speak with me at any time, just call. They are moving him to a private ward. Someone will come and find you and let you know where. You can see him then.'

Twenty minutes later she followed a nurse to the fourth floor and a private room normally reserved for Communist Party members. Hooked up to an IV and monitor, Misha lay there serene in a clean white gown and fresh head bandage. Viktoriya gently squeezed his warm hand and lowered herself into the leatherette armchair by his bed. What should she do now? The one man she would have naturally turned to for the answer was fighting for his life. And where was Yuri? No one had heard from him. She had to come up with the answer herself. Through the open door, Viktoriya took stock of two of Ivan's men, heavily armed, standing next to two police officers. She relaxed a little. Ivan brought her a bowl of goulash from the hospital kitchen.

'I've just heard the radio,' he said, 'it may explain Yuri's silence. The general secretary has been taken ill and Gerashchenko has temporarily stepped into the role.'

'I wonder how many people are buying into that?' she said. Did this spell the end of perestroika? Would they all soon be fleeing the country? She looked back down again at the face of her helpless friend and fought off the urge to cry.

'Come on, eat. You haven't eaten all day.'

Ivan was right. She was hungrier than she thought. After devouring the goulash, she pulled a spare blanket over her and fell instantly asleep.

Viktoriya woke with a start. At first she wondered where she was. Disorientated, it all came flooding back to her. She turned to look at Misha, unconscious in the hospital bed beside her. She got up and stretched her stiff limbs, rubbing her aching back and neck from sleeping awkwardly. Her watch said two in the morning. She walked to the open door.

'Would you like me to get you a coffee, Vika,' one of the two bodyguards asked.

'No, thank you,' she responded in a cracked voice, 'a glass of water would be good though.'

The guard disappeared down the corridor towards the small ward kitchen. It was then, with only one man left, she noticed they were missing.

'Where are the police?' Viktoriya asked anxiously. 'Weren't they supposed to have been on duty?'

'They left about fifteen minutes ago. They said their replacements would be here shortly,' the bodyguard replied, sensing that he had missed something.

'Where's Ivan?' Viktoriya demanded.

'Out in front of the hospital with the others.'

With a rising sense of alarm, she grabbed him by the arm. 'Go and find him.'

The second bodyguard came back with the glass of water. She took a long gulp knowing that it might be her last for a while.

'Vladimir, Kostya's men are coming.'

Viktoriya did not question her intuition. The

police had abandoned them, and they weren't going to be there when Kostya's men returned and the shooting started.

One guard here and around seven between the ward and exit, she thought; enough to put up a resistance but not to overcome a determined attack. There were too many exits, and there was no way they could cover them all.

Ivan appeared, breathless, gun in hand.

'We've got to get Misha out of this room!'

More bodyguards appeared. Moving Misha might kill him, but staying was certain death.

'Okay, Vladimir, we need to move Misha to another floor. Disconnect the monitors; be careful not to touch the IV.'

Vladimir waved at a colleague. Carefully they began disconnecting the monitor. A third man quickly arrived as a nurse responding to the flat monitor signal ran into the room.

'What are you doing? He's in *no* state to be moved!'

'The people who tried to kill him this morning are coming back for him now. They'll be here any minute,' said Viktoriya, grabbing hold of one corner of the bed and flipping the wheel locks with her foot.

The nurse looked terrified.

'We need your help,' said Viktoriya. 'We've got to get him off this floor, hide him.'

'There's an empty ward two floors down. I can show you,' she said, pulling herself together and checking the IV was properly in place.

'Thank you,' said Viktoriya. 'I'm going to ask you

another *huge* favour,' she pleaded. 'We're not staying in this hospital; it's too difficult to defend. I need you to come with us.'

'But I have a ward to look after… this is totally irregular… I am not a doctor. Where are you taking him?' she protested, no doubt frightened to be caught up in a street killing.

'There are other nurses on duty tonight. You are not on your own. I'm afraid I can't give you a choice in this but you will be well rewarded.' Viktoriya mentioned a number greater than her annual salary.

'Let me tell the other duty nurse. I'll need to get medical supplies to take with us. Where are you taking him?' she asked a second time.

'I'll fill you in on the details when we are on our way but you will need enough medical supplies for the night and tomorrow at least.'

Viktoriya turned to Vladimir. 'Go with her!' And to the nurse, 'Don't give your colleague any details. If the ward needs cover you can have them call one of the off-duty nurses. I'll make it well worth their while too.'

'Take him down to floor two, ward six. I'll be down there in a minute.' The nurse pointed down the corridor to the service lift.

The security men wheeled the bed out of the room while Vladimir and the nurse headed to the nurses' room.

Viktoriya walked back into the office and picked up the receiver and dialled. Come on, come on. The phone rang for a minute before it was wrenched out of its cradle. A breathless voice answered.

'Grigory, I haven't time to explain. Get yourself over to Morskaya.' She hung up without giving him the opportunity to respond, and dashed out the room.

★

The two men's transit passed unnoticed as they made their way up from the underground staff car park. Moving from floor to floor, gripping automatics concealed underneath green hospital orderly overalls, they headed for the fourth floor. It had not been difficult to find out on which ward Mikhail Revnik had been placed; one call to a police contact had quickly resolved that.

It took them less than five minutes to reach the lift and take it to the fourth floor. Overalls hanging loose and unfastened, fingers tightly round the trigger guards of their automatics, they exited the lift. It was empty; the hallway was deserted.

'Fourth floor, right?'

The other nodded and pointed at the room number.

The abandoned cardiac monitor stood there flatlining, making its singular high-pitched monotone.

'Somebody left in a hurry.'

Dashing back into the corridor, they almost bowled over a nurse.

'Where is Mikhail Revnik?' the first man asked threateningly. He edged out the barrel of his gun from under his gown. Her eyes travelled up to the lift floor indicator. It rested on two.

'We haven't got time, lady.' He raised the gun and put it to her head. 'Now where is he?'

She hesitated.

'I'm going to count to three and then pull the trigger.'

'It's probably the second floor... second floor, ward six,' she stammered.

Ignoring the lift, they took the staircase down to the second floor and listened for the sound of movement. A motorbike zipped by on the road below; a flashing blue light strobed the length of the hallway. Holding their automatics in front of them, they eased out onto the empty, wide, green-lino-covered walkway. Above them a faulty fluorescent light flickered on and off. Flattening themselves against the walls, one on each side, they edged forward, moving door to door, alert to any sound or movement. Two-thirds of the way along, they froze. A chair scraped against the floor. Silently, one of the men pointed to a ward door, three down on the left, very slightly ajar. It was marked with the number six. His partner a few feet ahead of him crept forward and squinted through the narrow aperture. The room was dimly lit. He could make out the edge of a hospital bed and the slim figure of a blonde woman leaning forward, plumping up the patient's pillow.

Where were the guards? His partner pointed to the swing doors further down. She must have stationed her guards on the other side. Their best escape would be back up the stairway. He held up two fingers indicating the number of people in the room, braced himself and kicked open the door.

★

A bullet hit him full in the chest, sending him cartwheeling backwards towards the door. Viktoriya was already on her feet by the time the second man rushed into the room; against the back light of the doorway he was a perfect target. Viktoriya squared the barrel of the Makarov to the silhouette and loosed off two shots in rapid succession. Still standing, a look of shock horror on his face, he raised his gun to exact his dying revenge on the woman he knew had killed him. The patient rose from his bed and shot him at almost point-blank range.

A bullet exploded from the chamber of the dead man's gun. Viktoriya felt a searing pain in her leg.

'You've been hit!' shouted Ivan, jumping out of the bed.

'It's all right, it's only a scratch… I can have this attended to later.'

They were still half deafened by the close proximity of gunfire. The whole episode could not have lasted more than thirty seconds.

'There'll be more from where they came from, and others outside. We've got to get Misha out of here quickly,' Viktoriya said, as two of their own men appeared from the corridor.

'We need an ambulance.'

Two doors down, a nurse attended Misha guarded by two security men.

'Where is the ambulance bay?' she asked urgently of the nurse who was clearly terrified by the thunderous exchange. 'Look, we are all going to get out of here,' Viktoriya reassured her, 'but you've got to focus now,' she said calmly.

'On the east side of the hospital.' The nurse clicked the ward phone disconnect bar up and down and was quickly put through to the ambulance bay. A voice she recognised answered. 'Albert, we have an emergency. We need to transfer a patient to the Aleksandrovskaya Hospital.'

'Okay, Ivan, let's clear the men to a less obvious distance for the ambulance crew and lock the other room. We don't need any more complications right now.'

CHAPTER 47

CHEREPOVETS

Yuri stood looking out of the window towards the runway and the fire crews still pouring water on the smouldering wreckage. Repair gangs cleared debris from the runway, filling gashes with steaming asphalt. A small crane manoeuvred itself into position and lifted a piece of wing that lay diagonally across the edge of the runway. A man waved it forward onto the muddy grass verge where it summarily deposited its load. There clearly wasn't going to be any investigation, not of any meaning. How long would it take before they had the airstrip operational, Yuri thought, before the military police arrived? At most an hour or two at the rate they were progressing. And when they did arrive, how would he be sure they were who they said they were and had not been despatched by one of the clandestine services?

The crash and his arrest were not a coincidence, of that he was certain, and if they had tried to kill him once, wouldn't they just finish the job? That would be much tidier than having a three-star general locked up in some prison or reinvented gulag. He had to escape, but how? He checked the window. Only a flimsy plastic downpipe, hanging off loose guttering, provided any means of descent to the concrete surface thirty feet below. And that was only if he could open the badly corroded window that had been glued into its frame with grey gloss paint. No, that would be fatal. The downpipe looked ready to detach itself from the wall without any help from him.

The sound of the door opening made him turn.

'Captain?'

Derevenko stood in the doorway, a parka jacket in his hand.

'Put this on, General.' Yuri caught it and quickly pulled it on. 'The major has given us a twenty minute start before he raises the alarm.'

There was no time to ask questions. Yuri flipped up his hood and followed Derevenko out the door. Save for a military jeep, the large open area between the building and the gatehouse was deserted, the guards gone. Fifty metres ahead, the security barrier stood raised and the sentry box abandoned.

For a moment Yuri wondered if it was a trap. Was it all part of an elaborate ruse? *Shot while trying to escape.* It would make life much simpler for whoever wanted him out the way. He looked over at Derevenko, who waved a set of car keys in the air.

'Courtesy of the major, General,' said Derevenko smiling.

'You do not have to do this, Captain; you don't have to get involved. You saved me once today already.'

'I think I am, General. They didn't mind killing me and my crew to get to you. That is what *that* was about?'

Yuri nodded. 'As sure as I can be.'

Yuri jumped into the passenger seat as Derevenko gunned the engine. Seconds later they were through the gate headed towards Cherepovets.

'So we can go any number of ways: Moscow, Leningrad, or east to Yekaterinburg. Russia is your oyster.'

'Derevenko handed Yuri a map from the side pocket.

'The MPs land in about an hour according to the major. They are going to be close on our heels.'

'I have a bad feeling about them.'

Yev pointed to the front compartment.

Yuri reached forward and flipped open the lid, picked up his automatic and released the magazine clip. It was fully loaded. The major had not let him down after all. Which way to go? Leningrad and Moscow were a similar distance, maybe five hundred kilometres, he guessed. North-west to Leningrad, Viktoriya and a boat to Finland, or due south to Moscow, and whatever awaited him there. Leningrad and perpetual exile; the capital, arrest or the chance to clear his name. There was no real choice.

'Moscow, it has to be, Yev.'

Derevenko nodded. 'Offence is the best defence. You can't play dead with these boys.'

Yuri opened the road map; west or east of the reservoir and Sheksna River? West was a little longer but took them out of the conurbation that much quicker, and if they had to beat a retreat they would be on the right side of the globe to head north to Leningrad.

'A114, then south, Ustyuzhna…'

'Kalinin, Klin…'

'You've got it,' said Yuri. He looked at his watch: it was nearly ten. 'We can switch driving after an hour or so. We don't want to be falling asleep at the wheel after what we've both been through.'

Snow began to fall.

'They said there was early snow on the way,' said Derevenko.

'Let's see how far we get?'

CHAPTER 48

Viktoriya watched the nurse and ambulance crew gently slide their hands under Misha and lift him delicately onto the hospital trolley. He had shown no sign of regaining consciousness. The nurse reassured her that this was intentional – a barbiturate-induced coma, she called it. The brain needed time to heal. All the same, she worried that her best friend might be a different person when and if he did eventually resurface. She bent down and kissed him on the cheek.

'Ivan, we need to split up, or they are going to spot us. You can lend me Vladek and take the rest of the men downstairs to the cars.'

Ivan extracted an automatic from his holster and handed it to her.

'I know you know how to use this. I'll see you downstairs by the ambulance exit ramp.'

Viktoriya donned a nurse's uniform and tucked her hair securely under a white cap. The nurse adjusted her apron.

'Perfect,' she said, smoothing the fabric over Viktoriya's shoulders. She handed her a mask and told her to hook it over her ears and pull it down so it partially obstructed her face.

Viktoriya saw Vladek on the brink of making some wisecrack.

'And no smart comments from you,' she said, smiling for the first time she could remember that day.

Vladek handed her gun back. She lifted her apron and secured it firmly under her belt and prayed she wouldn't have to use it for the second time that night.

'Are we all set?'

The nurse and two ambulance men nodded. Squeezed between a rock and a generous bonus, the two ambulance men had fallen quickly into line. Viktoriya would deal with the driver when they were safely on board.

The hospital was a maze of intersecting corridors. It was easy to become quickly disorientated. Viktoriya looked for a reassuring sign and began to worry that the nurse might have tipped off the police.

'Don't worry, everything is going to be fine... just get me back here tomorrow,' said the nurse, clearly sensing her anxiety.

Viktoriya guessed she was more used to dealing with critical situations than most.

Five more minutes of twisting and turning and they came out unopposed on the pick-up bay. An ambulance slipped the rank and stopped next to the trolley. Viktoriya warned the nurse not to say anything to the driver; their destination was the Aleksandrovskaya. Up at the exit, two armed men she didn't recognise had stopped an ambulance and were peering in.

'A lot going on… don't know what it's all about. The duty chief called the police but that was an hour ago,' said the driver.

The nurse slid in next to the driver and Viktoriya next to her by the window. Vladek jumped into the back with Misha and the two paramedics. The driver frowned, no doubt irritated by the number of passengers, switched on the blue flashing light, and drove up to the exit.

An armed guard stepped off the kerb in front of the ambulance. He was stocky, and Viktoriya estimated late twenties, with a shaved head and wearing a metal-studded black biker jacket. The driver wound down the window.

'We're in a hurry,' the driver complained. 'Get out of my way, you've no business here.'

The other guard came round to the driver's window and waved his gun at the cab.

'Not so fast, old man. Who have you got on board?'

The nurse leaned forward and gave a name, not Misha's. 'This is an emergency. We need to get our patient to the Aleksandrovskaya Hospital.'

Close up, Viktoriya recognised the gunman who had come round to her side as one of Kostya's men from the club. He clearly hadn't recognised her, but she didn't think it would be long before he saw through the disguise. She covered the side of her face closest to him with her hand and picked up a clipboard from the open glove compartment and studied it.

'Artem, go and check in the back.'

The man in front walked round towards the rear of the vehicle. Viktoriya rested the clipboard on her lap and felt for the handle of the automatic, flicking the safety catch to fire. Her left hand fell and gently pushed the nurse back an inch or two when the gunman looked back towards Artem.

The ambulance sank a fraction on its suspension as the second gunman clambered into the back. From the front, she heard him ask for the patient's card. Viktoriya tensed. He shouted the name out the back. It was the same name the nurse had given a minute before. The gunman stepped back a foot or so as his partner jumped down from the back and slammed the rear door closed. Viktoriya relaxed a little. He was going to let them through.

The driver reached for the handbrake as the gunman looked Viktoriya straight in the eye. A flicker of recognition crossed his face and he opened his mouth to shout. Viktoriya yanked the gun from her belt, leaned across the nurse and driver and shot him square in the chest as he struggled to turn his Kalashnikov in her direction.

'Let's get out of here!' she yelled.

The driver, needing no encouragement, floored the accelerator.

Kostya's man had virtually no time to react. Viktoriya watched as Ivan and two of his men appeared at the top of the ramp and cut him down.

They cleared the hospital, took the next corner

and slowed to a gentler pace. Ivan's second car tucked in behind.

'Why so slow?' cried Viktoriya.

'You want a dead-on-arrival, or not? Where are we going then? I guess it's not the Aleksandrovskaya Hospital.'

CHAPTER 49

NEAR KALININ

Yuri pulled up two hours out of Kalinin The snow that had been falling steadily until then had gathered pace in the last ten minutes. Twice they had nearly left the road, visibility reduced to a few metres. White powdery drifts leaned against the forest edge.

'What do you think?' asked Yuri. 'You're the pilot.'

'I thought you were the tank commander… this is pretty wild. Maybe we should pull up until first light. At least they won't be sending up helicopters after us in this weather.'

A dirt track led off the road into the forest. Yuri took it and steered the jeep through the thickening snow until he reached a second fork. Left or right? He plumped for right. No wonder this vehicle was called the goat, Yuri thought, as the tyres negotiated the thick snow and ice.

Surrounded by dense wood, three hundred metres in, Yuri found what he was looking for – a small log cabin, probably used by local loggers or trappers.

'Had to be something up here,' said Yuri.

Yuri climbed out of the jeep and flipped up his collar against the intruding snow. The cabin looked abandoned, but this late it was difficult to tell. He sniffed the air; there was no telltale smell of burning wood, no glow from inside. Derevenko got out the other side and shrugged his shoulders.

The pair trudged the final twenty metres to the raised porch.

'See anything?'

Yev rubbed off the ice etched onto the window and shone the torch inside. He shook his head. Walking back to the jeep, Yuri rummaged around the boot until he found the puncture repair kit, extracted a tyre lever and forced open the cabin door.

Inside, it was dry, if not spartan. A bunk, a gas cooker with no cylinder, and a small wooden table, covered in candle wax, with four heavily repaired chairs were the sum total of its contents. An old oil can, cut into two, sat on the dusty hearth of an open fireplace and served as a box for kindling. Yuri picked up a small brittle branch and snapped it in two.

Yuri shrugged. 'Probably better than the car. There's firewood under the porch outside. I think we're safe to light up.'

In less than ten minutes a roaring fire burned in the hearth. Yuri and Derevenko sat facing the heat, tucking into the piroshky pastries provided courtesy of the major. For the first time since the morning, Yuri relaxed. Maybe he could sit out the winter here, live the simple life, fish in the ice-covered river, hunt deer.

'Do you have a dacha, General?'

'No, but my grandparents and parents did outside Yekaterinburg, where I was born. It has gone now, but it brings back good memories.' Yuri thought of the lake and golden autumnal forest that rose from its edge and rolled back over soft undulating hills.

'Some history there.'

'My grandmother saw the Tsarina shortly before they were all murdered. She worked as a maid in a neighbouring house and heard the gunfire that night. Odd when you think of it. It wasn't that long ago, generationally.'

'And now, Moscow… where do you think we will go from here – politically, I mean?' the captain asked.

'I've been thinking the same question… the general secretary *is* the revolutionary now. He understands things have to change if the country is to move forward. And the communists? The smart ones – they understand he is their nemesis. They can't both survive. Have you been to Western Europe, Captain?'

The captain shook his head.

'Well, it's a revelation.' Yuri thought of his visits to Switzerland during the Afghan pull-out negotiations and the journey from there to Milan and RUI's office. 'The average citizen does not struggle for the bare necessities of life. More than that… the choice… the freedom… go where you want… buy what you want… of course, if you have the money.'

'And you, General, how are you caught up in all this?'

'I'm a *revolutionary*.' And he laughed, not quite having put it like that before. 'I'm not alone.'

'But one of the more... *influential*.'

'Perhaps.'

'Would you consider going into politics, General?'

'I don't think I'm quite ready for that.'

The captain passed Yuri the bottle of vodka. They were silent for a moment. Yuri took a swig as he leaned forward and threw another log on the fire.

'We could just sit this, whatever-it-is, out, General. Wait until the dust settles. You could make a decision then... stay or go. Rumour has it you have money... according to the major anyway... you could leave the country... but I suspect that is not what you are going to do.'

'True, Yev.'

He was not going to be an exile. He had to get back to Moscow, figure out what was going on.

CHAPTER 50

LENINGRAD

'No Adriana?' said Vdovin, clearly disappointed not to have seen her on his way down to Konstantin's office.

'She's doing penance, courtesy of the GUVD.' Konstantin decided not to elaborate. She was finished one way or another as far as he was concerned.

Vdovin shrugged and pulled a long face. 'Well it was good while it lasted, still—'

'So what's the state of play?' Konstantin interrupted.

'The general secretary is under house arrest at his dacha outside Moscow… and refuses to sign his letter of resignation… Ghukov has been replaced by Volkov, and the Americans have been told not to interfere in our European sphere. The deputy secretary is going to speak to the nation and give them the sad news that our general secretary is in a critical condition, which of course is true.' Vdovin laughed at his own joke.

'And General Marov?'

'On the run. The KGB is going to take care of

that upstart.' Konstantin saw the look of distaste on the general's face. 'Speaking of which, Misha Revnik is still alive.'

'Barely. I don't think he will be causing anyone any trouble soon.'

'Well, my friend is not happy.'

'You can tell your *friend* that everyone else on that list is taken care of. I have four people in a warehouse by Pulkova. They have no idea what is going on. I'll need to know what to do with them. They can't stay there forever.'

Vdovin nodded. 'You need help with Revnik?'

Konstantin did not want the military involved. There was money at Morskaya Prospect, tons of it. They'd sack the place.

'No, I'll deal with Revnik.' And Viktoriya, he thought. She had certainly given him a run for his money, proved more resourceful and lethal than he had anticipated. When she, her half-dead friend and general were gone, RUI would be his. It was more or less going to plan.

14 OCTOBER 1989

CHAPTER 51

NEAR KALININ

Yuri woke at first light and felt a powerful urge to relieve himself. Unzipping his sleeping bag, he rolled off the lower bunk and scrabbled around for his boots. He found them tucked under the bed and fished them out. Derevenko grunted, still asleep. Yuri decided not to wake him for the moment. He donned his parka and gazed out onto the clearing in front of the cabin. The jeep was where he had left it, its roof canvas still visible under a light sprinkling of snow. The snow must have stopped shortly after they had arrived. Tyre tracks traced their way back to the fork he had negotiated the previous night. He wondered how visible they might be from the main road.

Nothing to be done right now. He would wake the captain as soon as he was back. Fifty metres into the wood, Yuri stopped behind a large fir, unbuttoned his jeans and began to relieve himself on a small bank of snow drifted against the tree. He looked up at a crystal-clear blue sky, and, with a sense of relief, breathed in the morning air, watching his breath as he exhaled and the steam rise from the ochre indentation he was making at his feet.

The sound of feet crunching on snow made him look up.

One hundred metres down towards the fork, two men in parka jackets and fur ushankas crept up the drive. Yuri hurriedly fastened his flies and took cover behind the tree. He felt for his automatic and then remembered he had left it in the jeep. He cursed himself… so much for basic training.

He didn't have a lot of time. The moment the two intruders entered the cabin they would see his empty sleeping bag and guess where he was. Yuri estimated the distance to the jeep at fifty metres, about the same distance to the cabin door.

Squatting down, with the two men in front of him now, he began to circle towards the back of the cabin, using the trees and snowdrifts for cover. When the gunmen disappeared from view, Yuri sprinted the final thirty metres and flattened himself against the log wall, to the right of a small high-up window.

It was then he noticed the hatchet, buried in a wood block, placed next to a pile of neatly stacked logs. Carefully, he twisted it free. It felt heavy but familiar, just under a kilo, with a smooth wood haft. For the second time in less than twenty-four hours, he thought of his father and the dacha outside Yekaterinburg, splitting logs in late summer and stacking them in readiness for cold winter nights.

Bending down, Yuri loosened his laces and gently eased off both boots, making sure they didn't bang on the deck. They must be inside by now, he thought. As if in answer, Yuri caught the high-pitched screech of wood being dragged over wood followed by a heavy thud and a cry of protest. Yuri ducked under the window and edged his way round to the front porch. Raised voices emanated from the open cabin door. He could hear Derevenko arguing. Yuri weighed the hatchet in his hand. It might be Stone Age versus twentieth-century man, but it was the only chance he had... that they both had.

Bent double, Yuri raced under the front window to the door jamb and flattened himself against the side of the cabin. Where were they now? Front or back? He tilted his head slightly towards the open doorway. He could make out Derevenko's voice.

'Did you bring us any breakfast? We ate all our rations last night. I'm sure the general will be back in a second.'

'In the jeep,' replied a second voice.

Yuri stepped into full view. Derevenko sat at the table with two men Yuri now recognised as the co-pilot and navigator.

'Cometh the man, cometh the axeman... chopping wood, General?'

Derevenko and his companions began to laugh. Yuri swung the hatchet in front of him in mock attack.

'A pity, I was rather looking forward to using this. How did you find us?'

'We *borrowed* a jeep. There were checkpoints everywhere east of the reservoir so we took the

A14. We guessed you would head towards Moscow, General.'

'And you saw our tracks?'

Anatoly nodded.

'The *goat* has a pretty distinctive track.'

'We should decamp.'

★

With Anatoly and the navigator acting as point, the two jeeps headed back out on the road. Traffic was sparse; a freighter ploughed past them in the opposite direction and then a car.

Yuri tried to put himself in the mind of his pursuers. It wouldn't take a genius to describe an arc around Cherepovets. At least the two of them had succeeded in widening that circle by evading capture overnight, but if Anatoly and the navigator could find them, so could the military police.

'Do you still think they are going to be coming after us, General?' asked Derevenko.

As if in answer, a helicopter clattered loudly across the highway just above tree height. Yuri glanced up through the dense snow-laden overhang of trees and caught the tail of an MTV as it raced north. He guessed it would turn in about ten to twenty minutes and retrace its steps. They had to change vehicles, into something more anonymous than a military UAZ.

Derevenko flashed Anatoly to stop. The two vehicles pulled over, well under the forest canopy.

'We need to ditch these. We're an open target in a sky like this. You saw the MTV?'

They both nodded.

'They're doing a sweep. It's probably not the only MTV up there either,' said the navigator.

'Get everything we need out of the jeeps. Yev, you still have your uniform. Anatoly, go up the highway one hundred metres, and Stephan, one hundred metres downwind. When you see something coming, whistle.'

Yuri watched as the two men trudged off in opposite directions and took cover behind the firs that hugged the roadside's edge. Derevenko climbed into the jeep and turned on the engine.

They didn't have long to wait. Yuri heard a piercing whistle from Anatoly. Yuri banged on the canvas and Yev rolled forward, blocking the road in both directions. The dark blue Lada skidded inches from the side of his jeep. A heavily built man with wiry hair that stuck out from under his beanie, and wearing a tartan jacket, jumped out, furious at Yev's apparent lack of road skills. *What the hell was he doing blocking the road like that?*

Yev climbed out of the jeep as Yuri appeared from the roadside.

The driver looked momentarily confused.

'What's going on?'

He looked from Yev in uniform to Yuri in his civilian clothing.

'This smells fishy to me!' he shouted, raising his fists.

'Comrade, we need to borrow your car,' said Yuri.

Anatoly and Stephan appeared from opposite directions.

'*Borrow*? *Steal*, you mean.'

'No, comrade,' said Yuri, 'we are going to commandeer your very nice vehicle until we reach Moscow and then you can have it back.'

Yuri could see him hesitating.

'You really don't have a choice,' said the captain.

The driver, bug-eyed, turned full circle, looking from face to face before finally dropping his hands in defeat.

'Comrade, think of it as an act of patriotism,' said Yuri, holding out his hand for the key.

CHAPTER 52

LENINGRAD

'How is he?' Viktoriya asked the doctor when they were outside the office that now doubled as a ward room for Misha.

'I would rather he were in an intensive care unit, but his vital signs are good. He's young and he's strong.'

Viktoriya remembered the previous night and the anxious journey to Morskaya. The relief when they had finally pulled through the gates. Grigory had been the first to greet her. He looked pale and visibly rattled, and she had wondered whether he would be able to hold himself together. Ivan had appeared a minute later unscathed behind them and organised a temporary bed from the guardroom for Misha. She had rung the doctor as soon as Misha had been settled and organised for a hospital bed, equipment and medicines the next morning.

'He's safer here,' Viktoriya responded. Morskaya was more defensible than the security sieve that was the Mariinsky. There was only one main exit. And that exit was well fortified.

317

'He needs round-the-clock care. I can organise that for you,' said the doctor, making a note of things his patient might need.

'He is not to want for anything, you understand me?'

Grigory handed the doctor a brick of US dollars from the vault. 'Let me know if you need more.'

The doctor looked at the money, dumbfounded. Viktoriya doubted he had ever seen so much.

'One more thing,' said the doctor. 'Have someone read to him. A TV might be useful too. Stimulate the brain. Snap him out of his coma.'

'So what do we do now?' asked Grigory when the doctor had gone.

'We reinforce Morskaya. We have to assume Kostya will try again. Ivan has already contacted Roslavi.'

'And Moscow?'

'Who knows? There's not much we can do about it. Still no word from Yuri?'

Grigory shook his head and listed off the names of local political figures that had disappeared.

'Maybe it is "The End", the clocks are about to go back. It looks like Yuri is somehow caught up in it. I wouldn't blame you if you wanted to take the next plane out, Grigory. Wait it out. If it wasn't for Misha, I'd certainly think about it.'

To her surprise, Grigory shook his head.

'No, it's fine. Besides, someone's got to look after the bank. We're still trading.'

Viktoriya gave Grigory a hug.

What had happened to Yuri? she wondered when

Grigory had walked out of Misha's makeshift ward. Wouldn't he have *tried* to contact her by now if he could, or had he been disappeared, like those on the list of names Grigory had reeled off? She felt exposed. RUI needed a much stronger political base. Yesterday's had simply evaporated. The oil minister, Federov – in all the chaos she had forgotten about him.

She walked into Misha's office and picked up the phone.

'Alina, please put Stephan Federov on the line.' Viktoriya sat back in Misha's chair and wondered whether it would be Federov who took the call or whether he was part of the cull. She was relieved to hear his voice.

'Comrade Federov, I understand from the news bulletin that the deputy secretary general has assumed the post of acting secretary general.' She was conscious that Federov's line might be tapped.

'Yes, that's correct. We are all hoping for the general secretary's swift recovery,' he replied. 'I spoke with the deputy secretary this morning and he has assured me that this is hopefully only a temporary measure.'

Viktoriya guessed that Federov was repeating this with closet irony. This was going to be anything *but* temporary.

'He also assured me that there is to be no immediate change in oil policy.'

No interruption to oil deliveries from Roslavi, interpreted Viktoriya.

'I also have some bad news... Someone tried to kill Mikhail Dimitrivich yesterday.'

Federov seemed genuinely shocked.

'Who will be running RUI now?' he asked, concern in his voice.

'I will,' she reassured him; he would still get his cut. 'It's all legal. I am a major shareholder and the shareholder agreement provides for such an eventuality.' She had few illusions about Federov. Power and money talked. He wouldn't lose a minute's sleep if he were made a better offer elsewhere.

'And General Marov?' she continued.

There was silence.

'There is a warrant out for his arrest.'

'But they haven't caught him yet?'

'Not that I know. Last seen in Cherepovets. Beyond that, I really can't say.'

She put down the phone and wondered how long Federov would give her the benefit of the doubt, with her partners and allies fast disappearing. Maybe he had already made up his mind to shift his allegiance.

Ivan walked into the room.

'That was Maxim on the phone. The military have impounded two of our oil tankers at the border. Direct order from the new military boss in Moscow apparently.' He looked down at his notes. 'General... Volkov.'

CHAPTER 53

NEAR KALININ

'How far are we from Kalinin?'

Yuri was concentrating on the road, trying not to oversteer with Derevenko next to him, the two airmen in the back and the owner of the car between them.

'Twenty kilometres,' said the captain.

'We are going to pass close by Migalovo.'

Yuri nodded. Migalovo was the largest military air force base in Russia, home to giant AN-22s and IL-76s. If there was a general state of mobilisation, Migalovo would be the pulse.

'Let's see what's going on.'

'The place will be crawling with military,' Derevenko protested.

'It's east of Kalinin a couple of kilometres across the river; we can make a short detour.'

'You're the general,' said Derevenko, capitulating.

Derevenko would be as *wanted* as him now, all of them, thought Yuri, glancing in his mirror. They had thrown their lot in with him, on the unreasonable assumption that he could actually do something, somehow to turn the tide.

★

The outskirts of Kalinin reminded Yuri of the grim sixties' construction around Moscow. Prefabricated apartment buildings bumped into wide boulevards and elegant houses from another era.

Options, options? He racked his brain for an answer.

Yuri turned into a side street and stopped.

'Stephan, do you mind taking our guest out onto the pavement. With your permission, Captain,' Yuri continued when their passenger was out of earshot. 'I would like Anatoly to do something for me.' There was no way he could order anyone to do anything, not anymore. He looked at Anatoly's questioning face in the mirror and turned round to face him.

'I have *absolutely* no idea how this whole thing is going to play out, but I want you to take the train north to Leningrad, find a Viktoriya Kayakova or a Mikhail Revnik at RUI. They are business associates… and friends. I want you to tell them that I am alive and kicking but I need some support. Ask them to despatch two squads from Roslavi to the Leningrad Freight yard in Moscow and wait. Is that clear?'

'Yes, General.'

Apart from this aircrew, Yuri reflected with some irony that the only soldiers he could rely on at this moment were mercenaries, albeit Russian. He might not have a plan, but he knew from experience that opportunity was useless without the means.

'And one more thing,' it came to him, 'give them the name of Colonel Ilya Terentev. He lives on Degtyarny. He's an old friend – KGB – but I trust him with my life. If they need help he'd be a good place to start.'

Yuri looked at his watch; it was only nine in the morning.

'You can be there inside three hours by train.' The soldiers could be in Moscow around midnight if Anatoly were successful.

They waved Anatoly goodbye around the corner from the station and continued towards the embankment. Yuri pulled up for a second time and stared into a curtain of snow.

'We'll have to take the bridge to get closer,' Derevenko suggested.

Military vehicles poured across the iron bridge from every direction, tanks on trailers, artillery and troop carriers. Yuri found himself sandwiched between a public bus and a column of jeeps before turning onto a side road that skirted round the airport to the eastside.

There must be somewhere that gave them an elevation and a view of the airfield.

Derevenko pointed at a derelict-looking barn.

Co-opting their new charge, the four of them applied shoulders to the rotten barn door and splintered the lock from the wood. Yuri brushed the snow off his jacket and breathed in the stale smell of oily machinery and bat droppings. Derevenko shone a torch up at the empty hayloft four metres above them and then back down on the ground, searching for a ladder.

'There's nothing else for it,' said Yuri, after drawing a blank.

Yuri put one foot on their open palms, grabbed the edge, and hoisted himself up into the hayloft. He stood up and dusted hay and dried droppings off the front of his parka while his eyes adjusted to the light.

'Yev… bounce that torchlight off the ceiling, I can't see a thing.'

Yuri tested the decking with one foot gently applying weight, wondering if it would take his eighty-odd kilos. The wood groaned in protest before disintegrating with a loud crunch, sending a shower of rotten timber below.

'Are you all right up there?' Derevenko whispered loudly.

'I'll tell you in a second.'

Yuri wriggled his foot free.

'Dry rot,' he informed them, as though he were an expert on the subject.

Centimetre by centimetre, Yuri edged his way forward, gradually applying weight, testing to see if the floor would support him. When finally he grasped the sill of the hayloft window and looked out to the road and the airfield beyond, he was shocked by what he saw. Parked on the west side of the airbase, twelve Ilyushin-76s and eight Antonov-22s were being readied for take-off. Everywhere cargo trucks hauled artillery, tanks and ammunition into their vast underbellies. On the far side of the airfield, small loaders ferried H-20 nuclear missiles towards five TU-75 strategic bombers.

Yuri retraced his steps and lowered himself over the hayloft. Two pairs of hands reached up and helped him to the ground.

'What's going on?' asked Derevenko.

'World War Three… I don't know, but we'd better get out of here quick.'

Yuri gave the heavy wooden door a shove and stepped out into the cold.

The thump-thump of a MTV rotor was the last thing he remembered.

CHAPTER 54

LENINGRAD

'What do you mean we can't ship *anything*?' Konstantin complained to Vdovin.

'We've a general mobilisation under way; every available aircraft is commandeered for the airlift.'

Konstantin wondered what these clowns were up to. He had given his tacit support to a coup, not the invasion of Western Europe, if that's what they were planning. Were they completely crazy?

'Volkov is determined that the Communist government doesn't fall in East Germany. He's convinced the Emergency Committee to mobilise… as a precautionary measure.'

These things had a habit of taking on a life of their own, Konstantin thought. If the Americans suspected a blitzkrieg, they wouldn't sit still and wait.

'Can't you calm them down? You're a district general. You have influence, surely.'

Vdovin shook his head. 'Volkov is chief of staff now. He has the ear of the committee. And what's more I support him. Ever since our new general secretary wheedled his way to power, the Soviet Union has been the object of disintegrating forces. You've seen it yourself. It's falling apart. Well not anymore…'

'And how long before you have people on the streets?'

'The general secretary, I've no doubt, will be persuaded to resign. It will all be legal.'

'*Legal?*' Konstantin sneered.

'We are patriots, not traitors. Best you keep your head down, if you want my advice; it'll be over in a few days.'

Yes, they'd all be dead, thought Konstantin. They had all taken leave of their senses.

'I have to be going.' Vdovin got up and without further comment left the room.

Konstantin looked up at the wall clock: ten fifteen. He shouted for Bazhukov.

'We're grounded for now,' Konstantin informed him. 'Nothing in or out.'

'Customers are not going to be happy about that, boss.'

'You can tell them to write to the Emergency Committee with their letters of complaint… What's the latest on Morskaya?'

'Our men are posted outside. Doctors and nurses come and go. Revnik is still in a coma.'

Coup or no coup, he couldn't let Misha or his old flame survive now. They would only come back to bite him.

'And Viktoriya?'

'She's staying put with him.'

So there was no change. Konstantin knew there was no way they could storm the place; he'd looked at it himself. The gate was steel and concrete, and once in the internal courtyard they would be sitting ducks. He'd lose half his men. It had to be by stealth, not force.

'That friend of Adriana's, the cokehead, what's-her-name, where is she now?'

'Cezanne, she is upstairs.'

'Go get her.'

Konstantin stood up, walked round to the other side of the desk and leaned back on it. He tried to recall what Adriana's friend looked like: medium height, blonde, slightly wavy shoulder-length hair – no great looker but a great body. The men liked her and she liked coke – an ideal combination as far as he was concerned.

Cezanne walked into the room. Her fingers twitched nervously at the lapel of her silk dressing gown. She was different to how he remembered. Her hair was now an ash-blonde and slightly shorter than before.

'Come over here.'

'If this is anything to do with Adriana, I don't know where she is. I haven't seen her since she was released from the police station. Nobody has.'

And nobody will, thought Konstantin. She was helping prop up the foundations of a restoration project on Oktabrsky.

'Take off your make-up.'

He handed her a tissue and a pot of make-up

remover someone had left in his desk. 'This was probably your friend's; you might as well keep it.'

'She wasn't my friend really... we just watched out for each other in the club...you know...'

'I do, I do.' Konstantin grabbed the tissue from her hand and roughly rubbed off her make-up.

'Careful...what are you doing?' She flinched and pulled away. 'That hurts,' she protested.

Konstantin looked at her. She was exactly what he was looking for...ordinary, unremarkable... unrecognisable as the girl in the club.

'I've got a job for you. Do it right and Dimitri here will keep you in coke for a year. How does that sound?'

He held out a small bag of white powder and snatched it away when she reached for it.

'And what is it you want me to do?' she said, not taking her eyes off the polythene bag Konstantin held between his fingers.

'Deliver something, that's all.'

'Have I got a choice?'

Konstantin shook his head. 'Dimitri, do you think you can organise a nurse's uniform for Cezanne and a hospital ID tag.'

'No problem, boss,' said Bazhukov.

'That will be all, Dimitri, and close the door behind you. No, not you, Cezanne.' He handed her the small bag. 'Why don't you make yourself comfortable on the sofa?' He wondered if she would be as uninhibited as her friend.

CHAPTER 55

MOSCOW, LUBYANKA

Yuri came to with his head pounding. Where was he? A bare light bulb illuminated grey walls and a cell door. Was he back at Cherepovets? A stabbing pain made him reach his hand up to a spot just above his right ear. It was sticky with semi-congealed blood. Prodding around, he tried to determine whether his skull was broken and decided he was still, at least externally, in one piece.

Slowly, he righted himself on the bed. How long had he been here? He looked at his wrist where his Rolex had been and tried to remember. The thump, thump, the MTV, the military airbase at Migalovo – it all started to flood back. Where were the others?

He struggled to his feet and sat back down again as the room began to swim. Something had hit him hard. Gathering himself again, he stood up slowly and walked ten feet to the cell door and banged on the viewing hatch. There was no response.

Yuri sat back down again and poured himself a glass of water from a jug. At least he was alive, for the moment anyway. He fell back on the rough woollen blanket and tucked the pillow under his head. If only the throbbing would stop.

The sound of the lock being turned and the bolts sliding back made him sit back up. General Volkov walked into the room and ordered the guard to close the door behind him.

'For your head,' he said sympathetically. Yuri swallowed the offered painkillers and looked up at Volkov over the edge of his glass. He looked every inch the colonel general in full dress uniform.

'Where am I?'

'Lubyanka.'

Moscow, the KGB prison; at least he now had a geographical reference point.

'How long have I been out?'

'A few hours.'

Volkov pulled up a chair and sat down opposite.

'And my friends?'

'They no longer need trouble you... You have been leading us a merry jaunt, General. Quite resourceful... but then that is to be expected. But stopping at Migalovo... that was a mistake. You should have known better.'

'I seem to remember somebody else pointing that out.'

Yuri wondered what had befallen his companions and what it was that Volkov wanted that was so important for him to come in person. By the looks of Migalovo, he had enough on his plate.

'And General Ghukov?'

'Under house arrest.' Volkov looked around the windowless room. 'His quarters are a lot more luxurious than yours. Do you know the old joke, General?' Volkov continued. 'The basement of Lubyanka is the tallest building in Moscow... you can see all the way to Siberia.' Volkov laughed. Yuri looked at him stonily.

'And under what authority am I being held?'

'Military, Article 58,' replied Volkov, deadpan. *'Conspiring with the Western powers to assassinate Soviet leaders, dismember the Soviet Union, and restore capitalism.'*

'Bringing back show trials, General?'

'I am hoping that will be entirely unnecessary. Indeed it is my *fervent* wish that you return to the comforts of your luxurious apartment... at the earliest opportunity.'

'I have to say I'm confused, General. There I was thinking you were preparing for World War Three. I'm touched by your concern.'

'Marov, I don't doubt your military talents,' replied Volkov, clearly annoyed. 'Despite our past differences. The Soviet Union needs them right now.'

'Which Soviet Union is the question... yours or the general secretary's?'

Volkov extracted an envelope from his pocket, pulled out a sheet of paper and handed it to him. Yuri glanced at it. Headed *Declaration of the Emergency Committee*, it was signed by the deputy secretary, defence minister, chairman of the KGB, Volkov and three others.

'A declaration of martial law?'

'I'd like your signature on this, General.'

'Dignify your coup... I think not.'

Volkov looked irritated. Yuri could see him struggling to control his emotions.

'Marov, in case you have failed to understand the crisis we are in, the Soviet Empire is on the brink of collapse. That would be a catastrophe of unparalleled proportions. East Germany will follow Poland and so will the rest. NATO will be on our doorstep, as will be their missile shield... that can't be allowed to happen.'

'The general secretary does not agree with you. He is not prepared to see Soviet troops bloodily repress Eastern Europe – not anymore.'

'And the Americans... you are not concerned about them on our doorstep?'

Yuri shrugged. 'General, we have to let go. We couldn't hold Afghanistan, and if Eastern Europe rises against us, it will not be any different. We should learn from the British. They were smart, they had their last-ditch efforts too, but they knew when their time was up and withdrew gracefully.'

Volkov looked at him with undisguised disgust. He stood up and rapped on the door.

'I'll give you a little time to think about it... to reconsider your position... but not too long... or a headache might just be the least of your difficulties.'

CHAPTER 55

LENINGRAD

Misha blinked his eyes open. What was that noise, that flickering? His mouth was as parched as sandpaper. He looked about him, trying to focus. Everything seemed to be swimming around him. He closed his eyes, counted to ten and tried again. His eyes lighted on a plastic bottle mounted on a stand to the side of his bed. A tube with coffee-coloured liquid snaked its way into his nose and down the back of his throat. Another bag of clear fluid supplied a catheter to his arm. In the corner of the room a woman in a nurse's uniform sat watching TV, the volume barely audible. Sleep was dragging him down again, like a heavy irresistible weight. He refocussed on the screen; a group of men sitting at a table faced the camera. Who was the man in the centre? He was sure he recognised him. The deputy secretary general, Gerasim Gerashchenko, that was it. He shut his eyes and started to gently drift.

The sound of the TV being turned up hauled him back. His eyes darted along the line of grim-looking men. The third one from the middle wore a military uniform; next to him was a man in thick glasses. Where had he seen him before? He closed his eyes and began to float off.

He was running, sprinting full tilt down a wet street, grasping something tightly in his hand. Someone was chasing him, maybe more than one. He was looking for someone ahead but he couldn't remember who or why. He had to give her whatever it was in his hand. Yes, he knew it was a 'her' now, but he hadn't much time. In fact, no time at all.

His arm was freezing cold; a hand reached out and touched him. Startled, he opened his eyes. A nurse stood over him, syringing a crystal-clear liquid into the catheter. He looked back at the TV. He was sure it was important. He knew where he had seen him now. The nurse smiled down at him.

'You are awake,' she said in an unsurprised voice, as though he had woken from an afternoon nap and it was entirely expected.

He tried to say something but his tongue felt as though it was glued to the top of his mouth. The nurse reached for a glass of water, told him to sip and held it gently to his mouth. Misha grabbed her arm as a drowning man might a piece of flotsam. Sleep was pulling him under again. He had to get the words out. She bent an ear to his mouth, the words '*Safe… Vika… Yuri*' escaped. Misha, exhausted, surrendered to the beckoning deep.

CHAPTER 56

Viktoriya stared at the heart monitor and watched it describe a regular green ark across a black screen.

'How long did he wake for?'

'Only a few minutes. Going back to sleep like this is normal. It's the body's way of coping. He'll be in and out.'

The nurse gently tugged off the tape with tweezers and re-dressed the livid head wound.

'How did he seem, mentally?'

'Confused, but that is to be expected. He looked at me and his eyes focussed.'

'Did he say anything?'

'It was very indistinct... a few words. The doctor will give you a more professional prognosis... but this is all *good* news.'

Viktoriya looked at the TV set that had been pumping out propaganda all day long. The secretary general was still supposedly ill and unavailable for interview in his Moscow dacha. She wondered how many people were taken in by the new so-called Emergency Committee.

'Please try to remember what he said – it might be important.'

The nurse shrugged. 'As I said, it was difficult to hear, hardly a whisper... maybe your short name, *Vika, safe... Dimitri...*'

'Grigory?'

'No, not Grigory...'

'Vika, safe, Dimitri?'

'Yes, I think that was it.' She could see the nurse trying to remember, unsure she had repeated what he had said correctly.

Viktoriya told the nurse to contact her the moment Misha showed any sign of waking again and went back to her office.

'Alina, please can you find Ivan and Grigory for me.'

She stood by the long window she so often stood at, talking with Misha, and looked down into the yard. Two heavy machine guns, mounted on tripods, pointed at the gate. Around the internal balconies, men in thick winter gear, sporting Kalashnikovs, covered the machine gunners.

A cough behind her made her turn around.

Grigory stood next to Ivan in the doorway.

'We were in the vault,' said Ivan.

She waved them in and told them what had happened.

'That's great, wonderful,' said Ivan, and she could see him struggling with his emotions; he'd been an absolute rock since the attack. 'He'll be back in no time.' Grigory placed a supportive hand on his friend's back.

'Any news on the oil shipments?' said Grigory.

'I spoke to Maxim this morning. There is nothing he can do either. I'm going to have to go to Moscow and see Federov, try and straighten this out. When do reinforcements arrive from Roslavi?'

'Tonight, fifty men,' said Ivan.

There was a pause while they waited for her to say something.

'I've been thinking Kostya is not going to let this sit, whatever his motive might be. Knowing him as we both do,' and she looked at Ivan, 'he'll already have some alternative plan underway and he is unlikely to take prisoners… maybe you, Grigory.' She smiled. 'Where is he now?'

'At the airport,' answered Ivan. Vladek had been tracking him all day.

'Well, tell me when he is back in his office.'

'Why do you think Konstantin wants Misha dead,' asked Grigory, '… why now?'

Viktoriya had been asking herself the same question. Kostya did things for a reason: to secure his power base, further his business interests and punish transgressors. He did not perform random acts of violence or revenge. He was far too intelligent for that.

'What if it's *all* connected,' said Viktoriya. 'Yuri's arrest warrant and disappearance, the general secretary's illness, the Emergency Committee, Kostya's attack and the military stopping our tankers. Maybe Kostya is not the initiating factor, but somebody higher up the chain.'

'But then who?' said Ivan. 'Why would Misha present a threat?'

Viktoriya sat back down in the chair and closed her eyes. *Why? Why?* An image of Misha showing her the vault and the mysterious small safe swam into consciousness. What was so important that only the two of them had the code... although hadn't he walked off before properly telling her. *Safe... Vika, safe, Dimitri...?* Maybe it wasn't Dimitri, it was *Yuri*. She jumped to her feet. Maybe that was what Misha was trying to tell her.

With Ivan and Grigory in close pursuit, Viktoriya virtually flew down the stairs to the basement. Two armed guards stepped back from the vault door.

'Open it,' ordered Viktoriya.

Wordlessly, Ivan and Grigory punched in the dual access codes. Whirring and a loud clunk signalled success. Ivan rotated the large wheel lock and heaved open the door.

'I may be wrong but there *is* something important in here,' she said, facing the small wall safe – perhaps something worth killing for, she thought.

'Do you have the code number?' asked Grigory.

Viktoriya shook her head. 'Misha said I would know it. I suppose he didn't want to burden me... If questioned I genuinely wouldn't. Except I do... somehow. Just give me some space. I need to think.'

The two of them withdrew to the vault's entrance as she stared at the ten-digit keypad. It had to be a number they both knew, something special. She punched in his birthday, her birthday, long and short year date... that would be too obvious... her mother's, his mother's... nothing... Ivan's... Kostya's. There was a click and the door sprang a millimetre ajar. Misha's little joke, she thought, and smiled.

She waved over Ivan and Grigory and reached into the safe. Inside was a large sealed envelope. She picked it up and weighed it in her hands. Both of them looked at her expectantly. She shrugged. She had no idea what it could be. Grigory walked to the counting table and passed her a letter opener. She slid it carefully under the sealed edge and upended the envelope. Six large black-and-white photographs slid out onto the table. She picked one up and studied it. Two men stood on the embankment on that wet morning twelve years ago... how could she forget that day? She had kept the roll of film hidden for all those years... until Misha's first visit to Milan. She went back to the safe and felt for the negatives... nothing.

'Misha took these years ago, when we were teenagers, for some cloak and dagger guy who never reappeared... Do you recognise either of the two men in the photos?'

They stood staring down at the photographs she had neatly rearranged on the table.

'The man with the glasses looks sort of familiar, but this is years ago, people change,' said Grigory.

'Who?'

'The guy in the Politburo line-up they've been beaming non-stop today. I have no idea who is.'

That would make sense. Maybe Misha had witnessed something when he woke, recognised one of the men in the photo. But what was so important about these two men, these photos?

Alina materialised in the doorway.

'Vika, there's a man upstairs, says he needs to see you urgently. He has a message from Yuri.'

CHAPTER 57

Viktoriya threw clothes into an overnight bag, opening and closing drawers seemingly at random. When she had what she wanted, she carried the bag out into the living room and handed it to Rodion before returning to her bedroom and stripping off and passing her clothes to Alina, who had already taken off Vladek's coat and balaclava. Sliding back the wardrobe door, she pulled out a red G-string from the underwear drawer and flicked through the rail until she found the matching red corset. She held it up to the mirror. It would do fine. She stepped into the G-string and stood still for Alina as she buttoned the corset up from the back. She looked at herself again in the mirror.

'I need a belt,' she said, almost to herself. She rummaged through a chest of drawers and pulled out a narrow red patent leather belt and buckled it tight.

Viktoriya stepped into the bathroom and unzipped her make-up kit. It took a few seconds to find the foundation she was looking for – one a good shade darker than her everyday one. Pinning back her hair, she shook the small glass bottle before dabbing on its light creamy liquid with her finger and smoothing it with a brush. She used a dark blusher to accentuate her strong cheekbones and a bronze mascara for her eyebrows and lashes. She stepped back and looked at herself in the mirror before applying a dark smokey eye shadow and a contrasting bright red lipstick. Perfect. Finally, she combed her hair along a different parting.

'What do you think?' Viktoriya asked Alina as she slipped her feet into a pair of red stilettos.

'I hardly recognise you,' she said, helping her on with a short black satin wrap. 'Are you sure you want to do this?'

Viktoriya nodded. She looked out of the window to the wide pavement below. Four cars lay tucked in against the kerb, ready to take her back to Morskaya. A block down, another car – she could only assume it was one of Kostya's, keeping a lookout. Her small motorcade had surprised them, when the gate on Morskaya had been flung open for the first time since Misha's dramatic return. Men had rushed about in confusion. She had recognised several as Kostya's. Ivan, in the lead car, had given them just enough time to see that Misha was not with them.

Viktoriya turned back to Alina.

'Has Vladimir arrived?'

Alina nodded. 'He's in the living room.'

Vladimir had come separately by foot, hopefully unnoticed by Kostya's men.

Viktoriya donned her long overcoat, walked into the living room, picked up the phone and dialled her mother. She imagined the ringtone echoing in the communal hallway and prayed her mother was in. Come on, someone, *pick up* the phone.

'Hello,' said a familiar voice. It was her mother's neighbour.

'Elsa, how are you? Is my mother there?'

Viktoriya heard footsteps and banging on a door and then her mother's voice. She hoped whoever was bugging her phone was listening.

'Mother,' Viktoriya said when she answered the phone, 'I can't talk long.'

'Where are you? I've been worried about you? This new government, will that affect you?' She rushed out her questions without taking breath.

'Everything will be *fine*, Mother. I'm not staying at the apartment at the moment. Misha is not well.' She did not wish to elaborate and send her mother into panic. 'I am staying over with him at Morskaya for a night or two; I'm just headed back there now. I'll call you in the next day or so… and, mother, you *must* come and live in Leningrad.'

When she put down the phone she found herself staring at the floor trying to get a hold on her emotions. So much had happened. Hearing her mother's voice had brought her close to tears, unsettled her. Half of her even doubted she might see her again. Would anything ever be the same now? At that instant she would have given almost anything for her mother's warm reassuring hug.

When she looked up, three pairs of eyes met hers across the room.

Viktoriya forced a smile, picked up the hat she

had arrived wearing from the sofa and plumped it down on Alina's head, putting a finger to her lips as a reminder.

'Right, I think I'm ready to go back now, Rodion.' She locked the apartment door behind her, took the overnight bag off Rodion, and watched him and her new double and Vladimir take the lift to the car. Three in three out; she hoped they were counting.

Five minutes later, Viktoriya caught the elevator to the first floor and walked the last flight to the basement and service exit at the rear of the building. The cold wind hit her as she walked up past bins and rubbish piled high to the main prospect. Cars sped by. A taxi hove into view. She stepped forward and flagged it down.

'The corner of Liteyny and Kirochnaya.'

Viktoriya threw her bag into the back seat and slid in beside it. Ten minutes, she thought, and there would be no turning back. She reached into her bag and found the handle of the Markov and ran her finger along the silencer.

Snow had begun to fall lightly again. Staring out the window at passers-by, Viktoriya felt detached from the real world, out of synch with the everyday. The taxi stopped. She paid him and climbed out onto a virtually empty street. Two blocks up, she saw the entrance to Pravdy. Two armed men stood outside. One of them stepped out of the pool of light by the door and walked over to a car parked in front. There was loud laughter. He banged on the car roof and ambled back to his post. Viktoriya shivered.

Cutting around to a side street, she hiked two streets over before winding her way back to a narrow passageway that ran at the back of the club. She paused at its entrance. A door opened. Light flooded momentarily onto the street before evaporating. A girl in jeans and a heavy parka jacket with an overlarge fur collar trudged past her. Viktoriya flipped up her hood, slung her bag over her shoulder, walked up to the door and knocked. The door opened. A guard she did not recognise looked down at her with disinterest.

'I'm new,' she said, before he had a chance to say anything. 'I know where the dressing room is, Anna showed me yesterday.' Maybe it was because she had named one of the dancers that swayed him, her confidence or his complacency, but he nodded her through. The corridor was as she remembered: a black tunnel, low ceilinged, one person wide, lit only by small, dim sodium overhead lights that gave off an eerie orange glow. A girl approached from the other direction, on her way out; they both turned slightly and, without pausing, squeezed by each other.

Just before the dressing room and the stairs to the basement and Kostya's office, Viktoriya stopped outside the women's toilet, a cramped single cubicle. Thankfully, it was empty. She stepped inside and locked the door. Extracting the automatic from her bag, she stashed it firmly under her belt in the small of her back. Twice she drew and replaced it, making sure it didn't catch. Satisfied, she stuffed her coat in the duffel bag and crammed it into the small fitted cupboard under the sink.

A loud, sudden knock on the door made her jump.

'Hurry up, I have to be on in five minutes,' said a girl's voice.

Taking one final look at herself, she pulled the short black silk dressing gown around her, sufficient to obscure the gun, and opened the door. A girl she recognised but couldn't name looked at her.

'You new?'

'Sveta,' Viktoriya introduced herself.

'Well, don't hog the loo. There's only one between *all* of us girls,' she said, and pushed past.

Viktoriya nodded, suitably chastened. Up ahead she could hear women's voices and what sounded like an argument. Music from the club above throbbed through the ceiling. Heart pounding, she took the staircase to the basement and the narrow corridor to Kostya's door. A single guard looked her up and down. His eyes travelled down her bare arms and legs, and back to her gown, which hung provocatively open, revealing her corset and G-string.

'Konstantin sent for me,' she said in explanation. The guard bent forward to hear her above the din of the club immediately above the corridor and attempted to slide his arm inside her gown. Viktoriya jumped back and felt the automatic shift in her belt.

'I wouldn't do that if I were you.' She reached up to his face and stroked his cheek. 'Maybe later. What's your name?' she asked him.

'Taras,' he answered. He had large hands and a round face that glowed orange in the subdued light.

'Okay... Taras... Kostya doesn't like to be kept

waiting, you know what he's like.' Her hands went to her G-string. She adjusted the elastic lower on her hips.

Taras pushed open the familiar door to Kostya's office and closed it behind her.

Kostya looked up from his desk. He was pouring over some list or other with Bazhukov. They both seemed more bemused than irritated, no doubt wondering why one of the club girls had suddenly appeared uninvited. Bazhukov started to say something, but it was Kostya who reconfigured her appearance first. He looked startled.

'*Vika!*' he exclaimed.

Bazhukov went for the gun in his shoulder holster but he was slow. Viktoriya already had her hand on the Markov; she slid it out from under her belt and pointed it in his direction. Bazhukov took a step back and raised his hands.

'Kostya, keep your hands on the table where I can see them,' she said more calmly than she felt, 'and Bazhukov, you keep them up... I have to say I don't think much of your security.'

'So what is it you want?' Kostya asked coolly.

Viktoriya raised the barrel a fraction and squeezed the trigger. Bazhukov made a *pouf* sound and tumbled over the chair behind him.

'You'll need a new head of security now. That's for my father.'

Kostya's hands shifted down the desk a fraction.

'That's far enough,' she warned, and pointed the gun squarely at him. 'So explain.'

'Explain, *ah*... well it's nothing personal.'

'It never is with you, Kostya.'

'Somebody wants your friend dead... somebody high up. Until now it's only been *me* that has stopped them... but it's imperative now, you see. I have no idea why... you know, if it wasn't me, it would only be someone else.'

'And who is somebody?'

'The question I ask myself... KGB... the military... the new government.'

'And me... did that figure in *their* equation or *yours*? I thought we trusted each other... but then I should have known better. We are all means to your ends, aren't we, Kostya – every one of us, dispensable.'

'Are you going to pull that trigger?' he said, staring at the barrel.

'I'm considering it.' She took first pressure.

Konstantin tensed.

'Kill me and our friend dies.'

'Isn't it the other way round? Why is he suddenly *our* friend now?'

'You've made your point,' Konstantin said, looking at Bazhukov's body and the large red stain spreading over his shirt. 'Look, if you kill me they will just give the contract to someone else. They are not going to stop. Maybe it will be Vdovin and his merry men. He's not going to worry about losing a few soldiers taking Morskaya. Look... if the coup succeeds, the best you can do is get out of the country. If it fails – and these guys are crazies – maybe, just maybe, it will all stop. I can keep them satisfied for now, tell them Misha's in a coma and not going anywhere. Kill me and you've signed Misha's death warrant. Besides, did you think I had given up? You *know* me, Vika.'

Konstantin lifted his hands off the table and sat back in the chair.

There was a knock at the door.

'Call him in.' She hoped there'd be only one.

The guard who had tried to grab her walked in to deliver a message he had in his hand. She pointed the gun at him and waved him over to Konstantin's side.

'Quite a party now,' said Kostya, smiling.

'One last thing, and this is going to hurt, Kostya… Misha thought you might try something like this. That money you sent us – the *last* batch, all eighty-five million of it – it's sitting in an intermediary account in the Cayman's… I might just recall or divert it somewhere more useful.'

It was the second time in the last ten minutes that Kostya had looked shocked.

'Whatever happened to *my word is my bond*?'

'The same thing that happened to friendship… So here's the trade,' she said, waving the automatic at him. 'You stop whatever devious plan you have in train, your men remain strictly hands off Morskaya and Misha, and you escort me nicely out of the club.'

'And my money?'

'Let's see if you can behave first.'

Kostya nodded, picked up the phone and dialled RUI on Morskaya. Viktoriya heard Alina's voice answer.

'Alina, this is Kostya. Tell the nurses to throw away

all the injectables and ensure you get a fresh supply. Have your doctor check it over.' He replaced the receiver.

'It's a shame, Kostya, you could have been anything. Now both of you remove your guns and drop them on the floor. Use the tips of your fingers.'

Kostya nodded to the guard and the pair of them removed their automatics.

'Now, we're going to just walk out the way I came in.'

The corridor was empty. With Kostya directly in front, she walked her two captives steadily up the stairs.

'Get my bag, Taras.' She pointed at the toilet door. 'And now the back. Tell your man to down his gun.'

'You'll need to put your coat on, Vika.' She could hear the faint tone of amusement in Kostya's voice. 'And if you ever want a job…'

'Don't tempt me, Kostya.' She nudged him in the back with the silencer.

The man who had let her in backed away from the door as they exited onto the alley. Viktoriya thought how the scene might look to a passer-by: three men – and a woman, barely clothed, holding a gun.

She waved them back inside, kicked off her shoes and sprinted up to the main street. A black Volga screeched to a halt in front of her. Ivan threw open the door.

'Okay, the station. I need to catch that late train.'

Viktoriya cast one last look down the passageway at the lonely figure of Kostya staring back towards her.

CHAPTER 58

MOSCOW

Colonel Ilya Terentev gazed out the café window to the food queue across the street that had formed in front of a pop-up stall. Children tugged at their mothers' hands while the elderly stood patiently, inured to a crumbling system. All day, state television had broadcast pictures of the general mobilisation in response to so-called Western provocation. Was it going to be 1956 all over again? Thousands had died in Hungary. Yuri was right that things had to move on. But where had that landed his friend? Locked up in Lubyanka for anti-Soviet activity and, if the coup prevailed, it would get much worse. He gulped a mouthful of lukewarm coffee and grimaced at its bitterness.

The door opened. A man with a neatly trimmed beard and red scarf tucked into a dark grey wool overcoat stepped in, signalled the waitress for a coffee, and took the chair opposite Ilya.

'News from the front?' asked Terentev.

'None of it good, I'm afraid, Colonel.'

Terentev counted his good fortune. At least he felt could rely on his men's loyalty. Sticking together in an organisation as large and amorphous as the KGB was the first rule of survival.

'Our lot have the general secretary holed up in his dacha at Peredelkino. I sent Vasily there to check it out. Have you ever been there, Colonel?'

'Many times, with my wife. My friend has a dacha there.'

Terentev pictured its woods, small well-tended gardens and evening gatherings when dissident artists rubbed shoulders with the political elite.

'The Emergency Committee has not done itself any favours holding the general secretary so close to Moscow. How many men?'

'Forty... fifty... maybe more. No one gets in or out... under the direct command of the KGB chairman himself.'

'And General Marov?'

'General Volkov visited him this afternoon... came away furious apparently. It doesn't look like Volkov got what he wanted.'

'Support, I would guess,' said Terentev. Safety in numbers. Yuri would be a perfect addition to the list of conspirators. 'I doubt General Marov is going to be rushing to the cause.'

Volkov was clearly not as confident as he appeared. Terentev doubted if the new colonel general could rely on the undivided loyalty of every district general. Yuri might just give him the credibility he needed with the outriders.

'Are you reporting this up?'

Terentev shook his head. Where? If anyone found out that he was conducting a surveillance operation in Peredelkino he would land up in the same place as Yuri. The question was *what could he do about it, if anything*? The answer was plain enough, *not very much*. The deputy general secretary, secretary of defence, even his own boss were all complicit. Rumblings had not converted to people on the street... not yet, but then it had been less than forty-eight hours since the general secretary had disappeared from public view. The average citizen *wanted* to believe the Emergency Committee, but that confidence would soon evaporate if there were no sightings of the general secretary soon, and *then* what?

His junior officer sat waiting for instructions, staring out the window at the queue Terentev had been studying ten minutes before.

'Just keep me informed; any change, let me know immediately.'

For now, he would just have to wait.

CHAPTER 59

MOSCOW, LUBYANKA

Yuri relieved himself in the hole that excused itself as a toilet in the corner of his small cell, zipped up his jeans and pulled on the overhead chain. He needed more water; the jug by the table had run dry an hour ago.

Through a gap in the hatch he counted four cells opposite and, if he stood sideways, the solid reinforced door giving on to the narrow corridor.

'Derevenko... Yev!' he shouted. Silence. If they wanted to isolate him, he thought, they had done a good job.

He went back and lay on the bed and wondered whether Anatoly had got through to Leningrad and what Viktoriya would make of it all if he had.

He thought back to Smolensk. It felt like a lifetime ago when Viktoriya and he had wandered the streets in that early first winter snow, of how he had kissed her under the prying eyes of an elderly woman who sat on a chair at the end of her hotel corridor. He remembered how Viktoriya had looked at him with a mixture of suspicion and amusement. *You remind me of a wolf,* she had said randomly, looking at him with those icy-blue eyes. How off guard he had been caught by that remark and how much he had thought about it since: *predator, instinctual, powerful animal, threatening* were all epithets one could attach to the word *wolf.* When he asked her what she had meant, she had just shrugged. Maybe she was right, but he wasn't sure he entirely liked it either, not in the way she felt about him, anyway. But how else would he want to be perceived: a snake, a lamb…?

Neither of them had made any promises to each other when they had set off for their respective destinations the following morning: she to Leningrad, he eventually to Moscow; it had all been left hanging in the air, suspended, unresolved. If they ever met again, he wondered if she would pretend it never happened.

Yuri's mind turned to Volkov again and the other district generals. Had they thrown their lot in with the new chief of staff? Presumably they had by what he had witnessed in Migalovo, or was it an intended consequence of a general mobilisation, with no time for introspection or dissent. All the same, Yuri didn't think they would all be happy with it either. Ghukov was respected, but he did not believe Zhakov of the Far East district or Ivchenko of the Urals – who he got on with personally – would be eager to support a revived Communist government, not after the debacle of Afghanistan. General Alyabyev of Central Command Moscow, though, was that much harder to read. Older, no doubt approaching retirement, Yuri had little to do with him personally apart from staff meetings in Moscow. Alyabyev gave little away.

The sudden jangling of keys in the door made him sit up. The defence minister entered, followed by a guard with a jug of water, a bowl of something and a piece of rye bread. Were they trying to kill him with kindness now, he thought?

'General, please eat.'

The defence minister gestured at the bowl.

'May I say, General, I am deeply sorry to meet you under these circumstances.'

'Well that makes two of us, Comrade Dubnikov.'

Yuri had met the defence minister, Viktor Dubnikov, on several occasions, although it was Ghukov as chief of staff who met with him mostly. He was definitely communist old guard. In his sixties, Dubnikov had served Brezhnev before the present general secretary. Yuri guessed he was part of the political balancing act that the general secretary had needed to perform in the Politburo. Neatly dressed in a black suit, white shirt and red tie, the minister took the only chair and sat down. He removed a handkerchief from his trouser pocket and mopped his face.

'As I said, I am sorry to see you under these circumstances,' he repeated.

'We could take this conversation to a café,' Yuri countered.

'Well that would be awkward, I'm sure you will appreciate. Colonel, General Volkov has, I understand, been to see you. I just wanted to reassure you *personally* that should you decide to support the Emergency Committee, you would be well rewarded. You may have your personal difficulties with Volkov, but he does respect your military ability, he has told me so, as I do, I might add. We need talent like yours, General… How would second in command to the colonel general sound?'

'Comrade Dubnikov, I'm truly flattered, but *all* this can be easily solved. Let me see the general secretary. If he is ill, as you say he is, I will certainly reconsider.'

'I'm afraid that will not be possible. The general secretary is not receiving visitors, he is too unwell.'

'Why did I think you would say that?

'Comrade, I said this to someone quite recently, *do you want to be on the wrong or the right side of history?* Do you, Comrade Dubnikov?'

Dubnikov stood up, blue in the face, and banged on the door for the guard.

'I'm sure General Volkov pointed out that our patience is limited,' said the defence minister coldly. 'We need you final answer by this time tomorrow.'

Yuri stood up and took a step towards him so they were face-to-face.

'Comrade Dubnikov, I, of all people, am not someone who takes kindly to being threatened, remember that.'

The minister blinked and, without another word, left.

15 OCTOBER 1989

CHAPTER 60

MOSCOW

Viktoriya sat on her duffel bag outside Terentev's flat on Degtyarny. Six thirty in the morning and it was still dark. She had already worked out that the doorbell to flat five did not work and decided to wait fifteen minutes and see if anyone opened the main door before she started ringing bells randomly waking residents and drawing attention to herself.

Her sleep had been fitful on the Red Star from Leningrad. Travelling second class in a women's-only four-berth couchette, her only fellow passenger was a woman in her forties visiting family in Moscow. She did not proffer anything more than *visiting a friend* herself. What would she have said if she had told the truth – *taking photographs of indefinite significance to a KGB colonel*?

The door clanged open. Viktoriya jumped to her feet. A man, mid-thirties, sporting a military-style haircut and a canvas duffle bag hung off one shoulder, stepped onto the street.

'Can I help you?' he asked, looking her up and

down and the bag parked on the street. She had slipped on a pair of jeans and a blue cashmere sweater in the car before boarding the Red Star but had still not bothered to remove her make-up from the night before.

'I've come to see a friend. I'm from out of the city; his bell doesn't seem to be working.'

'If you don't mind my asking, who is it you have come to see?'

'Ilya Terentev.'

The man stared at her for a moment, sizing her up. She felt slightly unnerved.

'I'll show you up. I know where he lives.'

Viktoriya protested that that wouldn't be necessary but he ignored her. Extracting his key, he unlocked the street door and waved her in. There was nothing else for it. She picked up her bag, slung it onto her shoulder and let her hand drop inside.

'Please follow me,' he said politely.

'Second floor,' she said.

'Yes, number five. I know most of the people in this block.'

The lift was only fit for three people and felt claustrophobic with the two of them packed in so closely. She should have insisted they take the stairs, rather than be trapped in such a tiny space with a complete stranger. Still, it was only two floors. The door opened.

'After you,' he beckoned. It was still dark and the stairwell empty. 'Take a right.'

Was he really going to walk her to the door? she thought. They stopped outside number five.

A hand reached over her shoulder and wrapped on the door. She wondered how well this man knew Terentev. Her hand closed tightly on the automatic. It didn't feel right.

Footsteps sounded on the other side and the door opened. A woman with long hair, thirties, busy knotting the belt of a dressing gown, looked from her to the face behind.

'Natasha, may I introduce Viktoriya Nikolaevna Kayakova, late of Leningrad, probably the richest woman in Russia.'

She turned round to face her escort.

'Colonel?'

'The same… I didn't want to effect introductions in the street… this is my wife Natasha… and I think you can remove your hand from your bag now. I don't think you need a gun.'

More embarrassed that her manoeuvre had been so transparent than that she had taken the precaution in the first place, she let go of its handle.

'I don't normally look like this,' she said in her own defence.

'Please come in, Viktoriya Nikolaevna,' said Natasha.

The apartment was small but cosy. Several photographs of the couple were displayed on a dresser.

'Please,' gestured Natasha at the slightly worn brown tweed sofa. 'Would you like something to eat? Maybe freshen up?'

Viktoriya was not about to decline any of it.

'*Red Star*?' asked Terentev, almost a rhetorical question.

'Yes,' she said, 'no complaints… look, I'd love to have a shower, but before I do, can I give you this envelope.' She reached into her duffel bag, prised the inside panel off the base and pulled out a brown envelope.

'I received a message from Yuri yesterday… one of the men he's been on the run with… he wouldn't say from where or to,' – it seemed such a long time ago, she thought – 'he said I could trust you.'

'You can,' replied Terentev. He held out his hand for the envelope and she handed it to him.

'Twelve years ago – in fact, April 1977 – I was a student, my friend Mikhail Revnik—'

'—of RUI?'

'—yes,' Viktoriya continued. 'He took some photographs of two men on the Moika embankment. Some KGB type put him up to it, offered Misha a reward. We were *only* sixteen at the time… it could have been almost anyone. The trouble is, he was spotted… but he managed to fence it off on me before they caught up with him. Misha persuaded them he had thrown the camera into the canal.'

'Sounds very resourceful… and the man who had paid him to do it?

'He never reappeared. I hid the film for years and gave it back to Misha just before he travelled to Milan for the first time.'

'And he had it developed there?'

She nodded.

'I'd never seen the photographs until yesterday. I know Misha couldn't identify the people in them… well, until yesterday, when he came briefly out of his coma. Maybe he recognised someone… I don't know.'

'I'm sorry about Mikhail Dimitrivich. I heard the news. Where is he now?'

'In our own building in Leningrad… under medical supervision… don't worry, it's like a fortress… I can't help but think this is related.'

Terentev opened the envelope and spread the large black-and-whites on the dining room table. The photos were remarkably clear. She watched him frown and without a word pull up a chair as if to stop himself falling over.

'You recognise them?' she said.

'I recognise *him*.' Terentev pointed at the man with the glasses. 'Karzhov, chairman of the KGB, but not him, I've never seen him before. April 1977, you say?'

She nodded.

'Can I keep these… for now… I want to run some checks… under the radar?'

'Of course, that's what I hoped you were going to say.' Viktoriya stood up. 'I'd like to freshen up now, thank you, and then I want you to tell me what you know about Yuri.'

CHAPTER 61

Viktoriya stepped out of the small shower cubicle and towelled herself dry, glad to have washed the night away. She wondered if Misha had shown any further signs of improvement and whether Kostya would honour his side of the bargain. For now, she reasoned, it was not in his interest to do otherwise – there were at least eighty-five million reasons why he might hold back for forty-eight hours or so. And he was right. If the so-called Emergency Committee did wind back the clock and the communists regained the upper hand, she would be the one on the run. Exile would be the only option, the only one that didn't involve being incarcerated, or worse.

A knock on the bedroom door made her start. It was Natasha's voice.

'Coffee.'

The door opened a fraction and the welcome smell of coffee wafted into the room. She thought of mid-morning breaks in Misha's office, standing at the window observing the goings on below, catching up. She took a deep breath and held it, let go and took another before savouring her first bitter taste of coffee that day. She winced and closed her eyes, concentrating on the familiar caffeine rush, and immediately felt more positive. There was progress of sorts: Misha had woken, even if momentarily, and said something coherent, Kostya had been neutralised, for now at least, and she had arrived safe in Moscow and met someone Yuri told her she could trust. And on top of all that he had identified one of the players in the photograph as the KGB chair himself.

With her towel, she wiped the mirror free of steam and looked at her normal self, absent heavy make-up and her hair parted where it customarily fell. Quickly, she pulled on her clothes, jeans, a fresh T-shirt and sweater and with the dregs of the coffee headed back into the living room.

Terentev was talking to a man who must have arrived when she was in the shower. He nodded in acknowledgement but did not introduce himself. Two of the photos were gone. She assumed they were now stowed in his shoulder bag.

'If you will excuse me,' the stranger said, and let himself out.

Natasha handed her a plate of scrambled eggs.

'I have to be going too. Maybe I will see you again,' she said and followed the other man out of the door.

The colonel scooped up the remaining photos and handed them to her.

'No, please keep them; they're safer with you now.'

He disappeared into the bedroom and reappeared a minute later minus the envelope.

'So… where's Yuri? Please tell me what you can, everything,' she said, sitting back down again on the sofa.

Terentev sat down on the dining room chair opposite.

'Not good, I'm afraid. Yuri's locked up in the KGB prison in Lubyanka, the general secretary is under effective house arrest twenty kilometres south-west of Moscow, and General Ghukov has been replaced by a new chief of staff, General Volkov.' Terentev paused for breath. 'If that is not bad enough, the East German government is on the brink of collapse and there is a simmering mass uprising.'

'How do you think the new Emergency Committee will react?'

'Suppress it… start World War Three probably.'

'Not good then.'

Terentev smiled. 'Yes, I think that is a good assessment.'

'Can you do anything?'

'I may be a colonel in the KGB, but I have no political affiliations, money, or influence, to any degree… and I am up against some very powerful people, including the chairman of the KGB himself.'

'What about Yuri? Doesn't he have a following?'

'Not in Lubyanka… the old communist diehards are not giving up without a fight.'

'It would be interesting to know how much support this committee has from other ministers and how much they know about what is going on. Many of them are going to suffer – financially – if the communists gain the upper hand now. Do you know Federov?'

'The oil minister? Not personally.'

'He would be a good place to start. I spoke with him yesterday by phone, but he was necessarily circumspect… Do you have a phone?'

Terentev nodded.

'I am going to call him to arrange a meeting this morning at that café next to the ministry, you know the one. I'm not going to give him my name, but I'm sure he'll recognise my voice.'

'And you think you can get him to a meeting, just like that?' He snapped his fingers.

'Absolutely… if I know Stephan Federov.'

CHAPTER 62

Viktoriya remembered the café from her last visit with Federov: the French-style coffee bar and high stools, the mirrored wall behind, and low-hanging smoked-glass pendant lights. Terentev sat at the bar, facing the mirror with a clear view of the booth she had occupied in a corner out of sight from the street window.

She took a sip of the cappuccino that had been placed in front of her and thought back to her earlier call to Federov's office. At first she had struggled to be put through; his secretary had been understandably suspicious but Viktoriya had insisted. It was personal, she had said, Stephan would be *very* unhappy if she weren't put through *immediately*. Federov had taken the call. 'Federov,' he had said, his voice filled with suspicion. 'Stephan', she had replied, in the warmest voice she could muster. To his credit he had understood the situation immediately, played along with the demanding girlfriend routine and agreed to meet her at the café at ten o'clock. She looked at her watch: now, in fact.

On cue, the door to the café opened and Federov walked in.

At least he is alone, she thought.

'I thought you were still in Leningrad? How is Mikhail Dimitrivich?' Federov said as he slid into the booth next to her.

'Showing signs of improvement, thank you. Stephan, I appreciate the position you may be in, but some candour would be useful.' There was no point in asking Federov if she could trust him. A simple *yes* wasn't going to prove anything.

'There is more at stake here than simply our business relationship, as important as that is. I need to understand your position and that of your colleagues. The information I have is that the Emergency Committee has the general secretary under house arrest.'

Federov looked surprised.

'You are well informed… who is the man at the bar?'

'He's with me. He's totally trustworthy.'

He nodded. 'The Emergency Committee is not the Politburo. I have been told the same story as the rest of the public, although I know from my own contacts that what you say is true. The deputy secretary has assumed the levers of state, backed by the KGB chair and the defence minister. Those opposed have been detained or eliminated, like your friend General Marov, for instance. The Emergency Committee is relying on us to keep our heads down.'

'While it decides?'

Federov looked away.

'The opposition is too strong. It will be like Khrushchev. The general secretary will be replaced.'

'But it won't be so silent this time, not with Volkov about to risk a war in Europe.'

'No, it won't,' his voice trailed off. 'All I know is we haven't got long. There is a meeting of the Emergency Committee this afternoon. They are not going to let this drift, *especially* with the East German situation. I get the impression the general secretary is not going to resign through reasons of bad health either,' said Federov.

'What do you think will happen to General Marov?' asked Viktoriya.

'He'll have to fall in line or not, and if he doesn't… a posting to the Far East would be a good outcome.'

Viktoriya knew he was right. It was all or nothing for the Emergency Committee. They would have to legitimise their coup, and anything that challenged that legitimacy would be dealt with. The KGB was not squeamish about such things, arrests and payoffs would be the order of the day.

'And you, Viktoriya Nikolaevna, what will you do?'

'I don't want to think about that for the moment.' But she knew she would have to very shortly. Kostya would close in for the kill if the committee became the new government. Nobody was going to worry about the wellbeing of a wealthy street trader cum banker. Kostya would have delivered and no doubt be rewarded with RUI. It wouldn't take long to make back his lost eighty-five million.

The oil minister stood up.

'I have to be going, I'm afraid. If I can do anything

for you, I will. My advice to you is to follow your money out of the Soviet Union. Don't wait too long. And if Mikhail is well enough to travel, him too… even if he isn't, you will have to risk it.'

Viktoriya watched Federov exit the café as Terentev climbed off the bar stool and walked over to her booth.

'What did Federov have to say?'

'That we are all going to hell in a hand cart… there is no effective opposition…'

The door of the café opened and the man she had seen in Terentev's apartment that morning walked in. Terentev waved him over.

'Any joy?'

'I've given the photos to our best man; he remembers one or two operatives from that time. He knows it's urgent… and that if he gets caught it's probably curtains. The Emergency Committee are meeting at five this evening at the Defence Ministry. There is a broadcast booked for seven.'

The table fell silent.

'We need to get Yuri out of Lubyanka,' said Viktoriya. 'If the conflict widens in Eastern Europe he'll just be a footnote. Plan A was to kill him… they sabotaged his aircraft. There is no Plan B, not if he fails to support them and, knowing him as I do, he is not going to do that.'

The colonel nodded.

'I've been thinking, Colonel. I have twenty-five fully armed men at the Leningrad Freight yard on the outskirts of Moscow – Yuri's request before he was arrested. He gave no further instructions… I'm sorry I didn't mention this before…' said Viktoriya.

'Well, we can't storm Lubyanka. It's bristling with guards.'

'I've got another idea.'

CHAPTER 63

Terentev cricked his neck up at the clock set into the uppermost band of the yellow brick neo-baroque palace façade that was Lubyanka: midday. He cast a glance at Gaidar and the two men behind him dressed in military uniform.

'Ready?'

The three of them nodded. One of the soldiers rearranged his grey ushanka, making sure the red star faced forward.

With the two soldiers squarely behind him, Terentev walked into the high-ceilinged entrance hall he had entered a thousand times before. Failure, he knew, would also make it the *last* time.

Two KGB officers, standing beside a grey granite desk, barred his way.

'Colonel.' The nearest snapped to attention while the other stood stock-still, his hands gripping the barrel and stock of the Kalashnikov strapped across his chest.

'I've come to transfer a prisoner to Lefortovo.'

The officer entered their names in the log book, giving only a cursory glance to the official-looking paper Terentev produced from his inside pocket.

'Thank you, Colonel.' He saluted Terentev and Gaidar and stepped back.

Terentev led them left down the parquet corridor towards the rear of the building and the courtyard where the prison began, nodding occasionally at a familiar face. A second detail blocked its entrance. This time there was no salute. The officer in charge, a lieutenant, young, perhaps twenty-six – he had not seen him before – looked at him and his escort suspiciously.

'Can I help you, Colonel,' he asked. Behind him, three soldiers stood studying Gaidar and his men.

'I've come to transfer General Marov to Lefortovo Prison – orders of the chairman.'

The lieutenant took the transfer form from Terentev's hand and studied it before handing it to one of the men behind him.

'What unit are you with, Major?' said the lieutenant, directing his question at Gaidar.

'Kantemirovskaya Division, under Lieutenant General Tretyak.'

'General staff have assigned Major Gaidar to the transfer,' added Terentev.

It was normal for the military to accompany high-ranking staff officers.

'I haven't heard of any pending transfer of prisoner Marov, Colonel.'

'As you can see, Lieutenant, the order was only dated an hour ago.'

The lieutenant held out his hand for the transfer note. The soldier placed it in his palm. He studied it again. For a moment Terentev thought he might hold it up to the light, not that that would reveal anything. The paperwork was real enough; it was only the signature that had been forged.

'Why don't you call upstairs, Lieutenant? Third floor. I'm sure the chairman's office will confirm the transfer. Extension 363. We are in a hurry, Lieutenant.'

Sometimes events hinge on the simplest of turns, thought Terentev. If the lieutenant called his bluff, they were done for.

The officer studied his and Gaidar's faces before lifting the receiver and dialling.

'Detail to collect prisoner Marov.' The lieutenant turned to Terentev. 'Someone will be up to escort you to the prisoner shortly, sir.' The lieutenant snapped to attention.

Terentev cast a sideways glance at Gaidar, hoping that his relief did not show.

They did not have long to wait; a soldier led them down a narrow stone staircase. In the basement a wide corridor with cell doors extending either side reached to the corner of the building. Two plain-clothes officers emerged from one and walked past them. Terentev caught the sound of moaning from inside. They took the corner and stopped at a section protected by a steel-studded door.

'General... prisoner... ' he corrected himself, 'Marov is being kept in isolation,' the private said by way of explanation.

He stopped at the end door and flicked through the keys on his belt until he found the corresponding number to the cell door – 107 – inserted it in the lock and pushed.

★

Yuri looked up at the door as it opened and watched his friend and Gaidar walk in. The two of them were the last people he had been expecting to see. Terentev's and Gaidar's unsmiling faces warned him not to jump to his feet and grab them in a bear hug. Yuri noted the two soldiers standing behind Ilya and the prison guard.

'A bit cramped in here, Major,' he said, addressing Gaidar, ignoring Terentev.

'We have orders to transfer you, General, to Lefortovo.'

'Lefortovo? Am I a political prisoner now?'

Yuri had no idea about what was happening; he just had to trust in his friend.

'General, I am Colonel Ilya Terentev, is there anything you need to take with you?'

Were they really going to try and just walk out of here? Yuri thought. Was that the plan? Yuri stood up.

'I'm ready.'

With the prison guard leading the way, Yuri marched with Terentev and Gaidar directly in front of him and the two soldiers immediately behind. From their uniforms he assumed they were both Major Gaidar's men. Twenty metres down the main corridor they passed two prison officers leading a smartly dressed man in a charcoal-grey suit and tie.

He glanced up from the floor as they walked by and looked directly at Yuri. He had blood on his white shirt and his lip had been split; above his left eye a large livid swelling had begun to emerge.

Yuri wondered what had befallen Derevenko and Stephan. Were they buried somewhere in this hellhole? He wanted to stop and insist they found them, but he would only be putting other lives at risk. Ilya had managed to bluff his way in and presumably was about to bluff his way out. Stopping for passengers was not going to work.

Only the sound of their heavy footsteps marked the military procession. Yuri followed Terentev and Gaidar up the narrow staircase to the main floor. As they rounded the final corner and emerged into daylight, Yuri took a deep breath and slowly let the air out of his lungs.

A young lieutenant approached them. Terentev signed the release paper and they were through into the main corridor. Men and women in plain clothes and uniform bustled back and forth, throwing the occasional glance in his direction. Yuri wondered if anyone recognised him.

'We are leaving by the east entrance,' said Terentev over his shoulder. They took the next right down a service corridor and soon came out on the main corridor again but on the other side of the building. This was much less trafficked. Twenty metres along, three guards manned the exit onto a side street. They were deep in conversation. One of them noticed their detail approach and tapped his colleague on the arm.

'Colonel,' said the senior NCO. He saluted Terentev, clearly recognising him.

Terentev produced a duplicate of the release note.

The NCO was in the process of handing the note back when the wall phone rang. A private behind the NCO lifted the receiver from its cradle when the deafening wail of an alarm suddenly broke above them. Yuri looked up at the flashing box and back down again at the face of the soldier struggling to hear what was being said to him. Yuri could guess. The private's eyes darted from him to Terentev. Terentev stepped forward, ripped the phone out of his hand and kneed him in the groin. Gaidar and the two soldiers grabbed the other two, forcing them to the ground. They ejected their magazines and lobbed them and the AKs in opposite directions.

'Let's go!' Terentev shouted.

Gaidar pointed his revolver at the prone soldiers as two cars pulled up in front of the entrance. Terentev was the first to make it to the car door and fling it open.

'Get in!' he shouted to Yuri.

Yuri did not need any encouragement. He threw himself into the back seat, followed by Terentev and one of Gaidar's men. Out of the back window he saw the other two soldiers jump into the second car. His car lurched forward. Yuri turned towards the front and the balaclava-covered heads of the driver and front passenger. They took the first corner at speed and accelerated around the next.

'Where are we going?'

The figure next to the driver turned to face him. All he could see through the mask's visor were piercing icy-blue eyes and the twinkle of a smile around their edges.

'So glad you could make it, General. We're switching cars in two blocks,' said the now familiar female voice.

CHAPTER 64

Yuri gazed out of the Leningrad Freight first-floor window over the yard towards the gate, where armed security guards monitored traffic in and out. Terentev, Gaidar and Viktoriya sat expectantly across the table.

'So we have the general secretary under house arrest, the same for Ghukov, the Emergency Committee with the deputy general secretary in charge, and the defence minister, KGB chair and Volkov in support. No overt military support for the coup… but they *are* taking orders from Volkov,' reiterated Yuri. He had already established that Derevenko and Stephan were relatively safe for now inside a military prison on the outskirts of Moscow; the intelligence service had shown no interest in either of them.

'Yes, except, of course, the Emergency Committee is not painting this as a coup, but a necessary step given the condition of the general secretary,' chipped in Terentev, 'whose condition might turn fatal at any second.'

'Yes, and from what Federov has told you, Vika, the other government ministers are keeping their heads down seeing which way the wind blows.'

'Federov is certainly not going to stand up and be counted, not as things are,' said Viktoriya. 'The KGB and the army are going to be looking for you now. I can get you out of Moscow over the border in twenty-four hours if you want… that goes for all of you.'

'And you?' Yuri asked her.

'I'm staying put – at least in Leningrad with Misha.'

'What time is the Emergency Committee meeting?'

'Five this evening at the Ministry of Defence,' said Terentev. 'They are going on TV at seven.'

Silence descended again.

'Sergei,' Yuri said, turning to Gaidar, 'do you think you can get someone over to my apartment and smuggle out my uniform and a change of clothes. I need to get out of these,' he said, pointing at his jeans and soiled parka jacket. 'I don't think this will impress anyone.'

'I'll see to it straight away, General.'

He caught the flash of a smile on Viktoriya's lips.

'So, you are going to stay?'

'Do I really have a choice? These photos, Ilya, how important do you think they are?'

Terentev shrugged.

'And you say they are of the KGB chair, twelve years ago. What was he then?'

'A KGB colonel, foreign intelligence, spent time between East Germany and Moscow.'

Clearly, the photo is compromising one or both of the subjects. How many possibilities could there be?

Yuri thought. Was the other man a KGB mole inside one of the Soviet ministries – an informer? But what was so unusual in that?

Gaidar re-entered the room and took his seat.

'Thirty men?' Yuri said, looking in the major's direction.

Gaidar nodded.

'Well that should be enough. Is there anywhere I can take a shower, preferably hot, while I wait for my uniform?'

CHAPTER 65

Volkov received the news from the KGB chair in stony silence. How could someone just walk in and escort Marov out? But he wasn't just *someone*. Terentev was a KGB colonel. Karzhov had assured him that Terentev and Marov were friends and that they went back a long way; he did not suspect dissent went deeper. But how could he tell? Maybe it didn't matter; they had figured on opposition, planned for it and if *this* was the sum total of the remainder, it was an irritant and nothing else. Hadn't everyone important already fallen in line: the Politburo and the district generals... admittedly some with less enthusiasm than others. Besides, as soon as the deputy was confirmed as general secretary that would all change. The current general secretary would either resign, through reasons of ill health, or fall on his sword... or be pushed onto it.

After this evening, Marov and his merry men would be a mere side-story. Indeed, if Marov had any sense, any sense of self-preservation, he would be on his way out of the Soviet Union by now. General Marov – *defector*. It had a good ring about it.

There were more important things to worry about

than General Marov... or the wellbeing of the general secretary. The Western Army had been brought to full strength. The Americans could posture how they liked, but when the arrests started in East Germany, their promise of intervention would ring hollow. The US was not about to risk war.

Three o'clock... the car would collect him from GSHQ at four thirty and, at seven, perestroika and all the chaos that it had brought would be history.

CHAPTER 66

Yuri fastened the last button of his military jacket and looked at himself in the small dust-covered mirror balanced on the mantelpiece. The shower had been anything but hot, but he wasn't complaining. His hair and clothing had reeked of his Lubyanka cell, the odour of stale urine and mould. He hadn't been able to banish the smell, not until he had stood under running water for five minutes.

A knock on the door made him turn round. Terentev stepped into the room and gave him a mock salute.

'General Marov,' he said, looking him up and down. 'Quite a difference from when we picked you up, Yuri.'

Yuri could sense his friend was bursting to say something.

'What?' Yuri said.

Terentev placed one of the black-and-white photos on the desk.

'I think my man has had a breakthrough; it's only conjecture. He talked to one or two colleagues on the East German desk and they pointed him at a retired officer. He worked with Karzhov, didn't like him much apparently. This man said that at that time – 1978 – there was talk of someone on the inside high up in Soviet intelligence feeding information to the Americans. We also know from our own double agent at the time that the Americans had no idea who their agent's contact was on our side. An investigation drew a blank. One of the officers involved met an untimely end, found drowned in the Moskva. No one has sought to follow up since.'

'And the photo?'

'The retired officer recognised the other man in the photo – we only have his word; we can't run it through Lubyanka for now, for obvious reasons. He was an American CIA officer, a Tom Banner, arrested by us in the early eighties on spying charges, sentenced to life imprisonment but died in jail before he could be put up for one of our regular prisoner exchanges with the Americans – heart attack… if you want to believe that.'

'So you think it was Karzhov who was feeding the Americans?'

'It's certainly a possibility, working both sides for his own ends. Banner either never revealed his Soviet source or the CIA has chosen not to.'

'You mean he could be a sleeper.'

'Perhaps… or simply that they do not want to undermine other assets they might have in the Soviet Union… and they'll have them… best let him off the hook. Who's going to sell them information if there's a treason charge at the end of it?'

'And you think Karzhov engineered Banner's death to protect himself.'

Terentev nodded.

'Again a probability… he was frightened that Banner might give away his identity in return for freedom… maybe Banner was becoming impatient.'

'Okay… How about Peredelkino?' said Yuri. They only had hours before the Emergency Committee went on the air waves.

'Half an hour by the M1.'

'What about the back road – Michurinskiy Prospect – and you approach from the south? If you are stopped on the motorway there's nowhere else to go; I'm guessing you don't want a return trip to Lubyanka? Might take fifteen minutes longer… Does Viktoriya still insist on going?'

'No stopping her,' replied Terentev. 'They're her men too.'

'Okay, but I have to talk with her first. She needs to make a call.'

CHAPTER 67

The truck was more comfortable than she had imagined. Closeted behind boxes stacked to the roof, Viktoriya sat with ten soldiers in the back of an LF freighter. She stood up and looked through the clear oval plastic pane into the driver's cab where two other soldiers, in dark grey overalls, posed as LF crew. Outside, endless rows of anonymous red-brick tower blocks with white bay windows and covered balconies raced by in the fading light.

A car drove past them and tucked in between the two vehicles before pulling out again and overtaking. At intersections, military jeeps sat on wide grass verges watched them go by. She counted five in as many blocks, ready to shut down one of the city's main arteries at a second's notice.

She sat back down again on the cold corrugated aluminium floor, took off her jacket and folded it under her. Nobody spoke. This wasn't what her security force had signed up for at RUI, but from the occasional smiles on their broad faces she guessed that this meant more than the solid pay cheques and bonuses they had been receiving. Besides, weren't all their interests in the *new* Russia perfectly aligned. If the Emergency Committee succeeded in turning back the clock, most of them would likely find themselves back where they started – in the *real* army on no pay and no future, stuck in some backwater or attempting to put down restive East Europeans.

Gaidar cast a glance in her direction and at Terentev sat next to her. Until now, Viktoriya had not had much to do with him. Ivan handled security. But she could see why Yuri had placed so much confidence in him. Around her age, she guessed, maybe a little older, he had not let his rapidly growing private army atrophy. From what Ivan told her, it was better trained and armed than most regular units.

She looked at her watch. Fifteen minutes past five, sunset just after five thirty. Was it only this morning she had arrived in Moscow and this afternoon Terentev had managed to march Yuri out of Lubyanka? With a little luck and Kostya's reluctant support, the authorities might still think her barricaded in Malaya Morskaya.

Without any warning, the truck braked sharply, pulled left into a side street and abruptly stopped. Viktoriya stood up again and warily peaked out of the trailer window. A military jeep blocked their way. She immediately sat back down again and raised a finger to her lips, pointing to the outside. One of the soldiers flipped the safety catch on his Kalashnikov. Gaidar shook his head. Starting a firefight in the back of a truck would be as good as suicide, she thought. Viktoriya held her breath as the rear door creaked open and light flooded into the wagon. Someone shifted boxes, sliding them this way and that. No one moved. Terentev looked at her, unblinking, and squeezed her arm. It would all be over before it started, she thought, if they were discovered now.

The soldier shifting the boxes stopped and shouted the all-clear to another. The rear doors banged closed and the truck pulled out and turned once again onto the main road.

Viktoriya looked at her watch in the dim interior light. In fifteen to twenty minutes, roadblocks willing, they would be there.

CHAPTER 68

No one stopped him when Yuri entered by the main doors of GSHQ. Whether it was an inbuilt deference to uniform or tacit support he wasn't clear, but one thing he did know was confidence was everything… well almost… *carpe diem*, you either did or you didn't.

Suppressing the urge to break into a run, Yuri increased his stride, his metal-edged heels ringing out loudly along the flagstone passage as he hurried towards the communication room. His arrival was greeted with a frantic pushing back of chairs as soldiers and officers jumped to attention.

'At ease, men,' said Yuri, returning their salutes and turning to the duty officer.

'Lieutenant, put me through to the duty officer at Central District command.'

The lieutenant stared at him, frozen.

'General Marov, we thought you were under arrest.'

'I was… Lieutenant… didn't you serve under me at Smolensk – communications?'

'Yes, General, you recommended me for promotion to Moscow.'

It was coming back to him now.

'Yekaterinburg… you are from Yekaterinburg, my home city?'

The officer nodded. 'Yes, sir, well remembered.'

'Well, Lieutenant, I need your services now, and I haven't got time to explain.'

Yuri could see the officer hesitate before making up his mind.

'Yes, General.'

The lieutenant saluted him again before retaking his seat. The duty sergeant cast a wary glance in Yuri's direction and rotated the radio dial to the appropriate frequency.

'This is General Yuri Marov from the general staff,' said Yuri when the duty officer, a Lieutenant Orlov, responded. 'I wish to speak with General Alyabyev. Please put him on the line.'

'General Alyabyev is in a meeting, General. I have orders he is not to be disturbed.'

'Lieutenant, this is an emergency.'

Yuri could almost hear the soldier's mind whirring, calculating how much trouble he would be in for disobeying him or Alyabyev.

'Lieutenant Orlov,' said Yuri, exasperated, 'do you know who I am?'

'Yes, sir, of course'

'Well I intend to be around for a very long time, Lieutenant.' There was a pause. Everything depended on Lieutenant Orlov, Yuri thought – maybe the whole weight of the Soviet Union.

'I am putting you through now, General.'

'Thank you, Lieutenant.'

A few moments later, Yuri heard Alyabyev's disgruntled voice. Yuri imagined Alyabyev's face, the sardonic, slightly bored look he had seen so many times over the negotiating table that he had long since ceased to recognise as lack of interest.

'Yes, General, what can I do for you?' Alyabyev sounded tired. 'Aren't you under arrest, Marov?'

'Technically, yes, sir.'

'You're taking a big risk, Marov, walking into GSHQ and contacting me. Volkov will have you rearrested if he finds out.'

'He won't have to look very far, General. He left for a meeting at the Defence Ministry twenty minutes ago, and I plan to join him there after I finish this call with you. General, I need your help.' Yuri knew he didn't have much time. 'You *know* there is nothing wrong with the general secretary and that he is under house arrest in Peredelkino?'

'Marov, you probably know a lot more than me... we've all been kept busy with this mobilisation.'

'Well, I'm telling you, General, and my guess is that if he doesn't step down voluntarily, that will not prevent the Emergency Committee engineering it. You know what that will mean for him and for the Soviet Union.'

'You are talking about half the Politburo. Let's assume, General, you are correct for a minute. What do you propose to do about it?'

'General, you had a commando battalion the last time I looked at your dispositions, five kilometres east of Peredelkino. I have a squad of men on their way to his dacha.' Yuri looked at the wall clock. 'ETA ten minutes.'

'And you want to fight your way in?'

'No, General. I want you to deploy the battalion *around* Peredelkino. I'm *not* expecting your men to fight, General. But I do want you to block anyone coming in or out.'

'Volkov will consider this a mutiny.'

'He's going to be in meeting for the next two hours. Call it a military exercise, General. I just want them there until 8 p.m. You can retire them to barracks after that; three hours, that's all I ask.'

'Give me a minute, Marov.' The line went dead.

The sergeant looked from the lieutenant to Yuri, waiting for further orders. Yuri glanced at his wristwatch. What was Alyabyev doing now? Putting a call through to Volkov? Calling the military police? Maybe he had read the district general wrong all along, and Alyabyev wasn't a neutral and he had thrown his lot in with the conspirators. A minute passed and then another. Yuri expected the steel door to open at any second and for him to be led away.

There was a click on the line. Yuri looked over at the sergeant, who signalled Alyabyev was back on line.

'Yes, General?'

'General Marov, you have until 8 p.m. I hope I don't live to regret this.'

CHAPTER 69

PEREDELKINO

The freighter took a right off Borovskoye and north onto Chobotovskaya and the wooded outskirts of Peredelkino. Less than a kilometre now, Viktoriya thought. She wondered if Yuri had any success with Alyabyev. If he hadn't, they were all walking into a trap.

The vehicle lurched to a halt. She heard someone run round to the back and the groan of the rear doors as before.

'Okay, everyone out!' shouted Gaidar.

Viktoriya read the road sign opposite: Lukinskaya. To their right and left, dense woodland stretched in either direction. Around her, soldiers flexed limbs and checked kit as the truck completed a U-turn and headed back in the direction from which they had come. She stared at its retreating vermillion lights, momentarily mesmerised, as it faded into the rapidly descending darkness.

'Let's go,' she heard Gaidar say.

They headed left over a low wire fence and across

an open field where a flurry of early winter snow had thawed the earth to soft mud. They stopped at the forest edge – one last check. Gaidar gave the thumbs-up and they melted into the wood.

Fending off branches with her hands, Viktoriya tucked in close behind Terentev. Underfoot she felt the springy softness of pine needles and young saplings. Only the swishing and snapping of branches marked the phantom-like progress of their small column.

Two hundred metres in, they found the railway track they were looking for. They paused to get their bearings. Viktoriya pictured the map they had all memorised back at the yard. Michurinets and Peredelkino stations top and tailed the tiny dacha village. Terentev had made it plain they didn't want to land up at either. Both would be crawling with KGB troops. Across the open railway track, Viktoriya made out the lane that marked the outer perimeter of old Peredelkino; along its length, fruit trees shed the last of their cinnamon-tinted leaves.

They froze as headlights raced from the right. An army jeep carrying heavily armed KGB soldiers sped by, closely followed by a second. She imagined them turning right into Serafimovicha and left into Pavlenko, and the general secretary's dacha set back in the woods a hundred metres from Pasternak's.

Gaidar walked back towards her and Terentev.

'What's up?' she asked.

'Serafimovicha is swarming with KGB; one of the men has been reconnoitring ahead,' said Gaidar.

'How about we stick to the west of the village, make our way up through the wood by the river and work our way above Pavlenko before dropping down onto it?' she said.

'I should have remembered that logistics is your speciality... yes, that's exactly what I was going to suggest. We backtrack a hundred metres and cross here.' Gaidar pointed at the intersection of the railway track stretching east and stream running north. 'Five hundred metres up, we exit the wood onto *this* lane and walk up.' His finger skirted the lane until it intersected with another that led east. Three hundred metres along, it crossed Pavlenko.

A third jeep appeared, headlights on full beam, and disappeared towards Serafimovicha.

Viktoriya wondered whether the general secretary's captors were becoming twitchy. It was only an hour or so before the Emergency Committee was supposed to go on the air waves.

'We haven't got long,' she said, almost unnecessarily.

Spread out in twos and threes, they moved east as fast as they could until they hit the small stream that ran under the rail track and followed it north into the woodland beyond. A branch plucked Viktoriya's beanie off her head. A soldier behind her reached up and retrieved it.

'Let's stick close together now,' Gaidar whispered. 'Night visors, those of you who have them.' The undergrowth had become dense and impenetrable in places.

A soldier in front waved them forward. She stuck close to Terentev, eager to avoid twisting her ankle in some foxhole or having her eye poked out by a low-hanging branch. Squinting into the darkness, doing her best to shield her eyes, she swam forward, arms flailing.

Relief marked the edge of the wood as the forest canopy evaporated. Viktoriya took a lungful of cool fresh air as she walked down off a low bank onto the narrow lane she remembered from the map. Subdued street lighting illuminated a roughly made track. Opposite, ink-black windows of unoccupied dachas gazed bleakly towards them. Viktoriya shivered. A man grabbed her by the arm and pulled her back out of the light. A jeep crossed the lane two hundred metres below and disappeared. Nobody moved. They stood, silent, straining to hear the whine of an approaching engine or the murmur of distant voices. Viktoriya felt the warm breath of the man standing next to her and wondered if he could hear her pulse pounding in her neck.

A silhouette stepped back into the road. It was Gaidar. He signalled everyone to form a line behind him and murmured something to his sergeant. Viktoriya looked for Terentev and found him towards the end of the file standing next to the dehumanised form of a soldier wearing a monocular night-vision visor. She wondered if he could make anything out behind the blank windows: a resident's finger on the light switch, arrested by a band of heavily armed men emerging ghostlike from the black wood, or a guard calling the alarm.

CHAPTER 70

MOSCOW

Volkov looked at the assembled. Karzhov had walked into the room five minutes before and was deep in conversation with Dubnikov in the corner; the others had dotted themselves around the long mahogany table with papers spread out in front of them. Opposite, the head of the Peasants' Union worked his way through a long list of names. Volkov watched him studiously placing ticks and crosses against them, settling old scores, removing opposition. He passed the list to the interior minister, who edited it here and there before bagging it in his portfolio case and zipping it firmly shut.

'Everything in order, General?' he asked.

It was, apart from the whereabouts of that idiot Marov, but he did not have time to respond. The large double doors at the end of the room flew open and Gerasim Gerashchenko strode purposefully in. The deputy general secretary took his seat at the head of the table and called the meeting to order. Karzhov and Dubnikov hurried to their places, casting a glance in Volkov's direction. Gerashchenko looked pale, exhausted. Dark circles pooled under his eyes. How long had it been since they had precipitated this venture?' Volkov thought. Was it only three days?

When Gerashchenko spoke, he did so with the voice of a man who no doubt felt the weight and future of the Soviet Union upon him.

'Comrade Chairman,' he said, looking at Karzhov, inviting the KGB chair to speak first.

Karzhov picked up a typed sheet of paper and cast his eyes down the page.

'Deputy General Secretary, comrades,' started Karzhov, 'I can report that, as of this morning, internal opposition to the new government has been neutralised.' A good word, thought Volkov – *neutralised* – very KGB. 'Russians are giving us the benefit of the doubt for the moment, as are the other Soviet republics. Rest assured we will take whatever action is necessary to maintain calm.'

'And East Germany?' asked the interior minister.

Gerashchenko interrupted, 'I spoke with the East German premier an hour ago. He is confident that with our support he can reassert his authority.'

Our support? thought Volkov. *Two hundred thousand Soviet troops* would begin retaking the streets tomorrow.

'I know we can rely on General Volkov,' he added. 'Once we have re-established order we can replace the premier with a fresh face, not immediately. We do not want to be encouraging more dissent.'

'And the general secretary, do you have his

resignation in writing yet? We need to conclude this matter.'

'Within the hour, Secretary,' Karzhov said confidently; he did not elaborate. Indeed, none of them wanted to know the detail; that was Karzhov's responsibility. The general secretary would go quietly one way or the other, of that Volkov was sure.

The soft burring of the phone next to Gerashchenko interrupted proceedings. He picked it up. It must be important to have interrupted the meeting, thought Volkov. The secretary looked in his direction as he listened.

'General, apparently General Marov is in reception, demanding to join the meeting. I thought he was under lock and key?'

'That was the case until this morning. My men have been looking for him but it seems *he* has found us.'

'My men can rearrest him,' chipped in Dubnikov, looking at Volkov as though his men were incapable of that feat.

'He has warned me against that.' Gerashchenko shrugged. 'Let's see what he has to say; there can be no harm in that. Maybe we can win him over.'

CHAPTER 71

Gaidar was the first to spot the military checkpoint thrown across the wide lane above Pavlenko. Viktoriya counted five heavily armed soldiers standing behind a makeshift manually operate red-and-white painted boom. To the right, another soldier manned a heavy machine gun behind a neatly constructed wall of sandbags that curved protectively around him.

The soldier nearest the barrier shouted 'Halt!' as Viktoriya observed the man in his sandbag redoubt hunker down behind the gun and trail its barrel towards them. Gaidar's military uniform clearly confused them. One of the soldiers standing beside the barrier said something to the gunner. Grit and mud zipped around her a split second before she heard the deafening sound of the machine gun weave its deadly path. Viktoriya covered her ears and fought the urge to throw herself on the ground.

'Soldier!' shouted Gaidar, when seconds later the rapid *tuck-tuck* of the machine gun stopped. Their presence would no longer be secret. 'This is Major Gaidar of the Kantemirovskaya Division.'

When Viktoriya turned to find Terentev, he was

no longer there, nor was the soldier with the night visor. She quickly counted the number of heads she could see in the narrow beam of light that flooded towards them from the barrier: twenty men – that left Terentev and four others unaccounted for. She looked up at the two-metre-high bank of scrub and pine needles that followed the lane along its right side towards the temporary barrier and then back down the lane where they had just come and the ink-black forest beyond. *Where had they got to?* she wondered. She couldn't believe Terentev had deserted them.

'What are you doing out here, Major? Peredelkino is strictly off limits. You should know that? How did you get here?' Sound carried perfectly over the fifty metres that separated them. An owl cooed and then another a little further off. In the near distance, Viktoriya could hear the rising rumble of approaching vehicles.

'Throw down your weapons, Major,' the soldier ordered. Viktoriya watched the gunner tilt the barrel a fraction higher. They would all be dead in an instant if he squeezed the trigger.

'Drop your weapons, Sergeant.' It was Terentev's voice from behind the barrier. She looked up at the bank and saw Terentev and three other soldiers lying flat, their Kalashnikovs extended in front of them; a fourth soldier had his gun pointing directly at the back of the gunner at a distance of no more than ten metres.

'Soldier,' it was Gaidar's voice, 'Let's all remain calm. It's your commanding officer I need to speak with.'

As he finished speaking, a truck ground to a halt behind them and ten soldiers jumped down off the back board. A lot of people were going to die, Viktoriya thought, if someone lost their nerve. An eerie silence descended on the impromptu gathering as they faced off, soldier on soldier. Only the sound of the diesel engine ticking over disturbed the still night air.

'Major, it's me you need to speak with.' In the glow of the truck's headlights, Viktoriya made out the silhouette of the man who had spoken. 'I think it would be best if we avoided any unpleasantness.'

Gaidar lowered his gun and walked to the rear of his small column.

'You're not with Kantemirovskaya Division, are you, Major, if that's what rank you truly are?'

'Major Gaidar works for me,' said Viktoriya, before Gaidar had a chance to explain himself. 'And right now I represent General Marov.'

'General Marov?' He almost sneered. 'You are backing the wrong horse, comrade.'

'Viktoriya Nikolaevna—'

'Kayakova of Leningrad… ah yes. Is it the "Gang of Two"?' The colonel laughed. 'And what is it you are trying to do here? Recue our ailing general secretary? I've fifty men between where you are standing and his dacha. You are not going to get very far.' He took a step forward. Gaidar raised his Kalashnikov.

She could see now the three stars on his epaulette.

'Colonel, we are here simply to protect the general secretary. There is no need to spill Russian blood.'

He was smiling now as if she were deranged.

'*Protect*, doesn't he already have protection?'

'Colonel, I trust that is the case... just look at *our* presence as an insurance policy.'

Viktoriya looked at Gaidar, who had his barrel trained directly on the colonel. She had no doubt he would use it if he felt the situation were moving against them.

'*Nobody* leaves Peredelkino while the general secretary is held here against his wishes,' she said in a flat tone, 'you, your soldiers, *no one*. If anything happens to him, *you* will be held to account. Do I make myself clear?'

The smile vanished and his jaw tightened. Viktoriya prayed that Yuri's powers of persuasion had remained intact.

'And how do you propose to do that?'

'I'm surprised you aren't better informed, Colonel. If I'm right, a *spetsnaz* battalion is deploying around us as I speak... we are all hostages now.'

The colonel glared at her, his fists clenched. 'Corporal!' he shouted, 'put me through to Central District command.' A moment later he stepped into the cab of the truck and slammed the door shut.

The *whop-whop-whop* of a rotor blade made her look up as an MTV passed over them and headed in the direction of the dacha. Friend or foe? she thought. It stopped over where she imagined the general secretary to be and hovered in a holding position.

The door of the cab opened and the colonel climbed out. Ignoring the gun pointed directly at him, he walked up to Viktoriya and stopped. He stood there and looked at her for a moment, his face expressionless, exuding a deadly calm.

'My compliments, Viktoriya Nikolaevna, it seems for the moment you have the *temporary* advantage…'

CHAPTER 72

Yuri heard footsteps behind him on the marbled hall of the defence building and turned to see Dubnikov accompanied by two soldiers. Was he about to be rearrested? He had brazened it out so far. Soldiers, who he encountered every day at checkpoints around the Arbat, had been reluctant to challenge him so far. He might be at odds with the interim government, but that was it, for now it was only interim and here he was in plain view in uniform, acting as if nothing were amiss. He doubted the defence minister would be so reticent.

'General Marov, I offered to come *personally* and collect you. We don't want anything to happen to you like last time. Please come this way.' He smiled and waved his hand towards the lift.

There was no going back now.

'We are all in the plenary room,' Yuri heard Dubnikov say. 'I'm sure you know it well.' He did indeed, thought Yuri; he could have found it with his eyes closed. He'd lost count of the number of meetings he had chaired there under different circumstances.

'You've had a busy day by all accounts, General. I think General Volkov will be pleased to see you.'

'I am sure he will, Comrade Dubnikov.'

When they entered the room, Volkov was in the corner on the phone. Yuri prayed that Alyabyev had followed through. By the red-faced look on Volkov's face, he guessed he had. Volkov slammed down the receiver and retook his seat at the table.

'Apologies, comrade… It seems we have a problem. General Alyabyev has slung a cordon around Peredelkino – a military exercise, he says. I have ordered him down.'

Yuri saw Volkov cast a worried glance in Karzhov's direction.

'I'm sure this will only be temporary, General,' said Karzhov.

'I assume this is your doing, Marov?' said Volkov.

Yuri ignored him and looked at Gerashchenko.

'General, please take a seat, you are among comrades,' interjected Gerashchenko.

'Thank you, deputy secretary, but I would rather stand.' Yuri looked down the table, at the faces either side and Gerashchenko at its head. He had at least got this far without being rearrested. He wondered how the next bit would go down.

'So, what is it you would like to discuss with us that is so vital?'

There was little point in hedging around what he had come to say. Directness was the best policy. He needed to stay focussed… it was only him and them in the room… not the four thousand Defence Ministry staff on the other side of the door.

'I have come to demand that you release the general secretary while there is still time.'

He looked around the table at all the open mouths. Karzhov clenched and unclenched his fist.

'*Demand… Still time*,' scoffed General Volkov. 'Do you think that your little charade with General Alyabyev is going to change the course of history, that we are just going to let you carry on with your plans to defenestrate the Soviet Union? Haven't you done enough damage, General?'

'General Volkov,' interrupted Gerashchenko, 'please let the general finish.'

'It's been less than seventy-two hours since you reported the general secretary ill,' Yuri continued. 'You have time to pull back. We have *just* withdrawn from Afghanistan. You know the state of the army and the strength of public opinion. I'm sure General Volkov has made a good case for intervention in Eastern Europe, but the general secretary is *right* on this. If I am a judge of anything, Soviet troops are not about to begin street fighting in Leipzig or Dresden… even less East Berlin. And the West? You will drag them into a conflict they hardly have to fight… isn't our population already starving… Poland has gone, let East Germany run its course.'

'Glasnost… perestroika… hasn't it led us to collapse? This is just *defeatist* talk,' said Karzhov, looking around the table.

'The chairman is right,' said Yuri. 'Perestroika

has led us to the brink of collapse, but so have our previous failures.' He knew he was talking heresy now. 'I don't know how many of you have visited the West... their world is not perfect either, but it's a *long way* from ours. Perestroika needs more time... we have to be more open if we are to solve our problems. That is not defeatism... locking up Russian dissidents *is*. It didn't work in Poland and it won't work in East Germany.' Yuri paused and looked at the faces fixed impassively on him. Was he wasting his breath?

'Why are you here, General? Couldn't you be sunning yourself on the French Riviera,' said Dubnikov. 'Your business interests are no secret. Why don't you just get on the next plane and fly out of here... while *you* still have time?'

'I'm not going anywhere... nor is General Alyabyev,' he lied. He had no idea whether Alyabyev would withdraw or not, but he had to assume for now that they did not know either. 'If you wish to oppose the general secretary then do so openly – release him.'

Yuri extracted a large envelope he had folded into his pocket and slid it across the table towards Gerashchenko, who reached forward and grabbed it.

'Open it,' said Yuri, knowing this was his last gambit.

Gerashchenko pulled out three black-and-white photographs and dropped them onto the table. Yuri watched Karzhov change colour.

'What are these?' Gerashchenko asked, turning from Yuri to face the KGB chair.

Karzhov picked up one of the photos and looked

at a younger image of himself, together with another man on the Moika embankment.

'These are forgeries,' he fumed indignantly.

'Do you recognise the other man, Comrade Chairman, the man you are with? The year is 1977, if that will help jog your memory.'

Karzhov looked around the table for support, only to be met with stares of consternation.

'Who is this?' demanded the interior minister, pointing at the monochrome image.

'Comrade Karzhov?' invited Yuri.

'You'll pay for this,' hissed Karzhov.

'The other man in the photo was a CIA operative – a Tom Banner,' Yuri continued. 'He was imprisoned by us for espionage not long after this picture was taken. Soviet intelligence knew about an inside leak but couldn't identify the traitor, not until this photo, that is. The man who took it paid the price two days ago. Konstantin Stolin – some of you know him – tried to assassinate him.'

'His name?' asked the defence minister.

'Misha Revnik. He is alive, just. The agent who had him take this photo did not fare so well. Alexsei Baturin disappeared shortly thereafter; Tom Banner died in jail.'

All eyes were now fixed on Karzhov.

'He's lying... don't you see... I'm no double agent. What could possibly be my motive?'

'Key US intelligence information that helped you rise up the ladder... How many Russians did you betray for your own ends?'

Karzhov jumped to his feet. 'I want this man arrested!' he shouted, red-faced.

'Sit down, Mr Chairman,' said Yuri in a calm voice. 'Comrade Gerashchenko, may I put your phone on speaker. I have a call you need to hear.'

Yuri walked around to the other end of the table, switched the speakerphone on, picked up the receiver and punched in the international code. The number connected. *Pick up, pick up*, he thought. All eyes fixed on the phone.

'*Pronto*,' it was a woman who answered.

'Ilaria, please will you tell these gentlemen, in Russian, what you have on your desk and where you are.'

'Milan, General... I have four black-and-white photos on my desk – two men by an embankment.'

'Can you tell me, the man wearing the hat, what has he on his face?'

'Glasses, General... dark-rimmed glasses.'

'And the negatives of these photos, where are they now?'

'With a friend, who will release them to the international press if your general secretary is not freed by tomorrow morning or any harm should come to you, General, or in fact me or my associates.'

Yuri picked up the receiver and dropped it back in its cradle, ending the call.

'Comrades, do you wish to be associated with this traitor? If these photos are released, the Russian people will know soon enough that a key member of the interim government sold his country to further his career and even now may be supplying key information to the Americans. Maybe this whole coup – and that's what it is – is an American invention to bring Russia to its knees, to banish it for ever?'

For the first time, Yuri could see fear mixed with doubt on their faces.

'Don't think you are overreaching, General?' said Gerashchenko.

'I tell you, Comrade Gerashchenko, if we launch this repression, it will be the end, economically and politically – you will *all* be branded traitors by the people.'

Yuri looked again at Karzhov, who had turned as white as a sheet.

'Release the general secretary and we have a reset. I will do my best to intercede on your behalf; it cannot be in the general secretary's interests to advertise such dissension at the heart of his government – not in the middle of a crisis. That does not go for Karzhov; he is to be arrested for treason.'

They were staring at him now like rabbits caught in a headlight.

'And two other matters… you will release General Ghukov *immediately* and until such time as he is back at GSHQ I am to be made acting head of the army. General Volkov is to be relieved.'

Volkov looked across at Gerashchenko, his face filled with fury at the prospect of an end to his ambitions. 'Gerasim, we can face this down. We can't pull back now.'

'You can… that's the point… you simply have to give

the order,' interjected Yuri. 'Deputy Secretary, I suggest you speak with the general secretary yourself, in person, before he goes on the air waves. Make your peace.'

Yuri walked back along the length of the room and opened the double doors. Two soldiers appeared.

'Arrest Chairman Karzhov.'

The soldiers looked from Yuri to Gerashchenko, confused.

'Do as he says,' said Gerashchenko, capitulating. Gerashchenko switched on the intercom to the outer office.

'Anna, organise me an escort to Peredelkino. Comrades, if you wish to join me, please do. General Marov, I am appointing you acting head of the army. I emphasise acting.'

Yuri thought Volkov would charge at him. Instead, he slumped down in his chair and stared out of the window. Volkov turned and faced him.

'General Marov, I admire your courage, but it will be you, not me, that will ring the death knell of the Soviet Union.'

'No, General, you're wrong... time... and people like Karzhov.'

Yuri turned to the soldier standing beside him.

'Corporal, order me a car.'

Yuri turned back to Volkov when the soldier had disappeared.

'General Alyabyev will assume command of your group for now, until General Ghukov is back in post at least. It will be up to General Ghukov and the general secretary what happens next.'

All Volkov did was nod acknowledgement. Yuri wondered what the general secretary would do. Somehow he didn't think any of the conspirators would be serving prison sentences. Their abject failure should prove ignominy enough.

'If you will excuse me, General,' said Yuri.

Volkov stood up and without a glance left the room.

The soldier who had left two minutes before reappeared in the doorway.

'Your car, sir, it's waiting.'

Yuri acknowledged him and waved him to shut the door.

Yuri was alone again. He picked up the phone.

Two minutes later he'd been patched through to the KGB command post at Peredelkino. In the darkened window, all he could see was the reflection of himself, phone in hand, waiting, jaw clenched. There was a click on the other end. He lifted the receiver to his ear.

'General Yuri Romanavich.' He could hear the suppressed laughter in her voice.

'Viktoriya Nikolaevna,' he said, and saw his face break into a smile.

EPILOGUE

On October 18, the East German Communist Party, bowing to mounting clamour for change, replaced Erich Honecker with his protégé Egon Krenz. The new East German General Secretary, in a TV address to the nation, said that within the bounds of "continuity and renewal" the door was "wide open for earnest political dialogue." He also quoted Mikhail S. Gorbachev: "We have to see and react to the times, otherwise life will punish us."

A month later, the Berlin Wall fell, and with it, the East German Communist government.

MAIN CHARACTERS

Adriana	Nightclub girl
Agnessa Raskolnikova Agapova	Viktoriya's flatmate
General Alyabyev	Commander, Central
Ilaria Agneli	Italian model and buyer
Dimitri Bazhukov	Konstantin's second
Lieutenant Galina Biryukova	Volkov's adjutant
Luigi Crisi	Italian sales director
Yev Derevenko	Captain in the military air force
Viktor Dubnikov	Defence Minister
Stephan Federov	Minister of Oil and Gas
Major Sergei Gaidar	Commander of a private force
Gerasim Gerashchenko	Deputy Secretary General

Colonel General Andrei Ghukov	Chief of Staff
Karzhov	KGB Chair
Viktoriya (Vika) Nikolaevna Kayakova	Economics graduate
Yuri Romanavich Marov	Colonel
Ivan Antonovich Pralnikov	Mikhail's friend
Mikhail (Misha) Dimitrivich Revnik	Street trader
Konstantin (Kostya) Ivanivich Stolin	Mafia boss
Lev	Konstantin's debt collector
Najibullah	Afghan leader
Ilya Terentev	KGB Colonel
Grigory Vasiliev	Banker
General Vdovin	Commander, North West
General Volkov	Commander, Western Group of Forces